Delacroix was ~~lying on top of the car~~, his flaccid arms and legs hanging down oddly over the tops of the windows. He was facing up, the effect that of someone lying on top of a white coffin.

James Delacroix had loved that car. It was to die for.

I repressed a gag. "Can you tell what happened?" Albert and the boys could see the details I couldn't. I was shaking and my voice had picked up a tremor. "How did he get up there? Do you suppose he climbed up to do something to the roof and had a heart attack or something and just lay down till it went away?—only it didn't? Is he blue around the lips? Is there any blood?" I tried to sound efficient but the words were tripping out, falling over each other.

"Just the blood around the bullet hole," said Albert dryly. "It's a little blue."

"Bullet hole!"

"Directly into the heart, I'd guess. And one wound. Like an execution."

★

Previously published Worldwide Mystery titles by
JACKIE LEWIN

MURDER FLIES LEFT SEAT

DEATH
FLIES ON
FINAL

JACKIE
LEWIN

W⦿RLDWIDE⦿

TORONTO • NEW YORK • LONDON
AMSTERDAM • PARIS • SYDNEY • HAMBURG
STOCKHOLM • ATHENS • TOKYO • MILAN
MADRID • WARSAW • BUDAPEST • AUCKLAND

DEATH FLIES ON FINAL

A Worldwide Mystery/November 2000

First published by Thomas Bouregy & Company, Inc.

ISBN 0-373-26367-8

Printed in U.S.A.

For my favorite M&Ms—Miranda and Monica

ONE

THE LAST TIME I saw James Delacroix it was a scorcher, one of the hottest May Sundays I can remember. Actually, scratch that. Wishful thinking. The steamy May Sunday I'm talking about was the last time I saw James Delacroix *alive*. Alas, I did see him once again.

That Sunday, we were doing my husband Albert's thing, though he liked to think of it as a family outing. Right. Let me make it clear that anything to do with the Piper Turbo Arrow was an *Albert* outing. He lived to fly that plane. The rest of us, though invited, were incidental. These adventures had their moments, though I was always mortally sure that one day our luck would run out. We who are about to die salute you.

In any case, that weekend our destination was Carlsbad Caverns, land of the scorpion and bat, and so far our luck had been holding. By the time we arrived at Copper Creek, roughly the midpoint, we'd been en route for a couple of hours and were only too glad to land there for refueling. Approaching from the air, we could tell the airport was for the moment very lightly utilized. The VOR was perched nearby, sending its signal to guide us in via radial beams. Arlene, Albert's head nurse, always called it a witch's hat because it was a pointed cone, albeit white. A good witch, I guessed. The wind sock hung limp; a single small building poked uncomfortably out of the early

spring soil like one of last year's weeds that no one
had remembered to pull. It was joined only by a lone
hangar further down the road. No planes were parked
anywhere in sight. Still, Albert had dutifully radioed
our approach on the off chance that someone, on
ground or in the air, was listening.

He gave our new number, of course, but I hadn't
bothered to memorize it yet. Since our old plane,
Sweet Juliet, met its forced end on a mountain pass
last fall, I'd refused to bond with this new one. I knew
that the ID ended in Romeo, however, and that, in
flying parlance, stands for R. Not really appropriate,
since in the play Juliet outlived Romeo. Briefly. Very
briefly, actually. On second thought, let's forget this
whole idea. Anyway, Albert made our presence
known.

"Copper Creek unicom, landing advisory please."

The voice which responded was unhurried and non-
descript. "Four-six Romeo, uh, winds calm, altimeter
29.97. No known traffic."

"Which runway is active?"

"Your choice." No problem here, apparently, with
too many planes jockeying for position.

"Thanks. Four-six Romeo."

The radio voice didn't seem particularly interested,
certainly not what you'd call welcoming. No cheery
"G'day"'s. We were used to friendlier chats from
small-town airports. We knew, however, who it was
likely to be. We'd met the man a few weeks earlier.
We were pretty sure that voice was Delacroix himself.

Paul and Spence, our seventeen-year-old twins, had
been folded into the cramped backseat of the Piper
and desperately needed to deplane and stretch. Once
given the go-ahead, they emerged like clowns from a

circus Volkswagen, uncoiling to amazing full size and shaking out the kinks. Tall, adolescent-skinny, with the fair complexion and dark hair of their father, they looked more like each other than fraternal twins had any right to do. Where Albert had waves, starting now to fleck with gray, the boys' hair was straight. Spence had lately taken to sporting a ponytail, while Paul still made occasional trips to a barber, but otherwise their features made them essentially interchangeable.

"Wow," said Paul, doing a quick hamstring stretch against the side of the plane. "I didn't know I had so many muscles that could cramp."

"Yeah, Dad," added Spence, rubbing his calves. "Next time, how about a nice corporate jet."

Albert was frowning at a spot on the plane's well-waxed finish. He rubbed at it with a little spit and a finger. "You got it," he said absently. "The day I do a hostile takeover of IBM."

Heat made the air stand still, full of dust and haze and New Mexico spring pollens. The boys ambled off together in the direction of the squat beige building, obviously happy to be able to walk freely and hopeful that something interesting might await them despite all signs to the contrary. They were remarkably good sports about sharing their father's hobby *cum* passion. Better than I.

For me, the best part of flying small planes is when it's over. This was only a halfway point stopover to fill the gas tanks, but I take joy where I find it. I had climbed down via the pad on the wing and straightened out my jeans and white cotton camp shirt, damp from the combination of heat and nerves. Albert, as always, looked newly minted. My hair, finally released from being scrunched under headphones, was beyond makeshift repair. I needed to start over using whatever mirror was hanging in the little FBO bathroom. At least this single airstrip setup *had* an FBO.

Delacroix, we'd learned earlier, owned the FBO. Or, you might say, Delacroix *was* the FBO. In the counterintuitive language that passes for aviation lingo, Fixed Base Operator stands for both the business and the owner. Most FBOs sold fuel, sometimes food, sometimes memorabilia, and often lent out wheels for ground transportation. And most FBOs were staffed by pleasant people. Oh well, there are exceptions to every rule.

By the time Albert fooled around with the plane and retrieved some chocks for just in case, Delacroix was working his way toward us from the building. A large, husky man with a full head of yellow-white hair slicked back with something shiny, he was wearing old jeans and an older checked shirt, the sleeves rolled almost to the elbow. A significant paunch obscured the waist, hiding any belt he might have been wearing. From a distance, he could have passed for, maybe, sixty. Having chatted with him socially before, however, I knew that estimate was generous. Closer looks revealed broken blood vessels patterning their way across the broad nose, down the jowls, and on to the neck. The veins on his lower arms were ropy and varicosed, the knuckles of the hands showing arthritic changes. Seventy-five if he was a day.

Still, he looked strong and competent. In his own element, he was clearly more comfortable than he'd been when last we'd met. Then he'd been dressed in an obviously new dark suit chosen as appropriate for his daughter Arlene's wedding. A stiff shirt still showed wrinkles from its original folds. At the time,

I wouldn't have been surprised to find a price tag looping out from under his arm.

In person, his voice sounded warmer than it had on the radio. "Arlene called to tell me you'd probably be stoppin' here," he said as he covered the last few yards to greet us. "Dr. Beckmann, isn't it? And Mrs. Beckmann?"

"Albert, please," said my husband, offering his hand. He wanted to be one of the boys, he really did. Deep down, he craved the persona of a man who drank beer, owned a pickup truck, and sucked on toothpicks. As it happened, he hated beer, had never owned a pickup, and used toothpicks only for dental hygiene. And no matter how hard he tried, he couldn't refer to himself as "Al."

"And I'm Grace," I added, smiling. "Grace Beckmann. From Arlene's wedding."

"Sure, I remember." Delacroix shook both our hands and began shoving one of the chocks closer with his foot, tamping it against the plane's wheel. "Nice party. Good girl, Arlene."

"Best nurse on the service," said Albert seriously. "The absolute tops."

Delacroix nodded and promptly lost interest in discussing his daughter. There was business to be done. "You'll be wantin' to fill this up some, I'll bet. You want it all the way?"

"No, no!" said Albert, mildly alarmed. "Fill this baby to the top and we'll never get off the ground." He pointed fondly to the edge of the runway. "Those boys over there are ours. We're flying heavy today."

Delacroix looked over to the scrub beyond the airstrip where Paul and Spence seemed to be watching some form of wildlife inch along. I wondered a) if it was a snake, and b) just how poisonous a snake it was. The old man registered the boys, along with the fact that he wasn't going to make a very large sale. "Whatever you say, Doctor. So you think, what, half in each tank maybe?"

"That's what we had coming out. Otherwise, we wouldn't have stopped here. Could have made it to Carlsbad easily on a full tank, but not with four adults."

Delacroix meditated, glancing at the plane, probably estimating the number of gallons he'd be able to unload. He picked at a tooth while he considered his next step, bringing a flash of fire from the large diamond ring on his right hand. I took a quick look at the jewel. Diamonds are diamonds, after all, even when a guy's wearing them. The ring surrounding the stone was elaborately worked, scrolled gold outlined with dirt. Doubtless he never cleaned it. Strangely, the grime made the design more interesting, as did the fact that the diamond wasn't centered in the pattern. What on earth was this guy doing with a ring like that? Must have inherited it. Even denied a closer look, I knew he hadn't picked it up at Wal-Mart.

"I'll go get the gas truck. You folks feel free to freshen up there in the lounge. Boys too. There's coffee. Cold drinks in the machine. Bathroom's fairly clean."

He moved off toward the distant hangar, taking his time. I could tell we'd be here awhile. Age slows everything down. Old conductors use slower tempos. Old drivers rarely speed. Old FBO owners amble.

From the outside, the main building was a classic square, painted beige and missing large chunks of stucco. What remained was stained by years of dust and wind. The run-down look surprised me till I realized that when you're the only game in town it doesn't matter much how clean you keep the checkerboard. The only surprise was parked to the side, out of the sun where the finish was protected. A white Cadillac Sedan DeVille—a fairly new one, certainly no older than last year's model—sat smugly in the shade. Walking near it, we could smell the new-car leather through an open window. An original Magritte on the fly-specked wall could hardly have been more out of place.

Albert and I exchanged looks. "I wonder if he loans it out," I whispered. "Maybe we could find some excuse to go into Copper City." Little airports often have cars they let pilots drive, at least for a short trip to town. Without them, people who fly in are effectively stranded.

"He'd have to be nuts. Still…" He looked around. "I don't see anything else."

"So don't feel bad about buying only half a tank. He's not exactly starving out here. Did you see that rock on his finger?"

"Uh-huh. He seems a different kind of guy somehow."

We wandered into the lounge area, a small room smelling vaguely of Murphy's Oil, where the boys, having already arrived, had found the drink machine. They were chugging cans of pop and exclaiming over the oddities in a dusty glass case. The usual aviation charts, notebooks, and kneeboards were interspersed with postcards and books about New Mexico, none of them (except for the charts) looking newer than the 1970s. Two large hunting knives were in one corner of the top shelf, jarringly out of place. I wondered what use a pilot could possibly have for them. What fascinated the twins, however, were glass paper-weights containing embedded scorpions that looked lively enough to crawl their way out of the glass, through the back of the cabinet, and right up one's leg. I shuddered.

"Cool, huh?" said Spence.

"Terrific."

"He probably bought all this stuff when he bought the FBO and it's been sitting here ever since," said Albert, peering discreetly out the window to be sure Delacroix was still at work with the gas truck. "Arlene said he's been here about fifteen years. Lives right on the premises in a room at the back. Takes one lavish trip annually, but otherwise is happy here. Gardens a little. She thought he might be seeing a woman in town, but nothing too serious. Goes there for a meal now and then. And that's about it." He shrugged. "It's a life, I guess."

I could see, through several broken blinds covering the half-door, that he was working on our plane, re-moving a large hose from the opening in the wing. I'd already made a quick trip to the "fairly clean" bathroom and was now putting the finishing touches on something approaching a chignon. Long hair saves a fortune in salon money but it's a pain on a hot day. Simple to fix, though, so it suits me. "Can you even imagine the boredom?" I said, talking through a mouth full of hairpins. "I'll bet he doesn't get three planes a day."

"Oh, sure he does. This must just be a slow sea-son."

"Besides, Mom," said Paul, "maybe he likes it

this way. It's a perfect life for, say, someone practicing to be a Buddhist monk.''

"Or a Maytag repairman," added Spence.

"Or a guy in the Witness Protection Program," Albert chimed in, warming to the game.

"Sammy the Bull, running from the mob."

"Astronauts training for a solo trip to Betelgeuse."

"Maybe he…"

The words died fast when the door swung in suddenly and James Delacroix came in from the sun, panting slightly and wiping gasoline-scented hands on his pants. "Okay," he said to Albert with a nod. "That should do it."

They headed together to a desk at the back of the room to settle the account. The twins, who had pushed for a scorpion paperweight, scored, Albert adding it to the charges on his credit card. While the men huddled over the radio, presumably getting a weather briefing for the rest of the trip, I found the only comfortable chair in the place and flipped through the magazines unearthed from under a side table. *Armed Forces Journal. Newsweek,* dated 1986. An old *Life,* the full-size kind. I tried again. This time I found promotional material from General Motors, primarily on the Cadillac. At least it was newer than the rest of the reading material.

"Nice wheels you have outside," I said, prompted by the literature, to Delacroix as he and Albert returned from their duties. Even taciturn men will talk about their cars and their dogs.

Delacroix nodded, unsmiling. "It's what I want."

"And what you want is a new one every year, right?" I teased.

"About." He was serious. And he wasn't interested in adding any more information. He checked a stack of papers in his hand. Now that the gasoline sale was made, he didn't have to be sociable anymore and could revert. The default mode, I suspected, was silence. Interlaced with hostility. A phone suddenly ringing in the back of the room brought his head up and I thought I saw something—alarm, maybe, or fear—pass through his gaze. Afterward, I would try to remember just how he looked at that moment.

Albert, who'd been studying his charts, was distracted. "I think we'd better go. They're predicting a change in the weather later this afternoon and I'd like to be down before then. Where are the boys?"

In the background, I vaguely registered the sounds of Delacroix's voice rising and the bang of a receiver slammed down. "Outside. They're ready," I said, opening the door to a blast of heat. We were both half out when the old man's voice stopped us.

"Uh, wait a minute, please." He had materialized beside us and was holding out a manila envelope, sealed and taped shut. Apparently he could move fast when he had to. Or when galvanized by something, like a phone call. "You'll see Arlene when you get back, won't you?"

Arlene Delacroix Masters was chief nurse on Albert's medical service. Her recent marriage, followed by a two-week honeymoon spent Jeeping around the Sangre de Cristos, hadn't changed her career plans significantly. Of course, all else being equal, the head of the department would be likely to see her.

"Sure," said Albert, reaching for the letter. "Want me to give this to her?"

The man hesitated for a moment as if he had serious misgivings, hanging on to the manila envelope for a beat before releasing it to Albert's hand. Then his arms dropped awkwardly to his sides, useless with the parcel gone. "Please," he said finally. "Yes. It's just…just some music. For her."

Albert, if he wondered at all, asked no questions. He added the envelope to his collection of charts and the bag with the paperweight, and we headed back to the plane where the boys were waiting for their father to open the door and gesture them to the rear.

I was, as usual, the last one in and stood for a moment on the wing. Looking back to the unprepossessing building, I was struck by the image of Delacroix standing at the door. He was staring at us intently, the expression on his complicated face unreadable.

People have asked me since if he seemed frightened or distraught, if he was agitated, tense, showing signs of strain. All I can remember now after the fact is that he seemed, in a strange way, quietly resigned. If he was waiting for something that was going to happen to him, he'd been waiting for a very long time.

TWO

ALBERT'S WELL-TO-DO East Coast family was the reason we were able to live somewhat more luxuriously than most of his medical school colleagues. Those luxuries included, as I've mentioned, our own plane. Granted, as head of the department he commanded a very nice salary, but some of the better perks we owed to his frugal mother's textile mills and his father's savvy. Nothing like having stock in the family business.

Unlike Albert, I hadn't brought much of a material nature to our marriage. My mother, living now in a Baltimore retirement community, was at least self-sufficient. She'd learned, after my father's death years ago in an oil-well explosion, to juggle income and outgo till they more or less balanced. That trick pretty well wiped out any money remaining from insurance and legal settlements.

All that was left for me as an inheritance of sorts was Millie, Mother's onetime housekeeper who was mine now, whether I liked it or not. There was never any question that, having essentially raised me, Millie would come to live out her days in my house once my mother's home was sold. I called Mother long-distance at 7:15 every morning, the ever-dutiful daughter, and, after exchanging the bare-bones news of the day, turned the phone over to Millie. Then the two of them would dish happily in private for half an hour at the minimum, most of the time spent clucking over me the way they had a quarter of a century earlier. The phone bills were truly awesome. I'd shown a couple of them to Albert early on and he'd said, considering how happy it made the two of them, it was money well spent. Then he went out and bought hundreds of shares in the long-distance company we used. That way, they made us richer and poorer at the same time. Millie, come to think of it, was always a mixed blessing.

A mixed blessing isn't a bad description for Albert's love of flying either and the time I've spent sharing that passion. The turbulence we encountered for a while on the last leg of the trip that Sunday, for example, came down strongly on the minus side. I turn unfailingly white-knuckled once the plane starts to bounce around, which it usually does.

The Rocky Mountains make air rise across their high peaks. And then, because cold air sinks, the valleys cool faster than the peaks and that sets up what weather types call a pressure gradient. Makes clouds in the summer. Makes me a wreck in all seasons.

But then, our funky destinations are the good part. We've visited every point of interest, however remote, in a three-hundred-mile radius from our city, as well as more than a few of no interest whatever. Our aerial equivalent of blue highways. The few days we spent in Carlsbad that weekend, however, chalked up on the plus side.

The boys had been to a few minor caves, learned to differentiate stalactites and stalagmites (''C for ceiling, G for ground,'' they recited), but Carlsbad Caverns forever ruined them for lesser caves. Once allowed to enter, they trotted with the confidence of youth down through the dark limestone path to emerge, openmouthed, into a three-mile expanse of collected chambers, each more hugely exotic than the last. We, who were delicately picking our way, caught up with them and were awed and delighted. The massive sculptures were implausible, impossibly balanced. The half-light, heavy air, and constantly dripping water added to the sense of being someplace otherworldly and alien.

Paul was in charge of the information brochures and kept us, always behind, apprised of where we were. "This room is called Whale's Mouth, and you can see why," he whispered. Whispering seemed appropriate here. Even the clutch of rowdy five-year-olds we noticed in the lobby and who were now ahead of us seemed quiet and subdued. "Now I want to find the Hall of Giants." As if it could be lost.

The caves were an obvious success, even with our sons who are a hard sell. Much as they admired them, however, the real thrill of the area was the great exodus of bats emerging, as evening fell, from the mouth of the cave and out into the night. When 300,000 Mexican free-tail bats all decide to leave for dinner simultaneously, it is indeed a sight to behold. Someday, I hope, my boys will see the streets of Calcutta, Tokyo's Ginza, Shanghai during the Chinese New Year, maybe even Times Square at rush hour. None of those will surpass the congestion of the Carlsbad bats' night out, the whirring as they rise against the evening sky. The people around us were all transfixed, captivated by the spectacle, as were we.

We spent Sunday and Monday nights in town, wandering the shops and generally fooling around, a typical small-plane vacation. By 8:30 Tuesday morning, we were wheels up, destination Copper Creek for refueling and then home.

So much for the best-laid plans.

The little Copper Creek airport looked as quiet as it had on Sunday morning, the only difference being the gray skies and much cooler temperatures. At midmorning, the wind sock was blowing steadily east. I wondered if a front was coming in from the mountains and, if so, how quickly we could gas up, say hello to Delacroix, and get airborne and out.

Albert tried to reach the old man via unicom, but this time no one answered. "Out to breakfast, maybe," he muttered through the headset. "Hey, no problem," he assured me, noticing my raised eyebrows. "I'll land and see if we can scare him up."

"What do we do for gas if he's taken off for the week?"

Albert shrugged, checking the altimeter before starting his descent. "There should be some kind of contact phone number stuck to the wall someplace. Usually is, anyway. Don't worry. We'll unearth somebody."

I turned around to check the boys' seat belts. The twins were quietly absorbed, Paul with a paperback, Spence with an electronic game. I wish I could fly with such lack of concern. We didn't have headsets for them so they were clueless, oblivious to our plans. I motioned that we were going down and they dutifully stopped what they were doing and looked out the window, adding their body English to the task at hand. It must have worked. We landed smoothly.

The airstrip, under cloudy skies, seemed unnaturally deserted. Tufts of tumbleweed blew across the runway and into the scrub at the side of the ramp.

Once we emerged, I looked toward the FBO, waiting for the door to open and Delacroix to come ambling out, but there was only silence. The door itself, on closer look, was open, the broken blinds across the half-window, now driven by a stiff breeze, knocking against the glass. I was filled with a deep sense of misgiving, no less ominous for being for the moment unfounded. I wasn't alone. As we all stood beside the plane staring at the open door, no one said a word.

Finally, Albert cleared his voice. "Well, let's go see what's going on." He started toward the battered stucco building, the rest of us following a few feet behind.

"What's that?" asked Spence as we walked, pointing to a grassy area near the building. "Under there." Getting no particular response from us, he covered the twenty or so yards at a lope and bent to see for himself, parting the grass with one hand but not touching anything on the ground.

I caught sight of something shiny, reflecting the gray morning. "What is it?" I called.

"It's one of the guy's knives," Spence shouted back. "Looks like one of the ones he had in his case. Shall I get it?"

"No, don't!" I called to him, my anxiety rising again. "Don't touch it. For now, anyway."

"Why not?" asked Albert, ignoring my obvious mood.

"Just leave it," I said uneasily.

He threw his hands in the air, walking faster now. "All right. Okay. Leave it."

All four of us angled to the door and into the lounge area, walking tentatively. Despite the wind, the room smelled musty and unused. It felt a bit as if we were breaking and entering. "Jim?" called Albert. "Hello. Anybody here?"

"Look," said Spence, pointing to the case of merchandise. "Both knives are gone."

Whoever had taken them out had closed the sliding door behind the case. Nothing else in the case looked disturbed.

Albert walked toward the back of the lounge, shouting down the hall toward the rest rooms. "Delacroix? You here?" He waited a minute and tried again. "Jim?"

Nothing. I tried calling, my voice sounding harsh in the empty hall. Then I had a thought. "Why don't I go see if his car is there. He wouldn't go anywhere without that Caddie."

"I'll do it. You stay here." Albert brushed past me and out the door before I could protest, moving faster than usual. The three of us waited by the drink machine, the feeling of trespass still with us. The coffeemaker, I noticed, was on but the pot was empty. A black sludge had glued itself to the bottom of the glass. Automatically, I switched it off.

Then we heard Albert. A vague noise turning into something frightening, a guttural choked-off cry, came from the side of the building. My stomach went into spasm. We were out the door and racing in the direction of the corner. "No, don't come!" he yelled, but too late. He was running toward us, holding out both arms to keep us back, but all three of us ignored him, dodging beyond the hands that were grabbing for our clothes, trying to stop us. We made it, half tripping on each other, around the edge of the building and were right by the Cadillac when sight and smell assailed us.

Delacroix was draped across the roof of the car, his flaccid arms and legs hanging down oddly over the tops of the windows. His skin was as gray as the day, mottled with blue. My first thought was that this was somebody else because the diamond ring wasn't on his finger, but it was him all right. He was facing up. The effect was that of someone lying on top of a white coffin. Even standing on tiptoe I wasn't tall enough to see anything but his profile, but his eyes, as far as I could see, were wide open and staring at the bleak sky. Irrationally, it struck me that somehow it would have been even more horrible if, though sightless, he'd been forced to look directly into the sun. That he was dead was without question. That he'd been that way for some time was equally obvious.

James Delacroix had loved that car. It was to die for.

I repressed a gag. "Can you tell what happened?" Albert and the boys could see the details I couldn't. I was shaking and my voice had picked up a tremor. "How did he get up there? Do you suppose he climbed up to do something to the roof and had a heart attack or something and just lay down till it went away—only it didn't? Is he blue around the lips? Is there any blood?" I tried to sound efficient but the words were tripping out, falling over each other.

"Just the blood around the bullet hole," said Albert dryly. "It's a little blue."

"Bullet hole! No!" I stepped back to distance myself.

"Directly into the heart, I'd guess. And one wound. Like an execution."

The boys were uncharacteristically quiet. As far as

I knew, this was the first dead body they'd ever seen. Paul had turned quite white and was edging away. Spence, Mr. Cool, was inspecting everything with the sangfroid of a born detective. I couldn't believe him, but then I never could. My stomach had more knots than a sailor's manual. He bent down to look through the window of the car, craning to check the upholstered top.

"There's no hole through the car. I'll bet he was shot somewhere else and his body was pulled up there. But why?"

"And how?" asked Albert. "He was no lightweight. One man couldn't have lifted him alone."

"Maybe he was shot sitting up after he climbed up there," I added. "Though why? Why would he do that?"

"Any knife wounds?" asked Spence. "Don't forget those knives are missing. Or one of them, anyway."

"Can't tell. I don't want to touch anything."

Reluctantly, we left the body where it was and returned to the FBO lounge. I hated to leave him there but we needed help. As predicted, Albert found a phone number on a square of white paper tacked to a wall, called it, and told the story of our terrible discovery to the voice at the other end. The man turned out to run an auto repair shop in the town of Copper Creek but subbed with the gas truck for pilots when Delacroix was otherwise unavailable. He promised to send help and to come out himself. With some embarrassment, Albert asked him to please, if he had a chance, half-fill our plane so we could eventually get home. He knew how coldhearted the request sounded in the face of such tragedy but, under duress, made it anyway.

"I have to call Arlene," he said after hanging up, frowning and reaching for a small address book he carries in his back pocket.

"Shouldn't you wait till we get back?" I asked.

"Whenever that might be? Nope," he said over his shoulder, heading toward the phone in the back of the room, the one he and Delacroix had used together just a few days before. "She must be next of kin. She'll need to see to arrangements and tell the family. If there is a family."

Five minutes later he was back, shaking his head. "I tried everywhere I could think of, but no one can find her. Left messages all over to call this number, but we may not be here." He shrugged. "I tried. Don't know what else to do."

By the time the necessary people had shown up and performed their various unpleasant functions with the body, several hours had passed. After some debate about leaving the body untouched, the decision to bring it down from the car was pretty much unanimous. No one wanted to leave the old man's body up there a moment longer. We were asked to wait till the county sheriff could come from another town to ask us some questions. The boys had wandered off, fortified by machine-generated soft drinks and candy bars, the original shock behind them. We sat uncomfortably in the FBO lounge and considered our options. Thick clouds were gathering, darkening more ominously every moment. The prospect of flying in a thunderstorm had, to understate the case, no appeal to me whatever. Even Albert was wary of that much weather. Thank goodness.

"I think we'd better look for a place to stay in town tonight," he said, resigned. "Who knows when the sheriff will show up and besides, it's already too iffy to fly."

"From what I could see from the air, we're talking *small* town here. Want to lay odds on the possibility of a motel?"

"Zero to none. Maybe someone runs a B&B."

"And maybe cows fly at night when no one's looking."

Albert ignored me, thought for a moment, and then went out to find the owner of the auto repair shop who was, as requested, gassing us up. When he returned, he was studying a scrap of paper.

"Carla. Carla Correa, it says. She can put us up for the night."

"She has room for all of us?"

"Two extra bedrooms. Apparently she's done this sort of thing for stranded pilots before. Makes a few extra bucks and doesn't mind. Cooks well too, I guess. And Joe—he said his name is Joe, out there, the auto guy—will take us to town in his truck and give us a loaner till we can leave. He said we could take the Cadillac..." He paused for a moment at the look on my face. "But I said no."

"Thank you. Very much. Has anyone checked with this Carla?"

"Joe did, with a cellular. Everything's up-to-date in Copper Creek. She said fine."

The phone rang and Albert went back to answer it. When he returned, he announced that the sheriff was delayed and wouldn't be able to see us till tomorrow. "He asked if we'd please wait till then. I told him where we'd be. And encouraged him to make it fairly early in the morning so we can take off before the weather turns again.''

''He's from some other town. The county seat, wherever that is, but not from here. So how did he know this Carla Correa and how to find us?''

''I have a feeling everyone knows Carla. He told me something interesting, by the way.''

I waited. Why did he always want me to *ask* for the rest of the idea? Somewhere deep in him lurks a sense of theater.

He gave up hoping for encouragement and went on. ''Carla and Jim Delacroix were something of an item. I mean, to a point. She must be the woman Arlene said he was seeing a bit. When he wasn't at his post here, he could usually be found at her house.''

I found that disturbing. ''She could be a basket case by now, poor thing, since Joe's call. We shouldn't be staying there.''

''I asked the sheriff about that. He said she's a tough bird. Wouldn't pass up a buck.''

I thought about it. ''Well, you know it might be really interesting to talk to her. Maybe she knows who shot her boyfriend.'' I'd had a taste of solving a crime the preceding fall and found it strangely thrilling, admittedly in a horrifying way. Here we were right in the middle of another murder, or maybe some bizarre suicide, and this time I could be more objective, less emotional. Last time, we'd known the victim. Here, we'd barely spoken to James Delacroix.

''Why am I overwhelmed with a sense of déjà vu?''

''Beats me,'' I lied. ''Any chance we might be able to find lunch somewhere?''

The answer to that one turned out to be no. Murder details take time. By late afternoon, I'd given up on lunch and was looking forward to dinner. Arlene had called back and received the news. After the first few bad minutes, she agreed that she'd come down as soon as she could, though that might not be till tomorrow evening. Her brother would be of no use and besides, she had no idea how to find him. She'd have to wait till he called her for some reason to even tell him about the death. Albert assured her that nothing important would be done without her. That chore finished, we gathered the boys and were driven to Joe's garage where he gifted us with a thirty-year-old Chevy to use for the duration. My parents had driven such a buggy. I'd forgotten how large and comfortable old cars are. They just don't make 'em like that anymore.

The town had only one main street plus a few residential side roads leading off into the New Mexico scrub. Most of the shopfronts seemed to date from the early years of the century, though an occasional store advertised more high-tech items. The hardware store looked abandoned but the beauty shop next door was full. Someone was walking out, her hair tightly curled and sprayed. I wondered, as I often do on these flying trips to odd locations, what prompted anyone to choose this particular spot for a town. Water? Mining? Cattle? The tiny creek that gave its name for incorporation could hardly qualify as a major water source. In any case, the size of the community made our lives easier. Finding Carla Correa's house was no problem. Adjusting to the woman who owned it was a little harder.

She was standing on the front stoop of a sprawling

one-story house of painted wood, her arms crossed in front of her. Someone, during this complicated day, had suggested she was probably in her late forties or early fifties, but if so she was being unusually successful at keeping the years at bay. Shoulder-length hair was expertly streaked blond on blond. Her navy slacks fit perfectly over a full figure. Topping them was a blue-and-yellow paisley silk blouse tied in a knot at the waist. She looked too "city" for her surroundings. I could see why Delacroix had been attracted. It wasn't just good cooking.

We introduced ourselves all around and she invited us in. A heavy breeze blew through windows open in every corner of the house, promising the rain that still hadn't come. My first impression of the house's furnishings was that there was too much of them. I could smell something cooking, something redolent with garlic and onions and possibly chili peppers. My very empty stomach contracted with expectation.

We proffered our condolences and were amazed as well as relieved at the lack of emotion.

"We were friends, I guess," she said. "Though considering how long I've known him, I'm not sure I ever really knew him at all." She shook her head in wonder, the way one might do at seeing some unbelievable pet trick on TV. Then, having shown all she was going to of what was expected, it was back to business. "Why don't you put those duffel bags in the two bedrooms down that hall and come on back here when you're ready. I imagine you're hungry after all you've been through today. I'll have some margaritas ready for you, unless you'd like something else, and lemonade for the boys." She looked at them expectantly. They nodded, smiling shyly. "Dinner is chicken enchiladas and fruit salad. Nachos to start. Maybe, if I get ambitious, I'll do a flan for dessert.''

We thanked her and headed down the hall carrying the bags we'd remembered to extricate from the luggage compartment of the plane. Both bedrooms were spacious and very clean. I waited till we were in our room and the boys in theirs before whispering to Albert.

"Can you believe the man she was involved with was just murdered? This woman doesn't have a hair out of place, forget tears. What's going on here?''

Albert shrugged, his hands expressive. "Maybe this was a pretty casual relationship. Anyway, I suspect we'll find out soon.''

In fact, it took a while. Nothing about the murder was discussed over dinner, which was as good as it smelled. A Hispanic woman handled the kitchen and serving chores, but Carla Correa made it clear that the cooking was hers. She had changed to a hostess skirt topped with a black knit shirt. Around her neck was turquoise in profusion. I'd found something halfway clean to wear, but the gray linen pants were wrinkled. I didn't go with the meal.

Whatever style of food Carla had grown up with, she'd mastered Southwestern cuisine and decor beautifully. Wonderful Mexican paper flowers adorned the table as a centerpiece, substituting for the fresh blossoms I suspected would be there later in the summer. When the meal was over, she invited the boys to watch television in the basement. They happily accepted and disappeared downstairs. Not until then did she finally ask all the questions she'd apparently been holding back.

"So now, tell me please what really happened out

there. Joe was pretty brief and I don't interact too much with anyone else in town."

We explained, over excellent black coffee, how we'd found Delacroix in such a bizarre position, draped across the roof of his treasured car. The mental picture broke the reserve she'd managed until now. She buried her head in her hands and cried quietly. We sat for what seemed a long time, allowing the grief, if that's what it was, to fill her. After a final deep sigh, she sat up and wiped at her eyes with her napkin. She seemed embarrassed.

"Okay, so maybe we were closer than I let on a while ago. I knew something was wrong. He's been on edge for the last week or two. Ever since he got back from his daughter's wedding, really."

The woman serving the meal appeared to remove the water glasses from the table. Carla said nothing more till her help had returned to the kitchen. By then, the tears had been replaced by flashes of anger.

"It could have been anyone in his rotten family. Anyone but Arlene, I mean. He saw them all again at the wedding. Told me about some of it when he came back. His drunken son, refusing to say hello when he saw him. Guy's nothing but a bum anyway, lives on the streets. Some of his late wife's family snubbing him. Other people too, I guess."

"That's when you think his mood changed?" I asked.

She nodded. "Yeah. He was upset about something. So he probably wasn't any great shakes as a family man, but hey, you'd think they could forgive and forget at a wedding, for Pete's sake."

Albert was becoming uncomfortable with these intimacies. He usually telegraphs restlessness by check-

ing his watch. He was taking a surreptitious peek at
it now. "You know, Miss Correa..." He waited for
her to correct him with a Mrs., but when she didn't,
he went on. "You know, you really don't have to tell
us these things. We hardly knew the man. It was the
sheerest accident that we happened to be the ones
who found him. I'm terribly sorry about what happened, but maybe you should save these stories for
the sheriff. He's coming here tomorrow morning, I
believe."

She looked up under lowered lids, taking Albert's
measure. "I'm afraid you're going to have to hear
this."

"Why?"

"Arlene called me late this afternoon. Jim had
given her my number when he was at the wedding.
She said your wife was pretty famous around town
for solving a murder last year and that she wanted her
to try to solve her father's too. She'd been too upset
when you called her to talk about that. Probably
doesn't think too highly of the local talent. Could be
she's right. She knew you two would be staying here
tonight, so she asked me to tell you that she needs
your help."

Albert's eyes widened. "Oh, but surely that's
not...I mean, the authorities are the ones who need
to be in charge. Grace and I aren't..."

"No, Dr. Beckmann. Arlene was very sure. She
said you're her favorite doctor and she was pretty sure
she's your favorite nurse. You've worked together for
years. She said you'd do it for her, you and Mrs.
Beckmann. She knew you would."

Albert turned toward me, looking trapped. I couldn't help feeling a surge of energy. "Of course, Carla," I said, trying hard not to sound inappropriately eager. "We'll do what we can."

THREE

MORNING FOUND US, after breakfast, entertaining the sheriff in Carla's front room. He'd asked the boys to stay in case they had something to add, but all they really added was a certain grime. We hadn't counted on an extra day. Our laundry was being recycled since we hadn't brought many clothes, what with Albert frowning over every additional ounce of luggage. Have I mentioned lately the many joys of small planes?

Carla joined us also, and if the sheriff would have preferred her somewhere else, he didn't mention it. It was, after all, *her* house. I didn't think they *made* sheriffs as young as the slim, sunburned boy who sat before us. He was trying for a beard and so far all one could say was that it was a work in progress. Far from giving him the adult aspect he apparently craved, it looked as if it had been glued on for some long-ago Halloween party and was falling off in pieces. Being fair-haired didn't help. My boys, with their thick dark hair, could have made a better show of facial adornment and they were only seventeen.

Timothy something, I think he said his name was. Pells? Maybe. He didn't live in Copper Creek, didn't know Delacroix personally. I understood why Arlene wanted us involved. She must have realized that no one in what passed for local law enforcement had any personal interest in her father. Still, Timothy, boy sheriff, made some effort to ask us the right questions.

"I understand from Joe at the auto shop that you all saw Mr. Delacroix a few days ago when you landed at the airstrip." We nodded affirmatives. "Did you happen by any chance to spot anything missing when you came back this time? A cash box, maybe? Some object? Anything of value?"

"His ring," I answered instantly. "He wasn't wearing his diamond ring. Of course, maybe it was by his bed or near a sink. I take mine off sometimes. But he wasn't wearing it."

"You never said anything about that," said Albert, surprised.

"I forgot to tell you. But I'm telling you now, okay?"

The sheriff, feeling the interview getting away from him, did his best to recapture it. "Could you describe it, please?"

I thought for a moment, visualizing the piece I'd only glimpsed. "Very ornate," I recalled. "Intricately carved with some kind of design. European antique jewelry, I'd guess. A large circular-cut diamond set off-center." I looked at the boy hopefully. "Did you see it anywhere?"

He shook his head silently and I knew he was trying to picture something he could barely imagine. Apparently he gave up. "What else?"

"The knives, Mom," added Spence from a flowered wing chair in the corner. He was slumped in the cushions, an ankle propped on one bony knee. "Don't forget the knives."

"Knives?"

"Hunting knives," said Albert, sipping at the coffee he'd brought with him from the dining-room table. "Our sons noticed two of them in the case when we came on Sunday and they were both gone. Yesterday, Spence found one of them under a bush off to the side of the runway. In fact..." He glanced toward the wing chair. "We decided to leave it there. Grace did, anyway. So no one's touched it. None of us, anyway. You can probably find it without much trouble."

Knives were something the sheriff understood, something that could start his juices flowing. He excused himself to use the phone and we could hear him relaying instructions to someone about finding a missing knife under a bush. When he returned, Carla was waiting for him with a cup of coffee.

"Lots of milk, Tim. Figured you'd like that."

"Yes, ma'am," he said with the sweet smile he'd probably used on his third-grade teacher. "Thanks."

I thought it was time I took Arlene's instructions seriously. She'd asked for more help than she was getting. "Excuse me, Sheriff, but may I ask, did *you* find anything that might imply something was missing? I mean, we really didn't look through his things. Finding the body was about all any of us could handle for one morning."

He slowly tasted his coffee. Finally he said, "Well, I suppose it don't hurt none for me to tell you. Yes, ma'am, we did find things missing." He sat up a bit straighter. "We found everything missing. All the papers were out of his file cabinets, his drawers had been completely cleaned out, probably dumped out. Wallet was in his pocket, believe it or not, with the money in it. Don't know why the thief didn't take that too. I didn't know nothing about that ring, of course."

"His drawers. You mean his desk drawers? Or his personal drawers? Bathroom drawers? What?"

"All those. There wasn't nothing left anywhere. Hey, maybe he cleaned all that out himself. Maybe he was packing up. Did he say anything about moving?"

"Not to us. Carla?" Carla shook her head. I frowned, disbelieving. "Sheriff, we would have noticed if the place was the kind of mess you're describing. Could the robber have come *after* we left the FBO? I mean, it looked really undisturbed."

"You wouldn't have noticed unless you looked, ma'am. The drawers and everything was put back neat as you please. We looked 'cause it's routine. That's when we saw everything gone." He surreptitiously consulted a 4x6 card full of typing, a crib list of questions, I guessed. I wondered how long he'd had this job. "Back to your observations. Did any of you notice anything else of interest?" He looked around the room expectantly. "Anything out of the ordinary?"

I thought of the broken window blinds, the ancient magazines, the dilapidated building. What was ordinary?

"Grace?" prompted Albert. He deferred to me for critical details.

"Well," I said slowly, thinking. "There was the phone call." The sheriff's baby face showed a bit of interest. "He got a call just before we left for Carlsbad. He seemed to be sort of yelling but I couldn't hear what he was saying. He slammed down the phone. I think the call upset him. Maybe you can trace it. Sunday, around, oh, eleven or so."

He dutifully wrote down the information. "Okay, thanks. I'll do that. Anything else?"

I shook my head. Sure he'd do that. Just no time soon.

He polished off the cup of mostly milk and replaced it neatly on a painted wood side table. "Ms. Correa? Anything you'd like to add?"

Carla was still in her housecoat, a wonderful caftan of oranges and yellows. In the straight armchair from the dining room, she had the air of presiding over the meeting of the board, one located for tax purposes in the Caribbean. "I don't think so, Tim. I hadn't talked to Mr. Delacroix for several days. Of course..." The obvious suddenly occurred to her. "When did he die, do you know?"

I wanted to know that too. None of us had touched the body, so any stiffness or lack thereof would have escaped us.

"Monday night or early Tuesday morning, the thinking is. We may be able to get a better call on that when we hear from the coroner. By the way, Ms. Correa..." He stood, putting papers and a pen in various pockets. "Do you have a gun in the house?"

She stiffened slightly, sensing the implication. "Sure do, Tim."

"Could I have it, please?"

Carla disappeared for the briefest moment and returned with a small-caliber nickel-plated revolver. It must not have been far away. She handed it to the sheriff without comment. He looked it over, checking the chamber.

"I'll need to take this with me, ma'am."

"That's fine, Tim."

"Thanks." Then he bent to take his cup and saucer into the kitchen but Carla stopped him.

"No, no, I'll take care of that. You run along now."

He put the cup down, unsure of the next move. "Well, okay then, thank you. I'll be going." He looked with some embarrassment toward Carla. "All my condolences, ma'am."

Why is it, as a mother of boys, I feel this strong maternal sense toward all male young ones? This one was a sweetheart, reluctant to acknowledge that he knew about the relationship between his hostess and James Delacroix. Carla Correa, however, didn't share my tender feelings. Her eyes flashed. "Good-bye, Tim," she said pointedly.

Abashed, he fled the house.

The look on Carla's face was what I can only call complicated. Amused, all-knowing, worldly. Remember those figures in old-time arcade fortune-telling machines? Plastic women with scarves and earrings and a wise, mysterious smile? You fed them your coins and they came up with handfuls of answers. I knew Albert was anxious to leave as early as possible to avoid any afternoon storms, but I wasn't going till this particular seer told me what lurked in her crystal ball.

I grinned at her knowingly. "Just out of curiosity, was that your only gun?"

"Of course not. A woman out here alone? But don't worry, I didn't shoot Jim."

It was time to get rid of Paul and Spence. She wouldn't talk freely in front of kids. I shooed them outside, telling them a short hike would do them good before being cooped up in the plane, but Spence, at least, wasn't fooled. He glared at me just before heading out. Paul had never really been with the program. He'd been buried in a book about an Everest climb for days and was not in this or any other real world. Spence, on the other hand, was totally into the murder. He wanted to hear what this woman said. Intrigued by his interest, I promised myself to bring him up to speed about anything I learned at the first opportunity. After all, how often does your kid show any curiosity about parental doings? Even so, I chased them out.

Once they left, Albert made a point of doing the watch routine. "Can you hold this to half an hour or so? We still have to fly home."

"Sure." I looked to Carla for agreement and she nodded. "You don't have to stay if you don't want to, Albert. Carla and I'll be fine."

Faced with the possibility of missing out on something, a thoroughly hateful prospect, he backed down. "No, no, that's okay. You ladies do the talking, though. I'll just listen."

"We'll do that." Feeling the moving hands of clocks around the world all bearing down on me, I didn't waste critical time. "Tell me, Carla, when did you first meet Delacroix?"

She moved off the stiffer dining-room chair and claimed the wing chair Spence had vacated, settling in. "He moved to Copper Creek around, oh, fifteen years ago or so," she said. "I remember because that's about when I came here. Being the new kids on the block, we found ourselves thrown together now and then. Incidentally..." She studied her hands. "We weren't really, well...romantically involved.

People certainly thought we were, but in fact we weren't. Just wanted to tell you that."

Carla, I guessed, was a good bit younger than Delacroix. Of course, she could be lying about their involvement, but what would be the point? "Just good friends, huh?"

"I suppose. Not really that good. Sometimes I didn't like him much, wouldn't let him come around. He could have a pretty short fuse. Once we didn't speak for at least six months. But I usually gave in eventually. He was lonely, and I wasn't exactly turning the cream of Copper Creek society away at the door. You can't avoid a person very well in a small town."

Her caftan blended with the floral upholstery, making her face disappear into the pattern like one more flower. What I really wondered was what had brought *her* here, but I was reluctant to ask. "So...why did he come to this town? Any idea?"

"His wife had died quite a few years before. He was left with two kids, Arlene, who you know, and Del. His boy. I guess he waited till they were out of the house and then came here. The FBO and an old hangar were for sale and he bought them. Fixed them up once, I understand, though you'd never know it now. He bought other properties as well, a couple of buildings here and some in the next town over." She crossed her legs, apparently deciding whether to continue on the same track. "I always had the feeling he had a fair amount of money. Of course, he bought all those Cadillacs. But even without that, I knew he had rent and stuff coming in from a lot of places." She made a wry face. "Not that he ever paid me back for all the meals I made him. Once in a blue moon, he took me to the next town for a steak. Guy was cheaper than a three-dollar watch.''

"Any idea where the money came from?"

"Once he told me he'd hit it big in the city. Some major land deal, he said, that eventually became the city's general aviation airport. A lucky break. I think he had a smart partner. Either that or a rich one.''

The phone rang. I waited for her to answer it but she let it go. "I don't want to waste your time,'' she said in response to my raised eyebrows. "They can leave a message.'' I can never do that. A ringing phone, to me, is a royal summons, but then Carla and I didn't have much in common. "Well then,'' I said. "We were talking about his land deal.''

"Yes. He had a partner, he said. Couldn't have swung it without him. Marty something or other.''

Albert, up till now sitting quietly with his coffee, suddenly sprang to life. "Marty? Martin Hazlett?''

"Yeah, maybe. That sounds sort of right.''

He moved to the edge of the chair, pleased to be able to add something useful. "I know him. You've met him, Gracie. The guy's a legend of sorts. There's always lots of talk about him around the airport and the word is that he was involved in its development. It's a long story.''

That sounded like a bit of a leap to me. "C'mon, you don't know if it's the same man. Must be a ton of Martins or Martys involved in aviation somehow.''

Carla was chewing her bottom lip, waiting for me to finish. "No, your husband's right. Now that I hear the name, I recognize it.'' She shook her head, amazed. "Is this a small world or what?''

Albert had relaxed once more into his recliner and was staring out the window. "Flying is. A small world, I mean.'' I waited to hear more but that was it for him. Later, through headphones, I would get more of whatever story currently had him wondering.

I was feeling stiff from too much sitting. I'd thrown in shorts for the trip, hoping for warm enough weather to wear them, and had them on now with a pair of tennies, no socks. The welting from Carla's upholstery was etched into the back of my legs. As an excuse to move, I walked to the window to check for the boys, who were nowhere in sight. The skies had brightened since yesterday. In the distance were the rolling hills of New Mexico, dirt and scrub close-up, blending to a Georgia O'Keeffe landscape from here. I knew there were other houses around, but none were directly visible through the large front window. A lonely view. Not depressing, just empty. Why would a man with money choose this remote spot? Scenery alone wouldn't do it.

''Tell me about his family, or whatever you know about it,'' I said, returning to the chair and my concentration. ''I'm sure I'll have to call you later with all the questions I can't think of for the moment, but maybe we have time for a family history. Do we?'' I asked Albert.

''Ten minutes,'' he said, and meant it.

''Okay,'' said Carla, smoothing the caftan over pleasantly rounded thighs. The morning sun was kind to a face no longer young, softening the lines till they lost focus. I realized that this woman must have enthralled many men.

''You know Arlene,'' she began. ''As I said, he has one other kid, older than she is. Del, they call him. I think his real name is Gunther. Never met him.

The guy's a loser, a drunk. Called for money now and then. Jim had nothing good to say about him.''

"Ever talk about their mother? His wife?"

"Some. Lois was her name, I think. She died, don't remember of what, about thirty years ago. He had to raise the kids alone till they left home. She was his high school girlfriend. They married after he came back from the war."

I flashed on the old military magazines in the FBO. "The war, huh? Second World War, I assume."

"Right. Army. Bragged about being one of the men who defended Bastogne. He got ribbons and stuff for that. But the heroic part was later. Think he said he spent most of the war pretty well cooped up in England. Hated it. Said he was young then and wanted to see some action before there was no more action to see."

"So James Delacroix was a hero," I said thoughtfully.

"Well," Carla demurred. "Maybe yes, maybe no. I tried to look up his name once in a book about the siege. Quite a story it was, too. End of 1944, early '45. There were eighteen thousand men in Bastogne and forty-five thousand enemy troops trying to take them. Stubborn mules refused to surrender." She smiled ruefully. "Is that Jim or isn't it? But in any case, couldn't find his name in the book's lists. Of course, I may have missed it." She paused, her face darkening. "And he may perfectly well have lied about the whole thing."

What was she trying to say about a man who'd just been killed? Or executed? Did she ever like him at all? And who was she anyway? This was too much input for one morning. My head was reeling and we still had the rest of the flight ahead of us. I needed to process what we'd learned. We thanked our hostess profusely and, while Albert paid the tab, I collected the luggage, such as it was. My attempts to change all the beds were rebuffed. Maria Lena was returning to do the house, according to Carla, and would have been insulted.

Before we left, I put twenty dollars under the clock, which I suspected would not insult her at all.

FOUR

"PAUL, HAVE YOU called the camp yet? Millie, did the roofer ever show up and give us an estimate?" I checked my list, standing in the middle of our great room where we did most of our living. "Albert, are you going to be back for our dinner party Saturday night? And Spence, didn't you say your new sneakers—and I use the term advisedly for those canvas shoes that cost as much as our first house—had a cut in them?" I looked up to see if everyone was paying proper attention to me—and guess what? I was quite literally talking to a wall. Sunlight glinted from a polished rosewood desk, bouncing off a brass letter opener to spill across the Herez carpet. It was unnaturally quiet. Not a soul was left in the room. They'd all been there a minute ago. I felt like a general whose troops had hightailed it over the nearest hill at the first hint of danger. It figured.

All the details of a complicated household had now been delayed by two critical days. I'd expected to be home by Tuesday lunch at the latest. Instead it was Thursday morning and everything was running behind. We'd come back to dozens of messages, all transcribed by Millie, who never met a phone call she didn't like. Do not expect to dial our house and leave a simple, preferably electronic, message for any of us. There are enough phones around to make sure that Millie can grab one before the voice messaging can pick up. That way, everyone has a nice obligatory little chat with our housekeeper, like it or not. Occasionally, someone asks if there isn't something I can do about this. I just laugh.

We'd managed to talk to Arlene, no small feat since our trajectories were crossing. She was still in Copper Creek seeing to her father's final arrangements, staying, of course, with Carla. Albert told her about the envelope Delacroix had handed him to give to her and promised to leave it in her hospital mailbox. He repeated Delacroix's explanation, that it was music. The silence on the other end of the phone, he guessed, meant Arlene found that idea as farfetched as he did.

Leaving the package there for her was really no problem. Albert, still on his sabbatical, had no particular reason to go to the hospital, at least not for another month, when his sabbatical ended, but he tended to check in now and then anyway just to see what was going on. The Department of Medicine was in the capable hands of his second in command while Albert finished up the work he'd started late last year. The plan originally had been to study disease control in a third-world country, still unspecified, but things had changed. The third world, metaphorically speaking, turned out to be our own backyard. My mother had been nothing if not relieved.

The disease that had claimed Albert's total attention for the last half year or so was not exotic, unpronounceable, or rare. It was, in fact, ancient. The world had thought they had it licked. Then tuberculosis came back with a vengeance, sometimes drugresistant, sometimes AIDS-related, always deadly.

The scariest part, according to my husband, was

the new hot zone of virulent, drug-resistant bacteria
that had arisen over the last few years. While the
number of those cases had dropped in the United
States, they were on the rise in developing countries
and would spread worldwide in our lifetime without
serious intervention.

I had visions of Mimi dying in her lover's arms
while the gorgeous melodies of *La Bohême* emerged
from the pit. Thomas Mann's *Magic Mountain* was
on my college reading list. The real thing sounded a
good deal less romantic.

"A third of the people in the world carry the bacteria and predictions are that thirty million people
might die of it in the next ten years," Albert would
tell us, explaining why he was aborting our plans for
some memorable travel. "It's a lousy global epi-
demic. So I'm going to commute regularly to New
York, work with some people there."

"That's it? No Borneo, no Somalia, no...Ban-
gladesh?" We'd expected adventure, had already
looked into shots and prescriptions and airline reservations.

"It would have been India or Latvia or the Do-
minican Republic. And anyway, New York's an adventure!"

Yeah, right. Beaten out by the half *billion* people
expected to catch this disease in the foreseeable future. What a drag. But we'd met Albert in New York
three or four times during the last few months and
done wonderful New York things. As penance for our
lost *National Geographic* experience, Albert was terrific about getting tickets for sold-out shows and the
boys found great museums full of such things as float-
ing holograms and vintage television programs they

could call up and watch. But face it, it wasn't the same. Admittedly, I hadn't been altogether thrilled at the idea of spending six months under a thatched roof with two kids and no plumbing, but still I felt let down and let people know it. My family, pointedly I thought, gave me a T-shirt that said, "The more you complain, the longer God lets you live."

The change of plans meant I was constantly trying to remember Albert's schedule. We'd invited a colleague of his, Eli Finer, to have dinner with us and my unmarried tennis friend, Sarah Jane, Saturday night. My husband considered this sort of fix-up arrangement ill-concealed meddling and of course it was, but I still needed him to be there. Not in New York.

Now, with no one around to organize, and feeling overwhelmed, I sat down to consult my weekly calendar. I had a deadline coming up on an article about high-altitude adaptations, due at a sports magazine I sometimes wrote for. The twins were getting ready to start their summer jobs as junior counselors at a computer camp for elementary school kids and needed to touch base with the camp management before school was out for vacation. As the one in charge of logistics, I needed to be clued in. And, not incidentally, I'd just been given a murder to solve. James Delacroix had flitted in and out of my dreams every night since we'd found his body spread-eagled across the car. I usually dreamed he was driving a white Cadillac over a cliff. I'd wake up in a silent scream, trying to warn him. Arlene was a sweet woman, unassuming and competent. I wanted very much to help her and the longer one waited after a murder, the colder the trail became. And okay, I wanted the action. On those rare occa-

sions when there was any time left, I allowed myself
to have a life.

"Earth to Mom?"

I looked up at three young men, two of them mine.
I hadn't even heard them come in. All three were
standing in front of my chair at something like military attention.

I heard a voice ask, "Are you back with us?"

"Under duress. What can I do for you?"

Paul took the lead. "We wanted you to meet
Lawrence. Larry, if you want. Larry Leake. Only
we're going to call him Lawrence at camp so the little
kids will treat him like a genius, because he is one."

The boy was a good three inches shorter than the
twins, dressed in clothes so hopelessly square they
looked like hand-me-downs from some fashion-
challenged adult. His glasses were thick, enough so
that I suspected he'd be craving contacts soon if he
didn't already. A thin, long-necked boy with a prominent Adam's apple, he probably wasn't bothered by
calls from girls. I found it touching that my boys,
usually somewhat judgmental about looks and
clothes, had obviously suspended that judgment here.
Lawrence apparently had the one thing that mattered
more to them than cool duds. The boy probably knew
his way around computers.

I closed my calendar on a lot of unfinished business, stood up, and offered my hand. "How are you,
Lawrence? Do you go to school with these unfortu-
nates here?"

"Nope." "He doesn't, Mom." "No, ma'am."
They were all correcting me at once.

"Where then?"

"Rolands High." The nearby public high school.

Albert, an Easterner, had insisted on private school for our boys, but the public schools in the neighborhood were far from terrible. If Lawrence, aka Larry, was any example of Rolands students, I could only be favorably impressed. Something about the open way he met my eyes and answered my questions was poised and appealing. "Paul and Spence and I are all going to be counseling the first six weeks at Comp-and-Camp," he added. "If we survive the orientation."

"So you met there?" I asked.

"Not really." Paul was taking over since Spence, unexpectedly, had wandered off and was rifling through the mail, none of which could possibly interest him. "We met a while back. You know, he comes with his dad to spray our trees."

I remembered then, though only vaguely, that Albert had hired a new service recently.

"Leake Tree Service, Mom," prodded Paul. "That's his dad. Lawrence will be coming with him sometimes to help this summer too, when he isn't doing the camp thing with us."

"I'm Jesse Leake's son," added Lawrence hopefully. He wanted the name to matter.

"Of course I remember," I lied. I knew most of the people who worked all the various jobs for us in the growing season, but Albert had hired this one. The tree man, as best as I could recall, was a sallow-skinned guy with eyes that perpetually squinted, probably from spending his days with toxic chemicals. His son was a good deal better looking even with the Adam's apple and geeky clothes. Jesse Leake. Okay, I'd fix that in my head.

"Well, that's lovely. Is your dad into computers too, Lawrence?"

"No." He hesitated as though he wanted to add something more, but then thought better of it. "He...isn't." His eyes fastened on a photo of *Eight-two Juliet,* our deceased plane, framed on Albert's desk nearby, and he grinned suddenly. "He does that, though. He's been learning to fly for quite a while now. Doesn't have a lot of time for it, though." He seemed pleased to have found a connection. I hoped he felt that that similarity between us evened the playing field. Kids are not oblivious to status. Far from it.

Spence's voice sounded from across the room just as conversation was becoming strained. "Mom, I need to talk to you." The tone was laced with hostility. The other two boys looked at each other and tacitly made their move, exiting stage left.

I waited till they were gone and said pleasantly, "What?" My conscience was clear. I hadn't done anything to make him think I was more stupid than usual. In the eyes of a teenager, parents dumb down at the rate of ten IQ points an hour.

"You know I want to work on this murder." His voice was half an octave higher than usual, his regular stress indicator. "You promised you'd keep me updated but you haven't said a thing about what you learned after we left Carla's house."

I could no longer figure this child out. I never knew what would make him angry, nor was I sure of the proper response. Should I try to smooth things over or stand up to him? I played for time. "Just out of curiosity, why do you think you have anything to bring to this situation?"

"Why do *you?*"

"Because I've had a little experience in solving a crime. Because I'm a grown-up and have more life behind me than you do. Because I'm not going to be spending every day starting in two weeks teaching computer skills to rug rats."

"So. I have two weeks."

"Tell you what. You do something about that horrible hairstyle that belongs to guys I don't want to meet in a dark alley and I'll consider appointing you to the case." I felt like an inspector general, or more exactly like a rookie actor playing one in a community theater. I also knew that would stop him. He'd spent months growing that ponytail, shampooed it faithfully every morning, trimming the ends with small scissors between visits to the barber. I was asking a high price. Not that I cared if he wanted to play detective, really. It was one way to deal with the unexpected shock of finding a corpse. I just wanted... what? To regain my eroding authority over him?

Spence was stock-still. My ultimatum had clearly shocked him. "I'll...I'll think about it."

"Okay."

"*Did* you learn anything interesting from Carla? Or later?"

"Do you need the number of my hairdresser?"

He glared at me, at life, at the door, and charged out, turning in a different direction than the other boys had gone. His moods had become so volatile this year, I didn't know what to make of him. I wondered how Paul handled it, Paul who was so patient and basically sweet. They might look a lot alike, those two, but beneath the surface all bets were off.

As it happened, I *had* learned some good stuff from

Albert on the way home in the plane, things the boys couldn't hear because we were on the headsets. Between carving large loops around some weather cells he suspected of harboring thunderstorms, Albert caught me up on the man we were pretty sure was Delacroix's erstwhile partner. It was a fairly unusual tale.

It seems Martin Hazlett, the same man Carla Correa had mentioned, had been nearby in the airport store recently when Albert was buying the sectional chart that included Copper Creek. The High Flyer is a bright, modern, sunny place with lots of yellow paint on the walls and good vibes about it. People there are people who enjoy any purchase they make because any purchase they make has to do with flying.

Hazlett, who seemed to be listening to the conversation between Albert and the storekeeper, came over and introduced himself as owner of what everyone knew was the largest charter operation that flew out of our airport. He looked too young, according to Albert, to be chief honcho of such a big operation, but the looks turned out to be an illusion. The red hair and freckles softened wrinkles. Jowls were starting to form Friendly sort, though, according to Albert, with a youthful way about him, wrinkles or no.

"I couldn't help overhearing," he said with a touch of embarrassment. "You're going to Carlsbad, huh?"

"Mmm-hmm. Been there?"

"Oh sure. Many times. You going nonstop or are you touching down somewhere?"

"Probably in Copper Creek for fueling. We're flying heavy."

He laughed unpleasantly. "Great. Thought so. Say hello to the jerk who owns the place for me, okay?

Would you make a point of it? I'd really appreciate it.''

After that, it didn't take much to encourage the story. The men left the store together, found a perch on a stone wall overlooking several runways, and talked for quite a while.

According to Albert, Hazlett told him that he and Delacroix had originally planned to open a general aviation airport themselves. This was fourteen, fifteen years ago, before there was any such airport in the city. The land could have been had for very little at the time and then leased to a sizable list of aviation types who were salivating at the chance to build their dreams on the spot. There were no houses anywhere around then, no people to complain of noise or traffic, though that eventually changed. It looked like the perfect deal.

Hazlett had hocked everything but his Airedale to bring his part of the financing to the table. He'd borrowed from friends and family so mercilessly that people ran when they saw him coming. Delacroix, or so he'd said, had done the same. He seemed to have the money for his half of the deal, in any case. Hazlett didn't ask where he got it. They were close then, planning and talking big.

Until closing day, that is. When Hazlett came in to access the escrow account, the head banker rushed over looking very solicitous.

''Ah, Mr. Hazlett. You're back. I'm so sorry about your tragedy.''

Hazlett looked up from his briefcase full of paperwork. ''What?''

''Your mother. My assistant said you'd called to tell us you'd be out of town because she was hit by a car and killed. That's always so difficult, when no one is prepared for a death.''

Hazlett, wondering what in the world the banker was talking about, decided he had the wrong man and chose not to embarrass him. He simply asked for the money.

''But sir, of course it's gone. Your partner closed on that deal while you were out of town. Used all the escrow, naturally.'' Observing Hazlett's sudden pallor, he stepped back. ''He did have your power of attorney, you know.''

Hazlett didn't know. Had no clue. Turned out that Delacroix had closed on the deal himself a week earlier than planned, phoning ahead and using a forged power of attorney, and then swung around and sold the acreage to a third party who had been waiting in the wings. Same guy who owned the underlying land there now. If he suspected there was something not quite kosher about the deal, it was hardly in his best interest to ask questions.

Then Delacroix split. It took Hazlett a long time to discover the little FBO at Copper Creek, and by then he, Hazlett, had moved on to other things. His charter operation, for one.

''But that's outright fraud!'' Albert had cried, astounded at the story. ''Why didn't you have him arrested? Why didn't you sue the bank?''

Hazlett had hesitated, combing back the red hair with one hand. ''I had my reasons. Someday, maybe.''

The mouthpiece on my headset has a way of folding up, garbling speech. I fixed it, talking at the same time. ''Any reason you didn't tell me about this before I met Delacroix? The guy was obviously a sleaze, not to mention crooked as a pretzel.''

"Actually, I forgot," admitted Albert. "But maybe the whole story's a crock. Why wouldn't Hazlett have reported him? Too weird. I pretty much blew it off. Oh, and oops." Albert flinched. "I did forget to pass along that hello."

"Probably just as well, under the circumstances," I scolded. "But now we have our first serious suspect."

In fact, Martin Hazlett had just earned a prominent place on my list of people to interview. Soon. This man had a reason to hate Delacroix, albeit an old one, and he could fly. Reaching Copper Creek by car was only for retired people with lots of time and who were hopelessly lost. I really doubted that the killer, whoever he or she was, got to Delacroix by any means other than plane.

Delacroix's children were on my list too, which wasn't at the moment very long. One thing I learned last fall, however, was that suspect lists have a way of growing exponentially. A man's story is never, over a long lifetime, a simple thing, no matter how uninvolved with the world he wishes to become. That run-down FBO with its attached apartment certainly looked uninvolved. Maybe he had been in hiding, at least at first, from Hazlett. Was he in hiding from someone else as well?

In any case, the Hazlett story was a bartering coin, a little something to exchange with Spence for his long hair. I didn't know if it was worth a full-grown ponytail, but he wouldn't hear it until he'd hit the barbershop.

I told Millie about this devil's bargain over a Caesar salad lunch. Despite hating Spence's hair, she wasn't pleased. I could just hear what she'd tell my mother tomorrow morning, never mind that Spence was absolutely insisting that he be included. She'd say that I was exposing my son to grave danger just to enhance my reputation as a sleuth.

And who knew? Maybe I was.

FIVE

LOWER DOWNTOWN glowed with an early spring shine. Merchants had planted their big cement flowerpots, and red banners advertising a May arts fair blazed redundantly from every light post. I was happiest here with the lofts and shops, hotels and restaurants. Being a city girl at heart, I could feel an injection of downtown vitality drip into my soul. By noon, the streets would be filled with people pouring from their offices onto any patch of sun they could find, eating up the splendors of the season along with their lunch.

It wasn't till I veered vaguely north from the heart of town that the landscape began to shift, and when it turned bad it turned suddenly. A gentrified half block of picture framers and theatrical supply companies served as transition. From that point on, the storefronts lost their picture windows to protective boards and more than a few showrooms gave up any signs of habitation. Abandoned buildings have a certain desolation about them that no amount of sunshine can change. The same might be said of abandoned people. The area I was in now teemed with both.

I had to search for Del Delacroix here. It was the only place I could think of to look for a drifter. Arlene had dropped a fairly recent picture of the two of them into the mail for me before leaving for Copper Creek, and I had it on the seat beside me. Her brother looked the older of the two by at least a generation, even though I'd been told he was only forty, give or take. The face in the picture was surrounded by wispy thin hair of no definable color. His long, pointed chin sunk into his chest; the eyes that looked away from the camera were sad and rheumy. I wondered if I'd recognize him at all, even given the unlikely event that he was down here and our paths would cross.

Arlene had said to try the missions, the shelters, any organization that provided help to the homeless. She had no address for him. As many years as I'd lived in this city, I'd never really looked at these streets. I did now. Most of the shelters were within a few blocks of the glossy new baseball stadium, dotting the blighted streets. According to the papers, the neighborhood had had its share of murders and heroin crackdowns. I parked on a main street in front of a working garage, one of the few businesses in the area actually functioning, locked the car, and crossed my fingers.

The first sign I spotted was a large neon cross. It wasn't subtle. Well, I had to start somewhere. The front entrance was around on a side street and as I turned the corner to find it, I realized the door was ringed by some of the needier elements of society, all of whom were sprawled on the sidewalk and showing little or no signs of life. None, of course, resembled Del Delacroix. That would have been too easy.

The men were certainly not interested in me. I threaded my way through them, avoiding what little eye contact was offered me, and, Del's picture clutched in my hand, opened the metal door. A short flight of steps led me to the front desk, which was carefully ensconced behind a plate of shatterproof glass. No one was there, so I amused myself by read-

ing some of the many posted signs. A hand-lettered
card announced WOMEN'S RESTROOM OUT OF
ORDER. Under it was added in a different pen,
MEN'S TOO. It looked like it had been there a while.
A poster taped to the glass reminded any would-be
inhabitants that rooms came with obligatory early
morning chapel attendance.

A pleasant-enough-looking man came to the window and stooped to say hello through a hole in the
glass.

"Hi," I said. "Can you tell me how would I go
about finding out if a guy I'm looking for comes here?
Or is here now?"

The smile disappeared. "Nope, I can't tell you that.
We respect our people's privacy."

"Well…" I said, trying hard to find an angle. "His
father just died in another state and the family wants
him to know." It wasn't even a lie, actually. I had no
idea if anyone had told Delacroix junior about Delacroix senior, though I did have a pretty good idea that
he wouldn't be bereft to hear the news. I held up the
picture. "This is the guy."

The man, apparently a volunteer from whatever religious order was running the shelter, peered through
bifocal bottoms and shook his head. "I don't know.
Maybe he's been here, maybe not. Looks like a lot
of the men around this area. Trouble is, as it happens,
no one's in any of the rooms at the moment. Place
has pretty well cleared out for the day, it being nice
out and all. Maybe, if he were here, I could find him.
Folks'll be here for lunch pretty soon. Some are probably already lining up. If you want, you could check
just before we open the doors for the noon meal."

Dead end. There didn't seem to be much to be

gained by pushing harder. I gave him a business card
with my phone number, wrote DEL DELACROIX
across the top, and thanked him for his help. Outside
the door, the small crowd had grown. Newer arrivals
were actually on their feet and queuing up with a
quiet resignation. Passing them on the narrow sidewalk that led to the main street, I couldn't help edging
away, try as I might not to show that I felt I was
running an emotional gauntlet. I'd almost made it to
the end of the line when I felt a hand grab my shoulder.

"Hey, lady." He was young and walking on
crutches. "They got me, you see that? I was 'most
away and they got me back. Took my clothes. Left
me these shorts which ain't no good. You see that?"

I nodded, glancing at the man's new blue shorts
and his cast while edging away from his hand. I
smelled old tobacco and stale liquor. *Del Delacroix.
Ask him if he knows Del Delacroix. Ask them all.
Show the picture.* A few men in the long line were
watching. I thought about it and couldn't do it. Not
now. Not alone, surrounded this way. Outnumbered
twenty to one. Too chilling. Everyone with any experience in this part of town had assured me that
homeless people are harmless, wouldn't attack or
break into cars. It's easier to believe that when you're
in a comfortable leather chair chatting with friends
over a cold drink, surrounded by plumbing that
works.

I turned and tried not to run for the corner and on
to the main street with its welcome cars going by.
Stopping near a soaped-up window, I caught my
breath, annoyed that I'd let the situation intimidate
me. My red Aurora beckoned in the next block, wait-

ing to take me home. Across the street was another
mission. I was beginning to have the odd sensation
that it was me alone and without shelter for the night,
nothing standing between me and the mean streets but
one of these public buildings. I saw a mother with
several young children slowly making her way down
the next block. I desperately wanted to go home.
What to do? I swallowed hard and crossed the street.

Here I couldn't even get in the door. After ringing
repeatedly, a guard came to the entrance. I gave him
my newly created spiel, showed the picture, and tried
looking pitiful. He was helpful, answered most of my
questions, offered to page the man I was looking for,
but wouldn't let me in. I waited while he tried the
page a second time. Nothing happened. This was going to be more difficult than I'd expected.

"Our people are here for longer stays," he vol-
unteered when he returned. "Men that need a bed just
for the night sleep in a large dorm on the first floor.
Holds about two hundred when it has to. They have
to be out at five-thirty in the morning. Nice nights
like we're having now, they don't need the beds so
much. A good heavy rain or chill'll bring 'em in
though. You want to find someone like that, you come
here then."

I did the business card bit with him, sensing its
futility. I could just imagine standing by the door here
on a cold, wet, pitch-black morning waiting while a
couple of hundred homeless men peeled out the gate.
But obviously, that was what I was going to have to
do. Only not alone. I needed Spence. Albert probably
wouldn't be in town and if he were he'd have a fit
about the whole thing. Spence would love the adventure, but I'd used the long hair chip for this. I just

had to hope he'd care enough to hit the barbershop because, incredibly, I wanted him with me. Maybe I needed both of the boys.

By now, lunchtime, I was hungry and frustrated. I unlocked my car, looking both ways before opening the door. Once inside, I found a pinwheel peppermint in the ashtray. Not as welcome as a half-smoked cigarette would have been, but those days are over. I unwrapped the mint with one hand, a Houdini feat, and drove away from town, feeling greater relief with each mile I put between me and those pathetic streets.

The murder had to be put, for the moment, on hold. Time to give some thought to this dinner party I was having tomorrow night. Millie would do the cooking, but she insisted I plan the menu. Of course she could have done that too, and quite competently, but I think she considers it a learning experience for me. My personal and professional accomplishments are as nothing to Millie, who judges me exclusively on the merits of my domestic skills. Whatever, the supermarket stop took over an hour. I was concentrating on more than food.

Even so, I wanted the dinner to be nice—in every way. Sarah Jane wasn't a bad choice for Eli's blind date. Inspired, no, but not bad. She was originally a friend of a friend. I knew her primarily from my Tuesday-morning tennis game, but that was well enough for my current purposes. She was a little giddy, a little flirtatious, but I hoped for unplumbed depths. Whatever else, she was very, very attractive. A man could be pleased with her on his arm. She was, of course, happily single. Or maybe not so happily. She never talked about her ex except to say she was glad he never bothered to pay child support so she never ever had to say thank you to such a louse. Her finances were a subject of occasional gossip among her fellow tennis players, but we all agreed that somehow or other, it looked like she could well afford to support her own children without help.

The whole concept of a dinner party sounded truly bizarre after the morning I'd had, but that's the way it sometimes was with my life. I'd reserved a court at the club for Saturday afternoon with the idea of some mixed doubles followed by dinner at our house. Eli Finer, I'd been told, played tennis. Loved tennis. Originally European, with elegantly cut clothes and Old World manners, Finer was hard to visualize sweating or running down a lob, but Albert assured me he did both with enthusiasm.

He'd come as a visiting professor in the department and Albert had asked us to be nice to him. In the two months since he'd arrived, we'd had him for dinner three or four times. Millie loved cooking for him. This was a man who knew what he was eating, no small achievement in the fast-food world he was forced to frequent. He would take a mouthful of something complicated and taste it the way an oenophile tastes wine, eyes unfocused, all concentration on the tongue and palate. Millie would wait. Then, when he pronounced the morsel delicious, succulent, fit for a Michelin ranking, she'd break out in wreaths of smiles and hover over him for the duration of the meal. He was her pet.

He'd lost his wife and only child, a girl, in an automobile accident several years back. Why, then, not fix him up with Sarah Jane, at least in a casual way, and see if something clicked? Why not indeed. At least this time, a real dinner party, he wouldn't have to put up with our boys and their less-than-European manners. So Sarah Jane and Eli were coming Saturday night and I had to give the meal some thought.

I settled on a double rack of lamb, certainly an appropriate symbol for spring, stuffed with a pine nut dressing. New potatoes, fresh first-of-the-season asparagus, and a spinach salad should do it. Dessert would be a simple gelato. I'd have to stop at the Italian grocer's for that. A mini-antipasto would be nice with our drinks, providing I could find the right olives.

I couldn't help but wonder what the men outside the rescue mission were having for lunch today.

By the time I struggled home with all the groceries, Friday rush hour had begun, clogging up every artery to our neighborhood. Lately, it seemed, rush hour started earlier and earlier but particularly on Fridays. And particularly in May.

The twins and Lawrence, home after only a half-day at school, came out to shag the groceries. What better way to check out the new pickings and abscond with anything sweet. I always tried to make sure there was a reward for them in the bags somewhere.

I'd been so busy, I'd forgotten to look.

Then I looked.

Sure enough, Spence's hair was cut. Not shaved, not in-your-face cut, but cut.

He met my eyes over two heavy bags of groceries and I made only the slightest gesture of recognition, but it was enough. His mouth played with a tiny twitch of a smile. Then he headed toward the kitchen and I went to retrieve the phone messages.

"Your editor phoned," called Millie from the back of the room. "I wrote down most of what he wanted."

Most? Uh-oh. I went to find the message. I hadn't worked for this particular editor ever before, though I'd written some short pieces for his predecessor. Now this new one was asking for my ideas for illustrations and, if possible, could I take care of finding them? How do you illustrate high altitude? Clouds? Mountains? Tennis players gasping over an oxygen tank, high Rockies in the background? Little did this poor man know I had barely started researching this thing. That did it. The rest of the afternoon was going to be spent in my office.

I had all my papers arranged on the desk and was about to tackle an outline. I didn't always write articles with that degree of pre-organization, but some topics required it. This was one. Ah, but the best-laid plans. Albert chose this moment to come home from a flying lesson, full of unreleased tension. He was carrying his "hood," the piece of plastic that made him look like a bird with a surgically uplifted bill. When fitted on a student's forehead, the hood made it impossible to look out the window of a plane. That meant he was flying as if he were in a total cloud bank, unable to see the horizon, the ground, or anything else worth knowing. Albert was studying for his instrument rating. Gillian Morgan, his instructor, was the only thing that stood between him and death by pilot error.

"How did it go?" I asked dutifully, putting my work aside, I hoped, temporarily.

Albert threw all his flight gear on a mahogany chest, checked his watch, and headed straight for the pepper vodka. So what if it was a little early. "Let's just say, if I'd been alone in the plane and these had been actuals, you'd be out getting your widow's weeds about now."

"Tough, huh?"

"No kidding. This is one of the hardest things I've ever had to do. Gillian says I'll break through soon and think this is a piece of cake. I seriously doubt it. It just takes an unbelievable amount of concentration. You have to look at every instrument simultaneously. Practically."

"I hope she's very good at what she does. My skin washes out in black."

Albert paused to take a deep swallow of the spicy vodka. It seemed to help. "Gillian's great. She'll be a terrific airline pilot some day. I'd fly a DC-10 with her any time. She's very observant, detail-oriented. Nothing seems to get by her, though there are times I wish she'd miss a few of my more bonehead mistakes."

"Should I be jealous?"

"Absolutely. I'm mad about her."

I considered my late-afternoon glass of tonic and lime and decided in favor of it. Hardly civilized to let my husband drink alone. "Well, then, you can be jealous of me too," I said, chunking in the ice. "I spent my morning in the company of some devastatingly handsome drunks and derelicts today. They all thought I was really special."

That stopped him. No way was he going to let a comment like that go unheeded. And much as he hated what I was telling him, he insisted on hearing it all. When I was done, he slowly twirled the ice in his glass. The man was not happy.

"Why, Grace? Why? One of them could easily have jumped you. Is it absolutely necessary that you take such risks? I mean, what makes you think this is our problem? James Delacroix was a *stranger,* Arlene or no Arlene."

I didn't want to admit it, but this morning had in fact shaken me. "Well, maybe..." I began reluctantly. "Though you know I did tell Arlene I'd help." I held my glass between my knees, sitting on the very edge of the couch. "It's true, I probably should scrap it. I hardly know where to start. Okay, Martin Hazlett. I'll talk to him. That shouldn't be a problem. And he sounds like a man with motivation." I was talking more to myself now than to Albert. "You wonder how many other people our friend stiffed before he met his charming end. He probably made a habit of it. That story you told me makes Delacroix sound almost like a professional con man. But what I really need is to talk to his son and I don't know how to find him. He hated his father, that's for sure, and I'd have to know why. I need to peel this Delacroix guy back like an onion. Pull away all the layers and see what's left."

"Excuse me, but didn't you just say you'd think about scrapping this? Or did I dream that?"

"Think about it. That's all I really meant. I'd think about it." I stood up, returning the empty glass to the bar. "Now I need to hole up in my study for an hour and get this article organized."

"Go ahead," said Albert, placing his empty glass neatly beside mine. "I think I'll go see if Lawrence has come to play with me."

"Say what?"

"Lawrence Leake. The boys' friend. He's unbelievable on the computer. I love to give him a problem and just watch him work."

"Oh right. Lawrence. I've been meaning to ask you how you happened to hire his father."

"Met him at the airport, actually. When he told me what he did for a living, I grabbed him. And you know, those guys we were using last year were very erratic. Missed things. They let two of our locust trees out there in the back die off. He looked like a better bet."

"So now you like to play with his boy on the computer. How do your own sons feel about that?"

Albert, more mellow now that the challenges of the flight lesson were behind him, walked over to the back wall of the great room and switched on the IBM clone. "Doesn't bother them."

"Wanna bet?"

"No, really. They defer to him. Kid's father's a tree sprayer and he's a genius. Interesting situation. Talk about needing a therapist someday."

I started to gather up my life and prepared to hide out in the back of the house for an hour. Lawrence showed up, apparently by appointment, and I could hear him over in the corner with Albert discussing possibilities the way a chocoholic discusses picks for a pound of candy, but instead of marzipan and truffles, the choices they had before them were a world of Web sites, all of them of more than passing fascination.

"Well, Dr. Beckmann," Lawrence was saying, looking at all the hardware and caressing the keys simultaneously. "You said you wanted to learn how to access more sites on the Web and it looks like we can do all sorts of things here. Your computer's plenty fast, your modem's fast. We can have all sorts of fun. Were you ever in a war?''

"A war? Not exactly, no. I mean, I was drafted but as a doctor. Never left stateside. Why?''

"Well, we could have found old army buddies. So how about some movie reviews? Want to download graphics from the Louvre? We can get the best pieces from each floor and each department. Ever done a chat room? We could find one that talks about flying, I'll bet."

Albert laughed. "I have Gillian Morgan. I don't need a chat room."

I left my husband and his young tutor poring over the computer, sitting side by side, their faces paled by the ghostly light of the screen, and headed for my study. I could hear the whine of the mixer on high, Millie starting to make dinner in the kitchen. I decided I'd better detour to tell her we might have a guest.

One of these days I'll have to learn to be comfortable on the Internet. One of these days, I'll dress more beautifully than Albert. One of these days I'll play 4.5 tennis.

But it probably won't be any day soon.

SIX

"WHAT DID YOU DO to deserve Millie?" Eli Finer asked in his delicate accent, helping himself to another pair of medium-rare chops, the centers just rosy, from the rack of lamb. "You must have been kind to the needy in a previous lifetime."

"Either that or I kicked cats," I said so only the people beside me could hear.

"Grace!" said Albert, in the reproving tone he used with the boys when they were toddlers.

"Just kidding. I think."

We were, à la Martha Stewart, dining alfresco on this warm spring night. It had taken more than a few hours of hard work to bring the deck back to its fair-weather mode. We'd spent the afternoon sweeping away the accumulated grit of winter and retrieving cushions from the basement for all the iron furniture. The boys and their buddies, neighborhood kids plus Lawrence, were playing some form of soccer in the yard, but not near enough to disrupt the adult conversation. The sounds of their young voices served as a little night music.

The mixed doubles game had been only so-so. Eli turned out to be surprisingly competitive and Sarah Jane, used to the laid-back style of our Tuesday morning tennis, folded under the pressure. Even her comparative youth, and she was easily fifteen years younger than Eli, didn't help. Not that our visiting professor was ever the least bit discourteous, even when Sarah Jane gave up and refused to run down what was clearly a gimme. Correctly assessing the situation, he simply took over three-quarters of the court and, thus arranged, they played us from two down to a six-all tie. I decided if they won the tie-breaker, it would be a good omen for a possible relationship. They lost.

Conversation was better once the meal was over. As a serious epicure, Eli really wanted to concentrate on the food. I'd insisted that no one change, so we ate in our comfortable tennis togs. By the time Albert was ready to pour small brandies, the heavy meal, the relaxed clothes, and the mellow evening conspired to lull us all. Well, almost all. It was Eli who changed the mood. He'd simply been waiting for a quiet moment. "Arlene tells me you're working on her father's murder," he said, sitting the least bit forward in his chair.

Albert started shaking his head before the sentence was finished. "No, no, no, that's not true. Grace originally agreed to do a bit of detective work on it, but she's changed her mind now. Too busy." I loved the way he was speaking for me, but I was too full and comfortable to fight back.

Eli frowned, polishing his glasses very carefully on a corner of the napkin. "Actually, I'm sorry to hear that," he said. "I was hoping you two might be of some help to me."

The boys chose this moment to come clattering across the deck heading for the kitchen and some cold drinks. They returned with cans of pop and retreated to sprawl across the built-in benches at the other end of the deck.

"Hey, guys," I called, annoyed at the interruption.

"We could do without the pleasure of your company here."

"Mom, like we could care less what you all are saying," Spence shot back. "Just carry on. We'll be through in a minute. The grass is too wet to sit on."

I turned to Eli and, by extension, Sarah Jane. "Sorry. Spence has been an incredible pain lately." I was talking sotto voce but wouldn't have cared if Spence had heard.

Eli patted me gently on the hand. Since I first met him, I've been entranced by his Old World gestures and his soft, almost whispered voice. "It's all right, Grace. I understand what's bothering him. We had a bit of a talk before dinner. Everything will work out for the best."

I looked at Albert whose expression denied all knowledge, and then back at Eli.

"Later," Eli whispered. Then he went on as if no one else were there.

"The police have been to see me," he said, trying to sound casual. "Somebody, a guest at Arlene's wedding apparently, saw me arguing with this Delacroix person. Your corpse friend. They contacted the New Mexico sheriff and he asked for their help. They—the *politzei*, that is—decided they wanted to know more about it."

"Oh Eli, how dreadful!" I was truly upset for him, such a gentle man for a nasty confrontation. Or so he seemed. "I didn't notice a problem," I said.

Albert shook his head. "Nor did I."

Sarah Jane, not one of the invited guests at this mystery wedding, sat back and started playing with her French manicure.

Eli stared into the distance where thunderclouds were gathering. They were mirrored in his eyes. "The socially anxious Mr. Delacroix was wearing a ring that looked for all the world like one that had been in my mother's family for many generations," he said quietly. "Isn't that amazing? I asked him where he'd bought it and he became immediately hostile. Quite surprising, really. Started yelling at me that I was implying he was a thief and, of course, I'd been implying no such thing."

"I know that ring," I said. "I saw it once. Very unusual."

"And just like the one I remember."

"Maybe your mother sold it. Can you ask her?"

Eli looked down, his hands overlapped on the table. His voice was low. "Unfortunately, no. I can't. None of my family survived the war. I was sent away to Switzerland and eventually to England and then America. It took many brave people and a good deal of money to save my pitiful little life. The last hug I gave my mother...I was four years old. That was it, I'm afraid."

None of us said a thing. I noticed the boys on the other side of the deck were also quiet.

"The ring is gone, Eli," I said at last. "It was missing from the body."

He grunted softly. "Gone, is it? Ah, just as well. The thing is a Black Hand, a kiss of death." He became suddenly angry. "I hope it's buried deep in some filthy hole, some slimy pit, that it's irrevocably lost. My mother died in the camps. My aunt was captured by the Nazis in France because of it. And now Delacroix. And the police questioning *me!* I hope I never see the despicable thing again. Anywhere."

The sun had disappeared and with it the warmth of the day. It was still too early in the season to sit out after dark without at least a sweater. I went over to the boys who, judging from their faces, had obviously overheard the entire conversation and shooed them in to the house's lower level, leaving the great room for us. We wandered inside through the large wood and glass patio doors that led directly there, and settled down around the marble table. There was no way to retrieve a sense of Saturday night fun anymore and we didn't try.

Albert was looking concerned, the head of the department protecting his visiting professor. "Well, so what were you able to tell the police?"

Eli shrugged, thick eyebrows shooting up. "What could I tell them? I didn't know the man. I was amazed at his hostile reaction to my question about the ring. We argued briefly and that was it. A few angry words. The police seemed satisfied."

"Any idea who told them about you?"

"A relative of Arlene's, apparently. Her mother's sister, I think. She apparently overheard our conversation."

Sarah Jane was so out of the loop, her eyes were glazing over. Granted, she'd had some wine with dinner, but that wasn't all. Sarah Jane was almost always happier talking about Sarah Jane. That plus the fact that any chemistry between her and Eli had been left behind on the tennis court. This wasn't her night.

"I'm really beat," she said, yawning. "The game did me in. That and the wonderful meal. Would you hate me if I ate and ran?"

"Of course not," we all muttered very honestly.

"May I follow you home?" asked Eli, ever proper.

"No, please. I live just a few blocks away. As Grace knows." I had a hunch she wasn't very happy with me having fixed her up with a man so unappreciative of her charms. Maybe Albert was right about the sins of meddling.

We dispatched her with barely concealed enthusiasm, waving at the car till it was out of sight. Then we returned to the chairs and couches, adding a little brandy to the glasses.

"Okay, Eli, now," I said.

"Now what?"

"Now I want to hear the story of that aunt, the one who died in France. The one you say was killed by the ring."

Albert looked uncomfortable. "Maybe he doesn't want to talk about it. Maybe it's painful. Of course it's painful."

"But he has to tell us. He brought it up. You did, didn't you?"

Eli nodded. "You're right. I did." He sipped his brandy thoughtfully. I had the feeling he needed to talk, was basically grateful for the audience. "Sit back, though. It's not a pleasant story. And it's not short." As if to underscore its length, he sank deeper into the brown leather chair and cradled his snifter with both hands.

Eli's aunt, his mother's baby sister, had been a young married woman living in France when the war broke out, he told us. As Jews, she and her husband were of course worried, but as idealists and humanitarians, they knew they had to stay and do what they could in the face of what had happened to their adopted country. They joined the Resistance, miraculously surviving until 1944 in the most harrowing of circumstances. By then, however, they knew their luck was running out.

Being both Jewish and members of the underground put them in double jeopardy. They'd managed to get word through to family in the United States, the family that had by then taken the young Eli Finer into their lives, that, though they felt they were now in real danger, they thought they might be able to buy their way out of the country. Eli had arrived, by some miracle, with his family's jewels and some money hidden in among his things.

So, using the jewels and adding a respectable amount of hard currency from the American relatives, the family set in motion an elaborate plot. They sent a box of homemade *lebkuchen* to one of their own, an officer stationed in southern England. Under the cookies, in an ingenious false bottom packed with cotton, were the jewels and money. They had arranged for couriers to reach the young couple with the means for their escape.

The package never arrived. Or at least it was never received. The officer asked about it but could learn nothing. He reported it missing, did what he could to trace it with no success. It was spring. The Allies were gearing up for the D-Day invasion in June and the mails were disrupted, at one time completely delayed, at least for outgoing mail. He was, for a critical period of time, unable to tell the American family that the plans had gone awry and ask that they send another box if at all possible. In fact, he continued to look long after the invasion, long after the end of the war as well, but the package never surfaced. So much money, such priceless valuables, and they had completely disappeared.

In France, the amazing combination of cleverness and chance that had saved the young couple for four desperate years came apart. In a safe house, awaiting word from America, they were betrayed by a virulent pro-German neighbor who noticed strange comings and goings in the house next door. One morning she knocked on their door, asking to borrow a grater. They made the mistake of answering and that way she learned they were both in the house. When they went to get it, she stepped aside and the Gestapo forced their way in.

No one knew where they were taken or precisely what happened, and since they'd been so active in the Resistance, no one wanted to know. They were never seen again. Neither were the family jewels that had been sent to save their lives. Until last month, until Arlene Delacroix's wedding. Eli Finer, as a six-year-old, had watched while an interesting asymmetrical diamond ring was included in a mysterious package. He'd played with it for a minute, turning it to reflect the colors of the sun, before the adults had taken it from him.

He saw that ring again on the finger of James Delacroix. Or thought he did.

"Could you really be sure it was the same ring?" I asked.

He looked in my general direction, but vaguely. His hands opened in the universal gesture of bewilderment. "I don't...I mean, how can I be sure? We're talking fifty years ago, more than fifty. I was a child. But the ring made an impression on me, that I can tell you. Particularly when I saw the outrage and horror my adopted family felt when they learned that the package was lost."

Albert had listened to the story with his eyes closed. His Jewish father, he often told me, raised him with constant stories of the Holocaust. Lest he forget, lest he think for a single moment that being only half a Jew would have saved him had he lived in Nazi Germany.

"Memory is a funny business," Albert said at last. "Things that are fraught with emotion can be remembered for a lifetime, even when the things themselves are totally inconsequential. Personally, I believe that it was the same ring. You must trust yourself."

Eli stood up, brushing out the wrinkles in his finely tailored pants. He laughed bitterly. "Trust myself? Then what am I supposed to do? Dig up a corpse and shake it till it tells me how it got the ring? And where it is now? Come, Albert, Delacroix's death was the end of the line for this story. It's over. As is this delightful evening that I've just managed to ruin." He came over, taking my face between his hands and kissing my forehead. "Thank you, Grace. You're a beautiful woman and a charming hostess." He hesitated for a moment. "Perhaps not so good as a matchmaker, but you have many other skills. And tell Millie that her dinner was superb. And the menu perfect."

My menu, I thought darkly.

Albert rose to see his guest to the door, but held him back for a moment. "Eli, just one other thing," he said. "About Spence..."

"Oh yes." He started slowly toward the door, his hand on Albert's shoulder. "Your son doesn't want to go to college and can't find a way to let you know. So here I am and it looks like it's become my job to tell you. He says you're both totally into such things as entrance exams and applications and the like and there's no way you'll be able to handle the idea.''

"Oh, don't be silly," I said, moving with them toward the front entrance. "I'm sure you misunderstood. This is a kid who's a National Merit semifinalist. Of course he wants to go to college. Paul too."

"Paul, yes. Spence, no. At least not next year."

Albert found Eli's tennis gear where we'd stashed it and handed it to him, the racket cover and visor both marked with common sports logos. The man had spent as much time in Europe as he had in the States for the last three decades, but American brand names still delighted him. "And just when," Albert said, deadly calm, "did Spence tell you all this?"

"Before dinner. You were all busy in the other room. And 'all this' didn't take more than five minutes."

"Well, I'm sorry, but he doesn't have that option. Of course he's going to college."

I'd been quiet, trying to absorb Eli's statement as we walked through the house. What he'd said answered many questions about Spence's temper these last few weeks. I wasn't quite ready to back up my husband's fiat. "Now, Albert, we'll have to think about this. Don't make any more of these ex cathedra pronouncements till we have a chance to talk, will you please?"

He glowered silently.

Our fraternal twins had been a constant surprise to us since the day they were born. In some ways, they were no more like each other than any two brothers would be, but in other ways it was hard to remember they weren't formed from a single egg. Studies—and I read them all—seemed to show that the IQs of fraternal twins are closer to each other than are those of ordinary siblings. Forget genetics. Apparently, just being in the womb at the same time was enough to produce startling similarities. Paul and Spence were both bright, had IQs less than five points apart. From that point on, however... It looked like we had a problem on our hands.

The good nights were uncharacteristically muted. We waited till Eli's car pulled out of the driveway, then locked the door behind him. We were both too tired to talk about this bombshell right then, but it was clearly on both our minds. Albert left the lid off the toothpaste, for him unheard-of. I went to bed with my tennis socks on and had to climb back out to peel them off. The air from the open window smelled oddly chemical, wafting in from some unknown, toxic source. Nothing was as it should be.

But we were too tired not to sleep. The smell of smoke didn't become strong enough to wake us till after two in the morning. I found myself dreaming that I was barbecuing at the grill and the meat I planned to cook was sitting on top of a car, a big white car. A Cadillac. I kept reaching up for it but it was bloody and wet and kept slipping to the other side of the car roof, away from my hand. The piece I'd managed to put on the grill was already charred black, burning.

Burning. I sat up suddenly, pushing on Albert's back. "Wake up, quick, something's burning. Something's on fire."

Albert groaned and turned away. Now there was no question that the smoke was strong and close by. I shook him hard, then pulled his arm, pounding on his shoulder. "Wake up, darn it! We're on fire!"

That did it. He sat up wild-eyed. I didn't wait for the realization to completely sink in. Hitting the floor hard, I grabbed my robe, the old pair of loafers I use for slippers, and started for the hallway and the other bedrooms. "Call 911," I shouted over my shoulder. "I'm going for the kids." I paused then after all. I needed to be sure he was functional before leaving. He was certainly awake now. His body language had assumed a crisis mode, calf muscles visibly tensed as he swung his legs out of bed. Not until he actually reached for the phone, though, did I leave to rouse the boys and Millie. There was no fire on our level. I tore into the boys' rooms, letting the doors slam against the wall. That did it. They jumped up, startled. "Fire. Get up and follow me." Then, with the boys both close behind, I took the stairs at a flyover and knocked on Millie's door.

She grunted through the door and I could hear her muttering inside. "Get up, Millie, we're on fire!" Her door wasn't locked but no way was I going to open it without her permission. I'd learned that lesson as a child. Oh heck, yes I was. I barged in. "Come on, wake up. Answer me."

She sat up in bed, her gown askew. "What did you do now? Leave something on the stove? I told you not to put papers on those burners even when you think they're cool."

"Just get up, please? We have to get out of here." The smell of smoke was becoming overpowering. When I saw the first whitish curl sneak up from the floor, I panicked. "Now!"

Albert had materialized behind us, actually dressed in pants, real shoes, and a knit shirt. Nothing as inconsequential as a fire could alter his routines. As soon as Millie emerged in robe and slippers, we headed for the front door.

"The fire department should be here any minute if 911 doesn't blow it," said Albert, gazing as if fascinated by the smoke that filled the hallway. "I don't think this is just a little problem." *Gee, no kidding.*

The source of the fire still wasn't obvious when we burst through the door, being careful to close it behind us. Once safely out on the front lawn, Albert and I worked our way around, checking any suspicious areas. Millie stood nearly motionless, watching the goings-on, shaking her head back and forth. The boys were sleepwalking, barefoot, staring wide-eyed and seeing nothing. They took after their father in sleep habits. Essentially worthless till morning.

As soon as the two of us rounded the corner toward the back of the house, all questions were answered. Well, most questions were answered. The garage was on fire, positively roaring with flames. We could see the inferno through garage door windows we'd allowed to stay as clear glass. Albert had left his car outside on the circular drive, but my Aurora was engulfed. Good-bye car. The garage abutted the house, making it easy to bring things in directly to the kitchen. Making it easy for the raging fire to enter the kitchen. I heard the sound of a cracking glass as one of the garage windows disappeared and flames burst through, hot and angry. The heat singed my face and I jumped back. At this rate it wouldn't be long before it was good-bye house.

What happened next is still something of a blur. The fire trucks arrived, first just one and then in short order one more and an official fire department car. I had done what I could. The matter was now in official

hands. Albert went toward the trucks to talk to the
men, or maybe just to watch up close. Feeling silly
in my bathrobe, I moved away, finding a place to sit
under a small maple that had only recently budded
out.

I didn't want to be with the kids or anyone else,
not feeling like I did. The hissing of water on flames
roared like a cataract. Clouds of steam rose through
the night, blowing away from me and across open lots
around us. It was all just too much, not even counting
the murder. In just one night, we'd endured Eli's terrible story, the news about Spence, and now a fire
that might well have killed us all. If a breeze hadn't
blown the smoke through our open window, we might
not have realized the danger till it was too late. Of
everything, excepting our lives, that might have been
lost, I thought first of all our photographs. The twins
as babies and toddlers. Our histories.

How could a fire have started in our garage? Albert
was positively obsessed with keeping anything flammable away from the house. So what was going on
here?

Whatever it was, I didn't want to know tonight. I
couldn't deal with it. Tomorrow would come soon
enough.

SEVEN

THE MORNING PAPERS lay opened but unread in the front hall. In the dining room, one could smell fresh coffee but nothing else, no eggs, no toast, no sinful breakfast meats. Sunday was usually a special day in our house, the day when Millie retired to her room and left the kitchen to us. We cooked what we felt like without having to listen to our resident food dictator tell us how much cholesterol was in that piece of bacon, the bit of butter on our English muffin. But not today.

None of us had had much sleep. We'd all tried to go back to bed after the firemen left but I, at least, had given it up as a bad job around 5:30 in the morning. Albert, for all his later denials, was breathing a soft, even rumble as I got up. I tiptoed around till, assembled in jeans, a black T-shirt, and a pair of sneaks, I had on enough clothes to feel decent leaving the house. Then I slipped downstairs and crept out into the morning mist.

I wanted to see the garage by the light of day. Mistake. It was a blackened frame, the windows blown out, the brick as sooty as an abandoned nineteenth-century steel mill. On one side sat my charred car. I tried to remember what I'd left inside. The registration card, of course. Insurance info. Car phone. A handful of tapes, some show tunes, some jazz, one copy of the *Pirates of Penzance* we'd picked up—where else?—in Penzance. I'd miss that. I'd left the notes I'd taken on the homeless shelters in the glove compartment, as well as my own business cards, the ones I'd been giving out in hopes one would fall into Del Delacroix's hands. It was too early in the day to look any closer.

I felt myself tear up and swiped at my eyes in disgust. Other people might mourn a car but such nonsense was beneath me. Still, we'd been through quite a lot together, and I was truly fond of her, a gentlewoman's hot rod, so...red. No car for a wimp. I suspected there were other notes in there, scraps of paper detailing my plan of attack on the Delacroix case, for example. It was likely, and if so, that was another thing I'd miss. I tended to jot things down on a little memo pad I kept in the car. That did it—I was going to write things down in a rational, cogent way from now on and put the list where it wasn't likely to get fried.

By 8:30, the four of us were assembled in some form around the table, dressed but bleary-eyed. The boys were so wiped, they barely had the energy to grunt a "Good morning." Spence had his head down on the table. Normally, I wouldn't have let him get away with that but today wasn't normally anything. Only Albert looked halfway alert.

"The fire chief said we were very, very lucky that the fire hadn't spread to the house," he said, sipping carefully at the hot coffee. He alone had communicated with anyone in authority last night. The rest of us were content to learn whatever he'd heard at one remove.

Paul had found a slightly stale blueberry muffin in the kitchen and was nibbling away at the hardened outside. "Did he also say how we happened to be so *un*lucky as to have a fire in the first place?"

"He did." Albert hesitated a moment. "He said the fire had been deliberately set."

Okay, I wasn't surprised, not really. Not surprised, maybe, but shocked and depressed. Again my eyes brimmed. "How?" was the only word I could manage.

"A flammable liquid, something related to gasoline, probably."

"Did it lead all the way into the house?" Paul asked.

Albert obviously didn't want to answer that, at least not in front of the boys. He swallowed hard. Telling one's children the truth was a point of honor with him. Of course, not necessarily *all* the truth. Just no lies. There were times I questioned that credo and this was one of them.

"Yes, it did," he responded finally. "Your mother smelled the smoke before the door to the house caught fire. Millie, thank goodness, had locked up. Otherwise, whoever it was could have splashed the gas right through the kitchen and down the front hall."

That prospect had us quiet for several minutes. I doubt that any two of us were fantasizing exactly the same scene, but we all were busy imagining our own disasters. Albert broke into the silence with a voice a touch too hearty.

"I've already hired a private detective company to keep an eye on the house. You'll probably see strange cars around from time to time." He rubbed the bridge of his nose. "Also, the fire chief will be in touch with the police today, he said. He took a number of samples around the garage area and said he'd be able to tell us what chemicals were used in due course. I imagine we'll be hearing from someone soon."

Spence lifted his head at last. "So?"

"So that's better than nothing, that's what's 'so.' Don't you want to know everything you can? I suggested he contact Detective Morrisey."

We'd worked with the detective last fall when our plane had been stolen and crashed. He was one of the world's good guys.

"Of course," Albert went on, "I suppose an intellectual curiosity is one of the many things you've decided to scrap."

That dig made Spence take his head off the table and sit up. "Oh, right. I wondered when that was going to hit the fan. I guess Dr. Finer had a little talk with you last night."

"Didn't you want him to?"

Spence shoved his chair away from the table without answering and went into the kitchen. When he returned, he had a cup of coffee, something he never drank. He took a sip of it black, grimaced, and took another.

"Yeah, I guess. I did want him to. So, are you going to be okay with this or what? I'm not going and that's that." He waited five beats before going on. "I've really decided. Paul knows. He'll be your college boy, give you somewhere to go on Parents' Weekend."

Paul looked at his brother without expression. Obviously, he'd heard this before.

The conversation had managed to pull me from images of flaming holocausts. "Are we talking forever here, child, or just for the next year? And what exactly are you planning to do with the time you've just freed up?''

"I don't know. Maybe it's not forever, but I'm not promising anything.'' His look was purely defensive, daring us to cross a line. "As to the second part of your question, maybe I'll try to help you find out who shot that Delacroix guy. Or who tried to barbecue all of us last night. Or do you think that was the work of some dumb kids who were just playing with matches?''

I ignored the last. "And after you've solved all these high crimes and misdemeanors?''

Spence lifted both arms above his head in a bravado stretch, locking his fingers, and brought them down straight in front of his chest. Then he folded them around himself protectively. "Maybe work with a carpenter. Or a contractor. The school uses a handyman on a regular basis. Maybe they'd hire me.''

"And what,'' asked Albert, "do you know about being 'handy'?''

"I could learn.''

I looked at Paul who was quietly observing the scene. "How do you feel about this?''

He shrugged. "Whatever.''

The phone rang. And rang again. It took us a moment to remember that on Sunday Millie wasn't going to beat us to the receiver. Paul took it and handed the portable to his father who said something briefly and clicked off.

"Morrisey's coming. He'll be here in about twenty minutes, he said.''

That news effectively ended the first of our "Spence and College'' sessions. There would be many more to come. I hadn't even had a chance to ask him *why* he was doing this, but it all seemed inconsequential in the face of a burning house. We cleared the table, which wasn't much of a job since only Paul had been able to eat anything. I headed for the bedroom to change into something a bit more presentable and put on a little lipstick. Morrisey didn't strike me as a man who would notice the effort women took with their looks, but then again he wouldn't be oblivious as to the outcome. I wasn't sure why I cared.

I kept the T-shirt but caught my long hair in a twist and switched the jeans for a broomstick skirt. Perhaps the effort wasn't wasted, particularly since the skirt had a nice way of flattering my figure. I finished just in time.

"Mrs. Beckmann. Grace." Morrisey walked through the door and grasped my hand. "How lovely you look."

"You mean, considering that I spent the night like Cinderella, covered with ashes?" An inappropriate giggle escaped. I was really tired.

Morrisey was in a suit and tie even early on a Sunday morning. Perhaps he'd been making a bit of an effort himself. A small, compact man with gray hair and a serious demeanor adulterated by a twinkle, he'd originally reminded me of the high school teacher who taught me Cicero and Virgil. He followed us into the great room and perched on the edge of a large chair. The boys, to my relief, had disappeared. I seemed to spend an inordinate amount of time wishing they were somewhere else.

"My men are in the garage now taking samples of everything they can find," he began. "As you know, we suspect arson."

He waited for some response but we were too out of it to help.

"This feels a little like déjà vu all over again, but have you any idea why someone tried to burn your house down?"

It hadn't been that long ago that he'd helped us survive another threat to our lives. I wondered if he thought we were hexed. "Mm-hmm," I said. "Probably. We're working on another murder."

Morrisey's smile was half amused, half incredulous. "Surely you're not serious."

Albert began the story while I went to brew another pot of coffee and transfer some of Millie's homemade cheese rolls from freezer to microwave to plate. By the time I emerged with a makeshift breakfast for the detective, the story was just winding down.

"So that's where we are now," finished Albert. "This is way out of your territory, and, of course, it may have nothing at all to do with the fire, but that's what we've been involved with. Grace, really."

Morrisey took a cheese roll, broke it in half, and then put it down. He seemed to be trying to overcome a certain reluctance. "Not so far out of my territory as you think," he said finally. "That case has come to my attention despite the fact the man was murdered in another state. I happen to know that a warrant was taken out yesterday to search your colleague Dr. Finer's apartment because of the Delacroix incident. It should be happening this morning, perhaps right now. They waited till they could find him in."

Albert sat up so suddenly, his knee slammed the table. "Morrisey! That man is a visiting professor in my department! He wouldn't even be in this city if I hadn't invited him to come. How could you do that?"

He was more agitated at this news than he'd been last night when I told him his house was on fire.

"Now, now, Doctor, take it easy," said Morrisey. "We're not hurting him. We heard...well, we received a call about his behavior toward this Delacroix at a family wedding. According to the source, everything was missing at the Copper Creek FBO and they want to know what was taken. They're searching everyone associated with the case. The sheriff down there has checked with us. It's his case but we're helping."

Albert was glowering. He rose and began to pace. Then he turned to Morrisey. "Would you do me one favor, please? Would you call the station and see what happened? See if Dr. Finer needs me?"

It helps to have understanding friends on the police force. Morrisey went without hesitation to the phone on the other side of the room and when he returned, he was all business. "They've taken him into the station."

"Why?"

"Apparently they found one thing of considerable interest in his apartment. They found a ring. A ring they think belonged to Delacroix."

The ring! "What did he say?" My breath started coming fast. "How did he explain having it?"

"He apparently told the officers that he had no idea how it got there."

That did it. The fire had definitely receded to second place. Morrisey left his men working in our garage and, after introducing me to the man in charge, departed for the station. Albert, in his own car, followed closely behind. He wasn't about to let poor Eli face this nightmare alone. As for me, I had nowhere

to go and even if I had, I couldn't have gotten there.
There was this little problem about wheels. Second
on the to-do list. Call the insurance company and rent
or buy a car.

I'm an inveterate list-maker. No matter how dis-
organized, read frantic, my life, I always feel I have
things in hand if I can make a list and start crossing
things off. After watching the men leave for more
exciting venues, I went back to the dining room with
pen and lined legal pads, poured myself a cup of
green tea, and started writing.

The fire was line one. Find out who was trying to
burn our house down with us in it. The insurance
company was still line two. I decided buying a car
was a little precipitous for the moment and settled for
finding a rental yet again (I'd had to go this route
before). Then there was the article I'd been assigned.
Maybe the editor of the tennis magazine would let me
move the deadline back a couple of weeks. After all,
he had asked for all those pictures. Should I talk to
the school psychologist about Spence? He'd ask me
how I felt about my kids going dutifully to college
and I wouldn't be able to answer. Well, scratch that
for now. I decided not to give that meeting one of the
lines on my legal pad.

The garage would probably have to be rebuilt, or
if not, significantly repaired. I added the contractor's
name. We'd probably have to clear any reconstruction
with the police, maybe waiting till they were through
with the crime scene, but it wouldn't hurt to set up a
consultation.

I was beginning to get the kind of headache all the
tea and coffee I'd had wouldn't cure. Spence arrived

just as I was gagging down some Advil. He nodded toward the pad of paper, sliding into his usual seat.

"Have you added 'Solve the murder' to that list?"

"Not as such, no. I think that needs its own separate page."

He reached across the table, tore the page I'd been working on off the pad, and slid the tablet to his side. He gestured for the pen and I rolled it across. "Okay, there." He scrawled DELACROIX MURDER across the top, underlining it with a single broad stroke. "Now what are we going to do first?"

"We?"

"We."

I thought for a minute, rubbing at my thudding temples. "How about all the people 'we' need to interview? There's his son, if we can ever find him." I watched Spence write on the top line. "Probably it wouldn't hurt to talk to his daughter too. Arlene. Then Martin Hazlett, the man Delacroix cheated in a business deal." Spence had earned, through his haircut, the right to hear the Hazlett story. I briefly filled him in.

Spence's pen was keeping up. "Who else? Isn't there any more family? What about the woman who turned Dr. Finer in? Didn't someone say she was an aunt?"

How did he know about Finer? This child was hardly lacking in motivation when he was doing what he wanted.

"Yup, you're right. We'll have to get her name from Arlene. It's critical that we get a feel for his early life. Carla said he claimed to be some kind of war hero, but she also said he might have been lying."

"Don't forget Carla all but told us she keeps a bunch of guns around. We may not have to look too far into his past. His present could have plenty of problems. Don't write those off just because he was an old guy."

No older than I felt at the moment. "And maybe we shouldn't write off Carla either. At least not yet."

He put down the pen and shoved the legal pad across the table. "There you go, Mom. Doesn't it feel better when you have a plan of attack?"

The urge to make obvious analogies was strong upon me but I held back. "All right, Spence my love. It's a start. Where would you like to keep your list?"

"*Our* list." He ran his hand across the newly shorn locks just in case I'd forgotten my promise. "How about taping it to the bookcase in what you so colorfully refer to as the 'great room'?"

"Okay. And what would you like to call that room?"

"Anything else."

"That's not good enough. When you come up with something more descriptive, I'll consider it. Until then, 'great room' will have to do."

"By the way, don't underestimate the Internet. Who knows what we might turn up."

"What *you* might turn up. Good practice for your summer job. Personally, I'm not going near the thing."

"I'll draft Paul and Lawrence. We'll figure something out."

"Whatever."

He headed out with the list and a roll of tape, the difference in his walk notable. He strode, long-legged and sure, with a speed and direction I hadn't seen in over a month. Murder and arson were great motivators. Or was he simply more comfortable now that the college thing was out in the open?

My headache was starting to ease up, enough so that I decided to check the men who were still working in the garage. I could see at least two strange cars through the window and wondered what they had found to do for so long.

Three men were there when I finally wandered back out. It was still Sunday, though not a particularly warm and friendly one. White clouds, thick with possible rain, were forming over the mountains, slowly working their way east. A week ago today we'd left for Carlsbad. It didn't seem possible to have had so much happen in so short a time.

The garage looked, if anything, even more beaten up than it had earlier. A quick look at my car and I realized I could forget about finding papers or anything else inside. Too late for that. I went in, stopping the three officials in mid-operation. Two were from the fire department, one was police. We all introduced ourselves, after which I promptly forgot their names. One of them, the policeman, was the first to ask a question.

"Tell us, ma'am, why you have such a large quantity of herbicides stored here, could you? And what about all this glue and paint?"

I looked to see where he was pointing. Everything was in a storage area off the main garage, a clever small space we'd designed ourselves and which seemed to have largely escaped the fire. The herbicides were clearly marked. The rest I recognized immediately. "That stuff must have been left there by the tree men, since I wouldn't let them spray before a dinner party I was having this weekend. I guess they stashed their chemicals here rather than take them home. You can see, we have over a hundred trees. And these things, they belong to our kids. They used them in a couple of science projects for school. Bridge building and things like that.''

"You don't think, perhaps, that they might have been uh...sniffing this glue, do you?''

"Oh, heavens no.''

"It's not absolutely impossible, you know. Kids do crazy things sometimes.''

"Do you think their glue had something to do with the fire?''

The police officer glanced at the other men. They were stolidly noncommittal. He turned back to me. "We have to check all possibilities.''

I nodded, looking around at all the destruction. Garden tools, bikes, trash barrels, odds and ends like old sleds and balls, were totaled. My favorite red wheelbarrow had actually melted into something approximating modern art. It was too depressing. I thanked them for their efforts in our behalf and drifted back toward the house. The phone was ringing. I could hear it once I got close.

Albert was checking in, a gesture I appreciated. He must have realized how anxious I was to hear about Eli. "He's okay. Upset, and completely in the dark about that ring, but at least he can go home now. I'll take him. They're not charging him with anything, thank goodness. That's all we'd need.''

"What did he say about the ring?''

"That the cops found it right in his top drawer, under a few socks. It wasn't even hidden. He says it was planted. Had to be. Still, it was all he could do, he said, to let the police take it away. Once he held it in his hand, he knew it was his. His family's. His father's. It brought back too much.''

"What are we going to do for him?"

"I'm going to New York for the next three days. *You're* going to solve this murder. That should help a lot.''

EIGHT

"WE'RE VERY IMPRESSED with your son," I said to Jesse Leake as he wrestled heavy containers from the storage area off the garage. "According to my husband, he's amazing on the computer. And sweet, too. A good kid."

"Yeah." The tree sprayer was rubbing the fire ash from his hands to his pants, then going back for more barrels to roll onto the lawn. Until last night, there'd been a wall in the way. He stopped for a moment after the last barrel was out. "Good thing my stuff wasn't in the garage itself. Looks like you had quite a situation here."

Well, so much for his son. "I guess you could call it that. The police think it was arson. I don't suppose anyone else around here's had a fire, have they?"

Leake ran his hand through a graying buzz-cut, thought for a minute, and shook his head. "No one I work for. Sorry." He consulted a small spiral notebook that he kept in his shirt pocket. "So should we start on the back area today? The fire shouldn't keep us from working and no point in letting the trees die. I figure we have two days' worth of work here. At least."

"Whatever you want. Just work fast. I hate having those poisons in the air any longer than necessary. And, Jesse…"

He looked up from his notebook, clearly impatient to get started. "About Lawrence…"

"We call him Larry, my wife and me."

"Okay, Larry. Do you have any plans for his education? I mean, after high school?"

Jesse Leake looked at me warily, trying to decide where I was headed. "He'll go to work for me full-time, once he graduates. If he wants to go to college, he can earn his own way. Save up."

I thought of my Spence, so quick to give up an education Lawrence would most certainly jump at. "You know, we really have come to care about him. If he wants to go straight to school, and if, um, you'd let him go, we might be able to lend him... something." Albert could have said this with ease and poise. I, on the other hand, was horribly embarrassed but I wanted this man to know that we could help the boy.

I couldn't tell if Jesse was angry or humiliated. What he certainly wasn't was grateful for the offer. He came close to rolling his eyes, though stopped just short of that. He mumbled something I couldn't hear. Then, "Thanks. I think I'd better get started now. My men are waiting for instructions." He backed away quickly and disappeared around the side of a large truck.

"Thank you, Mrs. Beckmann," I muttered to myself. "You're *so* kind to be concerned." If I reported this conversation to Spence, he'd just say, "See? Not everyone's into this college thing."

I headed back to the house. Still Monday morning and already I'd accomplished quite a lot. Albert had left for the plane to New York. He'd be back Thursday. The boys were off to camp. Their counselorship, if you could call it that, didn't start for another twelve days, but they wanted to hang there anyway. School had only been out for a couple of weeks but they were already antsy. I'd called the insurance company and found the agent there very compassionate. She also sent over a rental car, which meant I had to drive the rental agent back to his office, but I had wheels again, such as they were. The car was clean, it was white, it was fairly new. I could live with it.

Millie was in the kitchen tackling the soot that had escaped into the house. The cabinets, not that far from the heart of the fire, were covered with a thick coating of black grease. She always enjoyed a large project and didn't stop her dipping, rinsing, and wiping, even while she talked to me. Happily, her energy was being spent on something other than quizzing me about the fire. "So how are we going to get groceries into the house, do you suppose? Track through the front door?"

"Oh, I don't know. We'll cope. We could always eat out." I knew that would get her.

"Lousy restaurant food?" She stopped squeezing the rag and looked up. "You can't let those growing boys eat stuff you don't even know what it is." She gave one more vicious turn to the rag. "They need wholesome food. They need home cooking." Translation: They need *my* cooking.

"Okay, Millie. Then we'll handle it. Are you under control for tonight?"

"Sure. I can get by for a week if you'll stop for vegetables and some fruit."

Was there some implied criticism there? I didn't normally buy enough fresh produce? Okay, I'm paranoid. Everything Millie says sounds like an attack to me, but that's probably more my problem than hers.

"Okay. But not till later. Right now, I'm meeting someone."

I wasn't going to tell her the person I was meeting didn't know he was going to be so blessed, that I expected to waylay him. I had to go out to the general aviation airport and hope to find him, but no point in burdening her with these details.

By noon, I'd maneuvered the rental into a parking space outside a flying club that was halfway between our hangar and the little sandwich restaurant that serviced the pilots and hangers-on. I couldn't be sure Hazlett would go there to eat, but it really was the only game in town, unless he brought his own lunch and he didn't seem the type to brown-bag it. I figured I'd go chat with Jack Potts, our general factotum and mechanic in the hangar we shared with one other plane. That way I could keep one eye on the door to the restaurant and wait for Martin Hazlett to climb those few steps in. Albert had found an old promotion piece with his picture in it as owner of Hazlett Charters. I was looking for red hair, fair skin, what seemed like a slightly receding chin. Someone who looked a little too young for the job.

Our Turbo Arrow, aka *Romeo,* was alone in the hangar when I wandered in. We shared the space with a beautiful Cessna 210, an arrangement Albert had recently cemented, but it was out. We didn't know the owners, so I was grateful not to see them now. I felt like small talk, but only with Jack—sweet, serious Jack. Jack Potts had recently, thanks in a roundabout way to us, come into a significant amount of money, but I knew it would affect his life not at all. I only hoped he was in his office.

He kept a small space adjacent to our hangar with

a desk and a couple of metal folding chairs. And, of course, a sink. Jack, whose work left him often covered in grease, was immaculately clean, washing his hands whenever necessary and sometimes when not necessary at all. If he had a touch of obsessive/compulsive behavior disorder, I didn't want to know about it. In fact, since to some extent a pilot's life depends on a compulsive mechanic, let's hear it for compulsion. There are worse faults.

I crossed the large gray cement floor of the hangar, stopping to pat *Romeo* on its nose. "Are you lonesome, old boy?" I asked it. "Missing your Cessna girlfriend?" I felt considerably more affection for the plane when its wheels were solidly on the ground.

"Mrs. B?" Potts's head peered around his office door.

"Hi, Jack," I called.

Potts disappeared and I could hear the sound of running water. When he returned, he was drying his hands on a paper towel, which he tossed in the trash. He walked over to my side of *Romeo* and gave it a pat of his own. "Had the plane washed and waxed last week. How does it look?"

"Better than I do. I wish someone would take care of me that well."

"Waiting for the doc?"

"Nope. Waiting for Martin Hazlett, who may not even be here today. Have you seen him around?"

"He was here earlier. Saw him at the FBO. Is he expecting you?"

"No. Just taking a chance at catching him."

Potts looked at me from under lowered lids. "About that murder you folks got involved in last week, huh? Guess you're kinda making a habit of solving things."

I walked to the large open doors and checked the restaurant steps. No one there. A couple were approaching the stairs down the long sidewalk, both dressed in jeans and carrying small blue flight bags, but neither was Hazlett. I leaned against the side wall where I had a clear view and settled myself for a wait. "What do you know about Hazlett, Jack?"

Potts retrieved a broom from the far corner and started sweeping the area near me. Might as well use the time profitably. Dirt blew in when the hangar doors were open and he certainly couldn't have that. "Probably nothing you don't already know. Seems like an okay guy, but keeps to himself. Made and lost a couple of fortunes, they say. His charter business does well. No problems there."

"How about personally?"

Potts shrugged. "Beats me. Guys around here, they don't talk about things like that." He paused, thinking. "There was a woman. Long time ago. There was some talk about that once. But..."

"Okay, Jack, don't worry about it. Now I know to ask him. Thanks." I shifted positions. Spending hours on a watch was the least appealing part of detective work, even for amateurs. I knew I'd never make it as a pro. "You can go ahead and do whatever I interrupted you from doing. I'll just hang around for a while."

My vigil was rewarded eventually, but not till almost one. Watching people come and go from the restaurant was making me hungry. When Hazlett finally showed, he all but ran the few stairs to the door. The sun caught the red hair just at the critical mo-

ment. I waved good-bye to Jack, who was chewing
on a sandwich from a paper bag, and jogged the fifty
yards or so to the café. I caught Hazlett in the lobby.

"Mr. Hazlett?"

He turned abruptly. Then smiled. "Hi."

"My name is Grace Beckmann. I wondered if I
could talk to you for a few minutes." He was really
quite attractive. Up close, I could see the freckles that
went with red hair and the very blue eyes.

"I'd ask about what but I'll bet I know," he said.
"You're the doctor's wife, I suspect, right? I've met
your husband. And everyone around here has certainly heard about your trip last weekend."

"You're way ahead of me."

"Come on," he said, taking my arm. "Have you
eaten? Let me buy you a sandwich. We can talk over
lunch, though I doubt I'll be much help."

I'd interviewed more than a few people over lunch,
but since I'd been writing articles at the time and the
interview was for professional purposes, I'd always
set a small tape recorder going right by the salt and
pepper. It usually picked up all the clinks and
chomps, background noises that drove me crazy.
Without it, though, I felt naked. Then again, I didn't
need verbatim quotes from this man. In fact, a recorder would certainly spook him. What I wanted
from him was strictly off the record.

We waited till we'd eaten, filling the time with
chatter about the aviation world. Much as I didn't
love actually flying, I could talk the talk. You can't
help but absorb all sorts of trivia when you're married
to a fanatic. When the waitress brought his dessert
and my coffee, I decided the time was right.

"What I'd really like from you, Marty, is every-

thing you know about James Delacroix,'' I began. By
now, it was Marty. And I wanted him at ease.

"You realize how old my experiences with him
are? I mean, it's probably been fifteen years or more
since we were 'in business' together. And I use the
term loosely.''

"That's okay. I'm trying for some deep background. I need to know more about him as a person.''

"As a person, he was an outright crook. Dishonest,
fraudulent, the kinda guy who'd sell his grandmother
for ten bucks.''

"Really one of your favorites.''

"Absolutely. And when I tell you what happened,
you'll understand what a peach of a guy he was.''

Apparently, for Hazlett, it was a colossal piece of
bad timing. He arrived in the city, a young man in
his early twenties, with dreams of a life spent around
airplanes and a nice six-figure inheritance tucked in
his back pocket. What was now this bustling general
aviation airport was then little more than a couple of
landing strips and a building or two. It took imagi-
nation to see what it could and would become, and
Hazlett didn't have it. However, he met a man who
did.

James Delacroix could see life's possibilities. He
had, in those days, a way of half-closing his eyes and
describing fantasy images to anyone who'd listen.
Pretty soon, the images were as clear as the six
o'clock news. He had some money, too. Not enough
to pick up all the parcels of land an airport would
require, but he wasn't broke by any means. The
young Marty Hazlett was dazzled by the wads of bills
Delacroix flashed around and grateful to be shown the

ropes by someone who seemed to know how to weave them.

Together, they went about the job of wooing the landowners, most of whom had been sitting on acreage that had gone undeveloped forever and were only too happy to divest—for a price. Delacroix was clever, his pitch perfected with time. When Hazlett added his inheritance and became an equal partner, they had what they needed. In time, they were ready to close on enough land for developers to expand the runways, add a tower, hangars, FBOs, flight schools, all the accoutrements of general aviation. They even had enough so that, should the opportunity arise, hotels could be built nearby to house the pilots who flew their own jets in for business meetings.

From then on, the story was the one I'd already heard from Albert. Fraud, deceit, a young man suckered by a semiprofessional con man. The deal had closed without him and the money was gone.

The betrayal was beyond comprehension, particularly to someone as trusting as Hazlett. It had, he realized, been almost a month since he'd seen his friend, though they talked daily on the phone. He went to Delacroix's office, then his apartment. All had been cleaned out. He raced to the county clerk's office and found the papers had all been signed by Delacroix alone. His partner owned enough land to build a major facility and he owned it alone. Hazlett didn't know then about the turnover or the third party who'd been waiting in the wings all along.

Cheated. Destroyed. Taught a lesson in duplicity he'd never wanted to learn.

"It took me quite a while to find where Delacroix had gone to ground. I realized I knew almost nothing about him, didn't know if he had a family. The banks had no forwarding address for him. They put his money into high-interest accounts which he would access now and then by phone, asking for checks to be sent to P.O. boxes all over the Southwest." He spooned some ice from his empty lemonade glass and crunched it in his teeth. "I found him, of course, eventually. Flew down to Copper Creek. He just laughed at me. It was all I could do not to kill him then and there."

His words hung in the air, perfumed with smells of bacon and coffee. The café had cleared out. We were the only ones still sitting, but no one was hassling us to leave. Through the large windows, we could see the private planes touch down and take off, their wings bobbling, sometimes identifying students at the controls.

"I know what you're thinking. And no, I didn't kill him. That was years ago."

"Have you seen him since?"

"No. And never wanted to."

"You could have sued him, had him arrested. Why did you just drop it? What he did was clearly illegal."

"More. It was immoral. It destroyed my faith. It destroyed my marriage. But there were...problems with the money I'd brought to the table. I couldn't bring the police into it."

"Not quite an inheritance from Grampa, huh?"

"No."

"Did Delacroix know?"

"Of course. At first, it was just dumb luck that he found me. Then he realized how to capitalize on the situation."

Well, well. I was peeling back the layers and find-

ing more than a little decay underneath. Onions and
James Delacroix. Both rotted from the inside.

"You seem to have recovered financially, anyway.
I understand you own your own charter service."

"Mm-hmm. But can you imagine how rich I'd be
now if I'd owned the land under this place?" He
smiled, the freckled face turning into a web of fine
wrinkles.

"And your wife at the time? What happened?"

He rose abruptly, his chair skidding back from the
table. It took me a moment to react, but then I got up
with him, staying at his side as he threw a bill on the
butcher block tabletop and headed for the door. We
were outside and down the stairs before he stopped
and looked back at me. I hurried to catch up.

"You really have to know what happened to my
wife?"

"No, not really. Not if you don't want to tell me."
I was embarrassed, the snoop asking unwanted questions, a social leper.

"If you're looking for a motive for me to have
killed the creep, sure, the answer to that question
alone would do it." He'd started walking again but
stopped suddenly. His body was lean and hard, the
hair glinting again in the sun. "She left me when the
money was gone. I'd promised to make us rich. She
wasn't into poor. Or struggling."

"Sounds like it wasn't that great a loss, a woman
like that."

"You think so? She was gorgeous, unbelievable.
Fabulously dressed. High maintenance and worth it.
I loved having her on my arm. Everyone stared."

Okay, it takes all kinds. Here was a man who could
let a minor fortune be lost to fraud and not pursue it.

Passive, able to be gulled and led. But apparently, thanks to Jack Potts, I'd stumbled onto the one thing Martin Hazlett felt strongly about.

He must really have hated the man who cost him his showpiece of a woman. Despite his denials, might the hate have, over time, become an obsession? A *murderous* obsession?

NINE

WITH ALBERT IN New York, Millie regressed into hamburgers and chili, even occasionally making pizza from scratch. The boys and I were in our element. We certainly didn't complain about roast chicken with French bread and a variety of fresh grilled veggies, an Albert-style dinner, but now and then fast food-style eats with a big salad were a treat. Happily, I'd stopped for produce at a farmer's market on the way home from the airfield.

Spence, of course, wanted to hear everything about my day. With his new, shorter hair, he knew I owed him. He could demand a full recital. The magnitude of his sacrifice was only too obvious to him every time he looked in the mirror. Not that I minded sharing things with either of the boys. It was refreshing to have these two almost-adult males to vent with. I told both of them about my interview with Hazlett, enjoying the role of talespinner and leaving nothing out. Neither could believe such naïveté in a grown man.

"Bummer. Hadn't he checked this guy out at all? I mean, someone must have suspected Delacroix was a sleaze." Paul was so logical, so organized, it was hard for him to imagine making such an error.

"Who knows? Probably no one had heard much about him, except that he had money to throw around. Hard to check on someone from out of town."

Spence paused for a moment before tackling his

second hamburger and stared blankly at his plate. "I can understand that. Lazy people *want* to trust. It's easier than doing the work of finding things out for yourself."

"Spence, my darling, you have the mind-set of a nihilist."

"If that means I don't like being told what to do, you got that right." He took a large, meaty bite. Millie's burgers never weighed less than half a pound. "By the way, did you ever call that sheriff in Copper Creek or wherever?"

"Well now, are you trying to tell *me* what to do?"

"Sorry," he mumbled. "But did you?"

"Well yes, actually." I wiped my greasy hands on a rust-colored cotton napkin that absorbed it all. "This afternoon. Took me a while to find him, since he seems to wander quite a bit."

"And?"

I reported as best I could on my conversation with Timothy Pells, whose telephone manner was as polite and diffident as he had been in person. His office turned out to be in a mid-sized town about a hundred and twenty miles from Copper Creek, meaning the Delacroix case was probably not first on his agenda. He had, to his credit, traced the phone call to the FBO that Sunday morning. When I told the boys the call had come from a pay phone on the north side of our own city, neither was at all surprised.

Spence reacted impatiently. "Well, Mom, you know whoever tried to burn us down must be here at least some of the time. Maybe he lives here and maybe not, but he hangs around. He has to."

"And you're so sure that our arsonist has something to do with the murder?"

"Of course," said Paul. "That's a given."

Okay, they'd accepted the idea, and with less problem than I had. I decided not to ask if the concept of a stalker bothered them. They'd just say that that was also a given. I had chosen not to burden anyone with my fears, but an image of the burnt-out garage popped unbidden into my head at all sorts of strange moments, bringing with it a racing pulse and turn of the stomach. Funny that no note or warning had emerged, no one eager to take credit for the disaster.

"Did the sheriff say anything else?" Spence wasn't letting go so easily.

"That Delacroix seemed to have been shot at close range with a large-size bullet. There were powder marks around the bullet hole. He didn't know either what Delacroix was doing on top of his car, but he thinks he was sitting up there when the shot was fired. That's why they haven't found the bullet. Is that weird? Oh, and yes, this is important. There were rope burns on his wrists. And he'd been stabbed, but only lightly. Multiple flesh wounds, but none deep enough to injure him. Quite a few times, though, as if someone were deliberately torturing him. Maybe trying to get something from him. Information or...something."

"How could we have missed seeing that?"

"The cuts were mostly on his back and thighs. Maybe whoever did it wanted to be sure there was no chance of injuring him accidentally. In any case, we wouldn't have seen them there."

"Wow!" Paul looked at Spence. "That's why

those knives were gone, I'll bet. And it was you who found one of them in the grass.''

Spence smiled, an unusual sight. He was really into this murder all the way.

''Incidentally, the sheriff did mention that the knife they recovered had been wiped clean of prints. The lab's still looking for any blood that isn't the victim's. And he also said we had managed to make such a mess of the ground around the car, no shoe castings were possible.''

''Oooh, guilt trip. And that was it?'' Paul prodded.

I looked out the dining-room window at a developing sunset, great swatches of gold and blue flung against the darkening sky, turning the mountains into an elaborate silhouette against the psychedelic light. Should I tell them about the rest? Oh well, in for a penny, in for a pound. ''I asked him if he'd tell me what he knew about Delacroix's relationship with Carla. If he'd heard anything. He did seem to know her, even though he doesn't live in their town.'' I'd be telling all this again to Albert when he called from New York tonight, but I was still relishing the novelty of talking to my own sons like peers. In most cultures, seventeen would be considered adult, but we hadn't quite reached that point.

''C'mon, Mom, you're making us pull this out of you.''

''Okay, okay.'' I folded my napkin and put it beside my plate. ''He said he'd heard rumors of some trouble there. That she'd had to run to the neighbors once or twice when he'd been drinking. A black eye, some cuts.''

''No kidding.'' Paul was truly surprised. Domestic

violence wasn't part of the twins' world. "She didn't look like the type to take that from some guy."

Spence grinned. "You did hear her say she owned a bunch of guns, didn't you? Maybe that's why. By the way, did the sheriff happen to mention if that little gun she gave him matched the bullet size?"

"Forgot to ask. Though he did say it was a big bullet."

"I suspect he'd have said if there was a match."

With so much to think about, we spent the rest of the dinner in silence. After thanking Millie, we all headed for the great room. Spence went straight to the list we'd posted. Hazlett's name got a check next to the entry. I didn't complain. There was nothing more we needed, for the moment, to ask him. But then, at the bottom, he underlined Carla Correa. He looked at me watching him.

"Maybe you can do that by phone, but it would probably be better to fly down there again."

"Oh, Spence." I dropped down on the couch. The last thing I needed was another bumpy flight in *Romeo,* and with the uneven landscape between here and Copper Creek, that's what it would be. I picked up a magazine and opened it at random. "Go to bed, child. Or go do whatever. Just let go of this murder for a while, will you please?"

Paul pulled at Spence's arm, leading him to the back of the large room and away from me. "C'mon, I've got some things I want to try on the computer." They, disappeared, the two moving in easy tandem.

I sat back and closed my eyes. Here I was, chasing the murderer of a man whose past was growing uglier by the moment. A cheat, and now a batterer. The man *asked* to be killed. Right now, I was too tired to care.

Tomorrow was Tuesday. Tennis. Thank goodness. I needed a little diversion. I made a fist, shook it in the general direction of the outdoors, and threatened the now-dark sky. *Don't you dare rain. Or if you have to rain, stop by 7:00 a.m.*

It listened. Big drops banged against the window all night but quit around four in the morning. I knew because, with Albert in New York, I slept fitfully. I missed his warmth and the reassuring rumble of his breathing. I wouldn't be too sad when this sabbatical was over and life returned to what passes around here for normal. In any case, when the rain finally stopped, I heard it quit and smiled. The courts would be dry in time.

Nine a.m. found us warming up, without Magda of course. Magda would saunter in twenty minutes late and without apology. Then we'd immediately start the game and she'd be none the worse for the cold start. Unfair. The least she could do would be to whiff a few balls as penance for her tardiness. Beebee Ballard, the financial wizard, shot a glance at me, rolling her eyes when we glimpsed our tardy friend struggling down the walk to the court, festooned with racket bag, purse, and shoes falling from her arms. All we could do was wave hello.

Once we started, the freshness of a spring morning invigorated us all. The trees around the court had leafed out and the beds near the clubhouse, which had been newly planted with bulbs last fall, were now rife with color. The air smelled of new life. I forgot my problems and played as hard as someone on the circuit. All of us, even Sarah Jane, were into the moment. She and I even won a set, no small accomplishment. It was all but impossible for anyone to win with Sarah Jane.

We gathered after the game on sofas around the clubhouse's soft drink machine, restoking our systems with fairly vile canned iced tea. News of the fire had obviously spread among our friends and the girls wanted to know all about it. I told them what I could.

"And what about Eli Finer?" asked Sarah Jane. I wasn't sure she'd want to talk about a date gone marginally sour, but she brought it up.

I didn't want to release any more information than I had to about Eli. The world didn't need to know that he'd been mixed up in anything unpleasant. I tried for innocence. "Regarding what?"

"Well, now really, Grace. Here you fix me up with a guy and you don't expect me to check him out a little? I heard that he had trouble with the police, that they picked him up because they found something incriminating in his apartment, something to do with your current murder." Sarah Jane's grapevine must be a thing to behold.

"For heaven's sake, woman, how do you get your information? You amaze me," I said honestly. "Where did you hear this?"

"From a source at the hospital. I go out sometimes with a guy in medical administration. Everyone's talking about it, since Eli isn't a regular. They're beginning to wonder if they hired Jack the Ripper as a visiting professor."

I shook my head and stared angrily at Sarah Jane, who was rapidly turning into my villain du jour. "Did he strike you as a murderer? That lovely man?"

She checked her cuticles. "Sometimes the nicest people…"

Terrific. Until this murder was solved, Eli was never going to be free of talk and suspicion. I got up abruptly and zipped the racket case closed, throwing the strap around one shoulder.

"Don't be mad, Gracie," said Magda. "I heard about it too and I've never met your doctor. People talk."

"People are idiots," said Beebee Ballard, the acknowledged brains of the group. She threw her empty can in the recycle bin and began to gather her belongings. "Look, if there's anything I can do, just call." She'd been a big help with our first murder case and it still thrilled her. "Particularly if money's involved."

"Money," said Magda wisely, "is always involved."

"Thanks. I'll do it."

I said good-bye to the girls, leaving them to continue the tennis postmortem without me, and headed for my rental car and home. I needed to regroup. My hand shook a little as I found the ignition and wedged in the unfamiliar key. It bothered me a great deal that people were talking about Eli, bothered me even more that someone had presumably planted a diamond ring in one of his drawers. Some malevolent presence seemed to be hovering around us and discovering too much about our lives. Look at the fire. I owed it to my family and I owed it to Eli to work harder on this murder. Arlene would recover from the loss of a father she saw only sporadically. Eli's life, on the other hand, could be ruined by this. I left for home in a brown study.

The boys, with Lawrence in tow, were on me as soon as I drove up, gravel crunching under my wheels. Now that the garage was history, I had to use the circular drive to park, making me feel like a visitor to my own house. Even worse, with that means of arrival, I could be seen and heard from all kinds of windows. No way of sneaking in unobserved.

"Mom! Mom!" The calls came the minute I stepped out of the car.

I extricated all the tennis gear, juggling parcels. "Wait. Hold it. Give me a minute, okay? I need to transition."

"No you don't," insisted Spence. "This is important. Del Delacroix called."

I stopped on the spot and leaned against the passenger side of the car. "He did?"

"Yeah. He said he got a message last night to call you."

Last night. What was last night? My head felt fuzzy and I wasn't thinking straight. Rain. That's what happened last night. "Oh wow, he must have checked into the shelter to get out of the weather. And whoever was in charge gave him the message, or maybe it was posted on a board. What did he say?"

The boys deflated like a landed parachute. "He said you couldn't reach him. That he'd call again after lunch. What if he doesn't?"

I wondered that myself. "Well, here's the drill," I said finally. "If he hasn't called by two, I'm going back down to the area near the shelters and cruise. He must be around or he wouldn't have caught the message."

"Then we're going with you." That, of course, was Spence. "Or at least I am."

"So am I," added Paul. Lawrence looked like he

wanted to join in, the third brother, but realized he didn't quite belong. He backed away, abashed.

"Actually, I'd like to have you with me, both of you, if you really don't mind. But maybe we'll get lucky and he'll call back."

Millie brought tuna salad on light rye, chips, and sliced fruit to the patio and we ate while we waited, the portable phone by my right hand. Seeing Lawrence with the boys, she didn't even ask if he was staying for lunch, just set another plate and added two large additional sandwiches. She loved strays.

I ate nervously, willing the phone to ring. The boys, too, were uncharacteristically subdued. The minutes ticked by silently. Millie cleared the table, with help from the Three Musketeers. I was afraid to leave my post next to the receiver, which I checked now and then for a dial tone. It buzzed when asked. Still it didn't ring. Finally, at a quarter to two, I gave up. "Okay, guys, looks like we're taking a trip downtown. You might want to make a pit stop before we leave. You won't have many chances where we're going."

Lawrence, seeing his favorite buds departing for the afternoon, thanked me politely for lunch and gathered up some books and a sweater he'd come with. "Mind if I get some things from the garage room before I go, Mrs. Beckmann? My dad said he thought he left some tools there."

"Of course not, Lawrence." I looked toward the garage, visible from here in the back. A van had pulled up near it earlier in the afternoon and our contractor had emerged, waving to us on the patio. He'd come, presumably, to take a measure of the damage (total) and replacement costs (enormous). I couldn't imagine that Lawrence would bother him.

Since the afternoon was rapidly disappearing, we waved good-bye to the workers and left promptly for that colorful area of lower downtown that I'd seen for the first time only a few days before. The boys watched from the car as we passed the empty buildings with their graffiti, the occasional man pushing his supermarket basket of worldly possessions, the boarded-up windows. This wouldn't hurt them, this glimpse of a deprived world. Too well brought up to stare at the stragglers on the street, they were nonetheless fascinated by a part of the city they hadn't known existed.

I passed Arlene's picture of her brother to the backseat and let the boys take a good look. "He's going to be hard to find, I'll bet. I don't even know where to drive, really, since I have a feeling the shelters don't get busy till mealtime and bedtime." We drove up and down the blocks, using the several shelters I'd visited as epicenters and cruising in ever-widening spirals. Except for a family with four tiny children walking quickly toward some unknown destination, no one was around.

Our pattern widened till, toward the west, we began to pass the upscale bars and restaurants around the new baseball stadium. I started to turn back toward the shelters. No way could Del Delacroix afford the tabs for such high-priced alcohol. Here, on a Tuesday afternoon with no game scheduled, the area was quiet but hardly deserted. Several sharply dressed young women were chatting outside a fern bar that specialized in red meat and good scotch. Late lunch, I gathered. On the steps in front of a remodeled office building, a man was sitting, his hands clutching a brown paper bag like life itself. I started to drive on.

"Mom, wait." Paul was turned on his seat, staring. "That guy."

I slowed the car, looked behind me, and carefully backed up, no small trick on a downtown street. "The one on the step?" I'd pulled up even with him, but across the street.

"Yeah. Him. Isn't he the one?"

The man with the paper bag looked up at that moment and met my eyes. The last thing I wanted to do was talk to him. The hair, the clothes, the obvious bottle, the barely concealed fury—this was someone to run from. It was all I could do to lower my window.

He called something to me that I couldn't hear. "Excuse me?" I whispered.

He raised his voice, which croaked at the effort. "I said, it took you long enough. All but put up a sign. Some dumb woman."

Paul, behind me in the backseat, had lowered his window too. Now he took over. "Are you Mr. Delacroix, sir?" Pure deference. Perfect.

"Hah! 'Mr. Delacroix, sir.' Yeah, that's me." He struggled up from the low stoop, package still in hand, and started weaving across the street. I had a momentary urge to gun the engine, burn rubber, and blow the place, but managed to resist. "You the broad left me the message? You the one want to talk about my old man?"

"Yes."

He'd reached the car now and had one hand hooked through the door handle. He leaned in. "Figgered you'd come lookin'."

I tried to keep from shrinking back. With the window open, I could smell his pickled breath. "You didn't call back."

"Oh, too bad. So park. You wanna talk, we talk. It'll cost ya."

"What do you want?"

"Lunch. A drink. In there." He pointed to the dark wood doors of the restaurant where the women were still in animated conversation. I could imagine how thrilled they'd be to see this bum walk in with us and ask for a table.

"In there?" I was sure he couldn't mean what he seemed to mean.

"Whatsa matter, lady, you got problems with that? Okay. I can go." He turned on his heel and started shuffling back across the street, oblivious to a car heading straight for him. The car swerved and braked, narrowly missing our little rental. The driver yelled something at our rapidly escaping quarry before going on his way.

"Wait, Del! Don't go. Just wait." I pulled into a spot on the street where a pickup had just driven off. If I'd had to cover another twenty feet, he'd have been gone. The boys barely hung on till the car was stopped. Then they shot out the door and raced across the street. No way could he have escaped them. They were suddenly positioned on both sides of him, ready to grab hold.

I took a minute to feed the meter, lock the car, smooth my hair, and take a deep breath. Then I crossed to the side of the street where rich sports fans fed and watered themselves before the game.

Okay, new inning. And the batter up was me.

TEN

SOMEHOW, THE RESTAURANT cum sports bar seated us. In the eyes of the restaurant manager, three decently dressed people must have balanced the one disreputable member of the party. That and the fact that it was mid-afternoon and the lunch crowd had largely dispersed. A fairly rowdy group of drinkers was clustered around the mahogany bar arguing noisily about batting styles, but otherwise we had the place pretty much to ourselves. We chose a corner table for four instead of one of the black leather booths, thus avoiding having to choose who would sit right next to our visitor.

Del Delacroix studied the menu with care, reading the small-print descriptions under every entree. When the waiter appeared, standing at a greater than usual distance with his pad and pencil, he was ready. He ordered a 12-ounce strip steak, au gratin potatoes, and julienned root vegetables with a lentil-barley soup to start. Add a shot and beer chaser and he was set. His ease of ordering surprised us—enough so that we hedged when the waiter turned to us. Having had lunch three hours earlier was a bit of a disadvantage but, for the boys, not an insurmountable one. They ordered designer pizzas, easily adding a fourth (at least) meal to the day. I settled for coffee.

"Looks like you know your way around good restaurants, Del." The truth, but I also hoped the bit of flattery would help. "Was your father a fairly well-to-do man?"

He was sitting directly across from me, his long legs stretched so far under the table that I couldn't help kicking his foot. He deliberately encroached on my space, a little game. He stared up at me from under lowered lids. "Was yours?"

The response took me back, but only for a moment. "All right, come on," I snapped. "We're here to find out what you might know about who killed your father. Don't jerk me around."

"Tell me again why this is *your* job. A broad and couple of kids."

"Arlene asked us to do it."

"That so?" He grunted. "Okay. For her, I guess." He twisted in his chair, trying to get comfortable. "So you want me to tell you who mighta killed him. Well, I'm not sure which of the gazillion people who musta hated his guts actually managed to take him out, but I'm just sorry I'm too much of a loser to have been the shooter. Ain't it always the way?"

The waiter brought his beer and a shot of bourbon, arranging them with exaggerated care. Del downed the shot in a gulp and signaled immediately for another. He watched till the waiter went for the reorder and then took a tiny sip of the beer. I could see what lay ahead.

"One more, Del. That's it. And you've got to eat when the food comes. I'm not wasting my time and money watching you get plastered."

His face got dark. He took a fork and, without a thought, bent it in two. Then he straightened it again, muttering under his breath. "All right, lady, then let's just do it. Ask. I'll answer. Talking about my old man isn't something I do for fun. Let's get this the heck over with.''

I glanced at my boys, taking strength from their presence. "All right. I can handle that. Now try answering my question. Was your father rich when you were growing up?"

"Yeah, I guess. Not that we, my sister and me and my ma, saw any of it."

"Then how did you know he had money?"

He shrugged. "Just did. Sometimes he came home with a big wad. Threw some bills at my ma and then left. Parts unknown. Those days, she'd take us for dinner someplace nice, us kids. He never went with us. She wanted us to learn how things were other places. My ma was a classy lady. Too good for that... But mostly, we didn't have nothin'." He threw down the second shot the waiter had brought and sat back coughing. "Askin' for things didn't do much good, mostly. Sometimes he'd buy us stuff. Usually he'd just get real mad. Finally we just stopped askin'."

I thought about what Carla had said. "Was he abusive to you or your mother or sister?"

"Abusive? Sure. Ya mean did he hit us? Ma and me plenty. Didn't hit Arlene much. At least, not while I was still home. Think he knew we wouldn't stand for that." He was quiet a minute. Then, "It wasn't just what he did with his hands, though. It was the things he said, the names he called us. The mean jokes he played. Promising to take us somewhere we really wanted to go, letting us get all excited, countin' the days. Then leaving while we were still asleep. Telling us when he got back how great it was, and wasn't it too bad we slept through it. When we cried, he howled with laughter. Things like that."

"Why didn't your mother leave? Take you kids with her?"

He shrunk down further in his chair, sending his feet directly between mine. I turned sideways and crossed my legs. He was somewhere else, looking down a crooked trail to a long-ago beginning. You could see his face respond to the memories playing like a scratchy eight-millimeter film in his mind. Finally, he said, "I guess she had no place to go. But…"

I waited.

"…but she was going to leave him. That's when he killed her."

The waiter chose that moment to arrive with the boys' pizzas and Del's soup. I caught the twins signaling each other, a tacit *Did he just say what I thought he said?* "I'll bring your meal in a minute, sir," the young man assured us all.

When he left, I tried to bring back whatever mood it was that had led to Del's outburst. "You were saying your mother was going to leave him?"

The man, his hands more or less constantly shaking now, nodded. He'd sat up straighter to eat his soup, allowing me to reclaim my leg space. Clearly, he was no longer in the mood to be interrupted. The soup took his full attention. He savored it slowly, tasting each mouthful. We waited quietly, the boys eating their pizzas, till he finished and put down his spoon. The soup seemed to change him somewhat, reminding him perhaps of other times. Or maybe he'd just been hungry. His voice turned mellower, more civilized.

"My mother was from a nice family. The old man used to rag her about that. Lois Gunther was her maiden name. That's my real name, you know. Gun-

ther. Kids started calling me Del. I liked it better'n
Gunther. She, my ma, was okay, like I told you. Was
the old man's girlfriend before the war. They knew
each other young, I don't know how. Then she waited
and married him when he got back and the war was
over.'' He paused, thinking. ''I used to ask her why
she married him. Why she didn't know what he was
like. She usually didn't answer. Once she said she felt
she owed it to him.'' He continued without a beat,
his tone flat. ''I hated that man more than anybody
in the world, more than Hitler. More than the meanest
guard when I did time. More than the devil. I still
hate him and he's dead. That don't matter. I hate him
dead too.''

''And he killed your mother.''

''Yeah.''

''You sure?''

He looked at me as if I were one of his street people off his meds. ''Of course I'm sure. I was there,
wasn't I?''

I had to force myself to sound casual. ''Want to
tell us about it?''

The dinner arrived at that moment, and instantly he
lost focus. Blast. I knew we were finished for now.
The boys, their pizzas eaten, made no attempt at chatter and neither did I. We waited and watched as Del
Delacroix cut the whole steak into pieces at once,
covered them with a blizzard of salt and pepper, and
chewed each hunk of beef with a certain dogged de-
termination. Then came the potatoes. He finished
them completely before starting on the vegetables. I
checked my watch. It would be nice to be heading
home right now, before the worst of the traffic started
to leave downtown, but there was no way to hurry

him. Not till every morsel was gone from the plate
and all the sauces mopped up with rolls from the basket did Del Delacroix wipe his mouth and look up
from the empty plate. He finished the last of his beer,
regretting the end of it. Then he sighed deeply.

"Thanks. Good meal. Always wanted to eat here.
Kept seein' fancy folks comin' and goin'."

I couldn't help smiling at his pleasure. "You're
welcome. Any time."

He pushed his chair back from the table. "Guess
I'll be goin' now."

That ended the smile. I was half out of my own
chair. "Oh no you won't. Are you kidding? Not without telling us how you think he killed your mother."

He appraised me silently. After letting me sweat
long enough, he moved the chair back to the table.
The food had taken the edge off the alcohol. His voice
was no longer slurred, the thinking process a little
clearer. However, talk was still something he obviously wasn't much used to. "Can't be absolutely sure,
of course. Ma's sister, Aunt Natalie, Nattie we called
her, believes like I do. Seems like he knew what she
was planning. She never told us kids, but we saw her
stashing our stuff in bags and putting them under
beds. She was down in the basement a lot, and that's
where boxes and a couple of suitcases were. I think
she was readyin' to light out. Take us with her. He
musta known."

"So what did he do? Or what do you think he
did?"

"Cut the brake cables in the car. Then sent her out
for some beer. We lived up a ways, top of a hill.
'Course, the car was such a wreck, they couldn't tell
if he'd done it. Didn't look, either. Thought it was an

accident. They wouldn't have listened to us kids any-
how, even if we'd tried to tell 'em.''

None of us said anything for quite a while. We
watched the late-afternoon sun stretch shadows across
the restaurant floor, dulling the wood's high polish.
The story was unprovable now, probably never could
have been proven, but it rang true. The man we'd
found dead was some kind of monster.

Eventually, Del told us more, about the bad times
and sometimes the times that weren't so bad. Teeth
that went unfixed and then trips to Disneyland. Sal-
vation Army clothes for the kids followed by expensive toys. They never knew what to expect. James
Delacroix was erratic. His inconsistencies were what
made life so unpredictable. After their mother's death,
the hitting surprisingly stopped. He and Arlene survived, with support from folks in their town. Both left
home as soon as they could, scattering to other cities,
but nothing ever worked out for Del. He'd started
drinking in high school, was a full-blown alcoholic
by his early twenties. No employer would keep him,
though he was a hard worker when sober. Arlene
went to stay with her Aunt Nattie once she was
through with school and, with her help, became a
nurse. Once gone, neither had much to do with their
father, nor he with them.

The boys had sat quietly, but now I knew they
wanted a turn. I was ready to call it a day, more than
ready, but they were just getting warmed up.

Spence was on the edge of his chair, elbows all
over the table. The waiter had brought the check without being asked, obviously hoping to get rid of us. It
wasn't to be. My son had questions of his own.

"What did you know about your father's experi-

ences in the war? Did he ever talk about it?'' Spence
asked.

Del looked a little put off, being questioned by a
kid. I thought he might not answer, but the question
must have intrigued him. ''Yeah, he talked about it
all the time. Biggest thing ever happened to him. Said
he fought in the Battle of Bastogne. Real proud of
that.''

I remembered Carla saying that she never found
any mention of him in the records of that battle, and
Spence obviously remembered it too. ''Think he was
telling the truth?''

Del frowned. ''Ain't got no reason to doubt it. Why
would he lie about something like that?''

''To make himself a hero? Pretend he'd seen action
he never saw?''

''Nah.'' The man shook his head. ''He said that
before that battle, he'd been stuck in England doing
grunt stuff. Mail room, kitchen. Hated it. Wouldn't
have told us that if he'd been lyin' about everything.
He was at Bastogne, I'm pretty sure.''

It was Paul's turn. ''Did you ever notice the ring
he wore, the big diamond with the strange design?''

Del looked at Paul, confused. ''Ring? He never had
no ring.''

''He did when we saw him.''

The man shrugged. ''Never saw it. 'Course, till the
wedding, I hadn't seen him in twenty years or more.''
He thought a minute. ''He had a box. Like a cigar
box, only bigger. I saw it once when I was a kid,
snooping in his stuff. There was rings in it. Bracelets,
chains, and stuff. Some coins that looked like gold.
Didn't mean much to me, but it did to him. He caught
me lookin' and about killed me. Told me if I ever

went near that box again, I could forget livin'. So I left it alone."

I sat back, slightly chagrined. My boys had done a better job than I had. It looked like they'd connected James Delacroix once and for all with Eli Finer's family jewels. What's more, they'd placed him in a mail room. I couldn't wait to talk to Albert and tell him what we'd learned.

The bar was starting to fill up in earnest now. It was happy hour, people were coming in from work, the television was picking up night games from the East Coast, and the mood was energized. I paid the check and we all started to file out. The group that had been drinking in earnest since before we'd arrived were settling up and heading for the exit also, making room for the newcomers. Unfortunately, we reached the door at the same time.

"Nice date you got there, lady," said a thickset man in a plaid shirt. He was having trouble walking without holding on to the wall. His three buddies faked a laugh.

I'd been fishing for car keys but looked up, startled. "Are you talking to me?"

"See any other ladies?"

Trouble. I chose not to answer. I pushed through the door quickly, keeping an eye on the boys, who were right behind me. Our guest had already gone through but was waiting.

This time, with us all on the sidewalk, they started on Del. "Lookin' good, fella. Get that outfit at Saks?"

One of his friends, a baby face, said, "Yeah, he did. Trash sacks!" They all guffawed.

I just wanted to get out of there, but wasn't willing

to leave Del alone. I touched him on the shoulder and whispered, "Come on. Come with us. I'll drive you wherever you want."

The bar jockeys weren't going to let go. "Hoo boy, better take her up on that. Maybe she likes 'em a little shabby."

He might have shrugged even that off, being more sober than usual after his dinner, but then the plaid shirt made the mistake of giving him a shove. Not a particularly hard shove, but it caught him off guard and he staggered. That did it. It became suddenly clear that men like Del didn't survive on the streets without learning a few tricks.

He whirled around on one foot while the other knee smashed into the beer-distended belly of the man who'd shoved him. It looked like tae kwon do, only not so graceful. The plaid shirt doubled over, holding his middle and gasping. The other three, not overly quick on the uptake, realized a fight was on. By that time, Del had grabbed Baby Face by the hair and forced his head down to meet a knee on its way up. The smack made me cringe. I heard something crack. One of the remaining two, a burly guy in sweats, spun Del around and swung a practiced fist at his nose. Del managed to dodge, deflecting the blow to his shoulder, but it landed hard and he winced.

My sons, counting the odds and deciding four against one was too much even for someone with street savvy, jumped into the action, pulling the bigger men away from Del long enough for him to catch his breath. Paul caught someone's elbow just below the ribs and gasped. Spence put a hammerlock on the man who did it, slowing him down longer than I would have guessed he could have done. The boys,

tall and thin, probably weighed together not much
more than the biggest of the drunken creeps. A quick
scan of the area turned up nothing I could use, no
rocks or steel pipes. *Blast.* I thought about screaming,
but realized all that would do was distract the boys
when they needed to keep their heads. Instead, I
looked wildly about for some help, preferably a cop.
People were driving by, slowing down for a look, and
then speeding on. I yelled for them to get help, gestured at the knot of angry men, but all that only scared
them off. *Chickens! Fools!* I looked back at the fight,
by now a wild morass of arms and fists, but then
stopped trying to intervene. Something had changed.

I saw the plaid shirt suddenly fly through the air
and land heavily on the sidewalk a good five feet
away, an ear scraping painfully against the rough cement. Moments later, Baby Face was hurled into the
street, making a car screech to a halt to avoid hitting
him. Neither man, I knew, was likely to come back
swinging—on the outside chance that either one was
able to get up at all. They looked half dead.

My boys, pretty messed up themselves, had left the
center of the battle and were walking toward me,
watching over their shoulders at what was left of the
fight. Del was enjoying himself now. He had one of
the remaining two drunks up against the freshly sand-
blasted brick and was steadily punching him out. The
other member of the party seemed to consider some
action and decide against it. Instead, he took off down
the sidewalk, moving fast despite a new limp. Del
stepped away from the man he was working on. The
guy, no longer held up by the lapel, slipped to the
ground. The incident was over.

Under the tattered clothes, the old beard, the

rheumy eyes, Del Delacroix was strong enough to fight off four angry, boozed-up men. A lifetime of drinking hadn't done much to affect his strength. He rubbed his shoulder where he'd taken the hit, moving it around several times. Then he looked around for us.

"Sorry about that. Happens sometimes," he said, starting to walk off.

"Are you okay?" I called.

He stopped briefly and then was on his way, tossing a "Fine" behind him. Some people had emerged from the restaurant and were seeing to the injured men while I watched. By the time I turned back to Del, he was gone.

Both twins had torn various items of clothing. Paul had an angry red mark on his chest right where it could be seen with an open collar. It would be a humdinger bruise by morning. We were going to have to do some fast repair work before walking back in the house where Millie could notice what had happened. I didn't want this incident reported on the morning phone call to my mother, and I wasn't too thrilled with the idea of telling Albert. I should never have exposed them to such danger. Still, I was proud of the boys.

"Mom, did you see what Del could do?" asked Paul.

"And do you realize what it means?" added Spence. "That guy was like some kind of superhero. He's the strongest man I've ever seen."

I checked them over, probing Paul's injury. "I saw it. Impressive, but why do you think it matters that he can fight like that?"

"Because he's strong enough to do what we

thought no one could do. If he wanted to hoist his father up to the top of the car, he could do it. By himself. Heck, he could probably toss him to the top of the World Trade Center.'' Spence tucked his shirt in absently. ''And he thinks that man killed his mother. Motive. And ability. Both.''

Paul made a face. ''Nah. He's kind of a nice guy.''

''When he's more or less sober. But what about when he's really drunk? People change.''

The argument went on throughout the trip home. We were able to clean up and change clothes before facing the rest of the world, but somehow the boys looked a little the worse for wear. Millie served us dinner without a word, but I had a feeling she knew perfectly well that something had gone wrong. Odds on, I'd hear about it in the morning.

ELEVEN

WEDNESDAY DAWNED bright and promising as I began charting my mental to-do list. Albert would be home tomorrow. I hated his four-day trips and wanted him back. My article needed writing. Millie had a string of phone calls for me to return, so dealing with them would have to take a certain priority, particularly since one of them was from Detective Morrisey. The boys were heading to the camp today, planning to use the powerful computers available to them there to try tracking Delacroix's tour of service. I hoped they'd manage to do whatever was expected of them by the camp management as well. They were, after all, being paid to work, even though the term hadn't officially started.

Millie had served breakfast this morning in silence, her face stony. The twins, insensitive males that they were, noticed nothing, rushing through cereal and juice and heading out.

She waited till they were gone before launching her projectiles. "So are you going to tell me what happened to those kids or are you going to pretend the bruises I see on them were caused by falls off bikes?"

I bolstered myself with a gulp of coffee, flinching at its heat. If Paul and Spence had just worn long-sleeved, high-necked shirts, Millie wouldn't have seen a thing, but I forgot to warn them and it was, of course, May. "Yeah, um, okay," I stammered, nodding. There went the bright start to the day. "Well, we had a little…uh, happening yesterday. Nothing serious.''

She put down the cloth she'd been holding, a kitchen towel, actually, and leaned against the edge of the dining-room table. That placed her above me, reaffirming her dominant role. ''Did this 'happening,' perhaps, have something to do with our fire? Or the case G. Beckmann, girl detective, is working on? Or the fact that we have the cops calling here again?''

I sighed. ''Oh, Millie, give me a break. Do I have to tell you everything that goes on in my life?''

She fooled with the towel in her hand, twisting it into a ball. ''No. But if you don't, I'll find out for myself.''

She would too; I never doubted it. Like the time in third grade when I'd managed my first—and last—attempt at shoplifting. There was simply no hope for me with this woman. So I told her everything.

She mulled the story over for a minute or two before a tiny smile played at one corner of her mouth. ''Really waded in there, did they?''

''Mm-hmm.''

''How about that.'' She stared off and I assumed she was mentally rehashing the scene. Then she said cheerfully, ''More coffee?''

I couldn't believe it. She was actually pleased. Wonders in this house will truly never cease. After I declined her offer, she collected the boys' plates, swiped at the table with the towel, and returned to the kitchen humming something under her breath. I felt like a biopsy had just come back negative.

Still chewing my English muffin, I adjourned to my desk in a corner of the great room and flipped through the message slips I'd been handed last night. A few

I didn't need to return. Gillian had called to remind Albert of his Friday lesson under the hood. I'd leave that on his dresser. An editor from a magazine I'd never worked for had phoned and requested I return the call next week since he'd be out of the office till Monday. I do love it when new magazines call me out of the blue for an article. So gratifying, such warm fuzzies. Maybe I really had achieved a small reputation. And maybe this wouldn't be one of those editors who insist on three rewrites just so they think they're doing their job. At moments like this, I wasn't ready to stop freelancing.

The photo I'd left for framing, said the message, was ready. That left the only other call of real interest, which was from Morrisey. I'd return that and then call Arlene Masters, nee Delacroix, for an appointment to talk.

Morrisey was away from his desk but only for a moment, according to the young woman who answered his phone. He'd call back as soon as he returned, she assured me, because he had something he wanted to tell me. I sat back in my desk chair and decided to wait for the call before initiating any others. It always irritates me when I try to return a message that was just left and the line is busy. I was glad I waited. Morrisey was back on the line in no more than three minutes.

"Will you be there for half an hour or so?" he asked, ignoring telephone niceties. No hello, nice day, how're you doing.

"I can make a point to be."

"Great. There's something I want to discuss and I need to look in your garage. I don't suppose there's any chance your tree sprayer is around today?"

"What garage? I don't have a garage. And the sprayer may show up. I don't think he finished yesterday, at least not completely. Why do you want him?"

"I'll tell you when I come." He hung up abruptly.

Okay, I'd have to wait for his info. Meanwhile, I could finish my phoning. I left a short message on the new editor's voice mail confirming that his call had been received and that if it was about an assignment, I'd look forward to working with him. I hoped I didn't sound too jazzed, but fresh challenges were always exciting.

Then I called Arlene. She happened to be at the nurses' station at that moment, so I didn't have to leave yet another message and then stare at the phone. She was more than willing to meet with me. In fact, try thrilled. My call, she said, meant I was actively working on her father's murder and that's exactly what she'd hoped was happening. We decided to shoot for the hospital cafeteria around three that afternoon when it was fairly quiet. She could probably squeeze out half an hour. She offered to bring the contents of the envelope her father had sent home with Albert on the off chance it was important somehow, but I was nervous about that. This was the last communication she would ever have from her dad. I didn't want to spill a cup of coffee all over something that she might consider precious. I suggested she make a copy and she agreed.

With serendipitous timing, Morrisey showed up just as I'd checked off the last of my "to-do"'s. He declined Millie's offer of something hot or cold to drink, waited till she left the room, and sunk tiredly into the oversized couch. When he pointed to the chair across from him, I came over, perched on the edge of the cushion, and waited.

"We have a confirmation from the fire department on the chemicals that were used to start your fire," he said without preamble. "It looks like it may have been a crime of convenience."

"What does that mean?"

"Primarily that someone was in your garage looking for an opportunity for vandalism, saw all the flammable chemicals in the corner, and seized the moment. That's what they say was used on the floor leading to your back door, something called a surfactant. Used to make pesticides cling to leaves. The same product your tree man left in that area off the garage."

"Now wait, do you actually know he used that particular chemical or are you just thinking he might have?"

"Here." Morrisey opened his briefcase, fished around for a moment, and came up with a photo. "This was taken the night of the fire."

The picture showed the recessed area of the garage, the part that had escaped destruction. Canisters and sacks were pushed into a corner. The words CAUTION and WARNING could be seen here and there. On one can, large enough to contain five gallons or so, the print was red and large. It said DANGER.

"Boy." I shook my head. "I had no idea sprays like that were flammable."

Morrisey leaned over to point to the DANGER sign in the picture. "Obviously, that stuff is, and that's the surfactant I was talking about. According to the fire people, the rest of the chemicals will burn, but not easily. They're oil. Like motor oil. You can light it and it'll burn, but to get it started, you'd have to hold, like, a cigarette lighter to it for quite a few seconds."

"I can't imagine arsonists use oil to start fires."

"They don't. Most of the time, they use gasoline. Ordinary gasoline is so volatile, you bend down to start *that* with a cigarette lighter and you'll go up yourself."

"And this surfactant stuff?"

"Every bit as volatile, according to my sources. And that's what was used on your house. They've analyzed the traces they found."

I started chewing on a cuticle, a bad habit. "How could they know? Whoever did it, how could he have known that the mess in that corner could be used to burn us down? I didn't know these were flammable materials. Why would anyone else?"

Morrisey crossed his legs, propping one ankle on his knee. I'd never seen him make himself so comfortable. "All he'd have to do is see the DANGER sign. And besides, my dear, not everyone can afford to hire these jobs out. Some people actually deal with garden sprays themselves. They have experience. They know about such things. Incidentally, you might want to talk to your tree man about the wisdom of leaving products like that in the garages of people who hire him. He should have known better."

I could feel my anger growing. That jerk, leaving something around that could have killed us all. Why did Albert hire him? His due diligence was usually better. To Morrisey I only said, "So that's why you wanted to talk to Jesse."

Morrisey shook his head. "No, not really. I'll say something if you want, but telling him off is your job. I want to talk to him about the state of the containers right after the fire, whether or not he could tell if someone had been in them. Any chance he's around now?''

"Don't know. Let's look.''

I led Morrisey through the glass doors to a deck and the yard. It was such a mild day, a breeze carrying the fragrance of new growth, that once out I knew we'd never want to go in again. The detective glanced toward what had until recently been our garage. "You're right. Looks like it's a little too late.'' The cleanup work had already begun under the contractor's lead and there was essentially no longer anything left of the building. All the spray containers were gone.

I was about to agree when I spotted movement in the far northwest corner of the yard. Jesse. I recognized the shirt. He seemed to be packing up his equipment and didn't notice us. I called to him as loudly as I could but he didn't react, continuing on with his methodical cleanup work.

"Here,'' said Morrisey. "We'll try this.'' He dug around in his jacket pocket till he found what he wanted.

I looked and had to laugh. "A whistle? A detective with a whistle? You're kidding.''

"You think? Watch this.'' He put the silver whistle between his lips and let loose with a blast that flushed birds from their hiding places. We were suddenly surrounded by the frightened flapping of many wings. Even insects seemed to spasm into motion. The noise reached Jesse, whose head picked up instantly. When he saw us, he nodded and gestured that he'd be right there.

Morrisey wiped the whistle off against his jacket

and returned it to his pocket. "I've had that since I was a kid," he said, mildly embarrassed. "Gift from a buddy."

"And you love blowing it."

"I do."

Jesse Leake, dragging sacks and hoses behind him, reached us, bending down when he arrived to organize his belongings into a pile. Then he wiped his hands on gray cotton pants.

"You wanted me?"

I introduced Detective Morrisey. Leake nodded silently, his watery eyes alert. When the detective asked him about his stock of pesticides, he was ready with an answer as if he'd just been waiting for an authority to inquire.

"Yeah, I noticed someone had been in my stuff. It was messed up some. I leave things real neat so I know what I got."

"Could you tell if they'd used up quite a bit?"

Leake rubbed a hand across his short gray-blond burr. "Not really."

"Any reason you didn't report it when we were here last?"

Jesse Leake shrugged, jamming his hands into both front pockets. "I meant to say something. Then I decided it weren't worth mentioning."

What a wonderful guy. Our house almost gets burned to the ground with us in it and he doesn't think something that critical was worth mentioning. I was already in a state over Jesse Leake. Ever since our talk about Lawrence, I was steamed and getting madder by the moment. "So, tell me, why did you leave something that flammable in our garage in the first place? Do you do that routinely with your other clients?"

His hands came out of his pockets and rose to chest height, palms out as if to ward off a blow. "Okay, you're right, it was a dumb thing to do. I almost never leave that stuff behind on a job. Usually I finish, but you have too many trees. That night, I figured, shoot, I won't drag it all home. Be back early next morning. Stuffed it in that little space off the main garage."

"And that was the only time you ever left materials behind?"

"I swear. The only time."

Morrisey clearly wanted to talk to him a bit more and I sensed the conversation would proceed better without me. I wandered off, checking the progress of various bulb flowers that were in various states of maturity. When I noticed Morrisey was done with Leake, I returned.

"You're through now for a few months, I assume," I said to Leake.

He was all business now. "Yes, that's a fact. Unless you see something I missed. Keep an eye on those foxtails," he said, nodding toward the offending trees. "They get mites sometimes." He pulled paper from a shirt pocket and started totaling up some numbers. "I can have a bill for you in a minute if you want. Pay me now, or whenever." He licked the point of the pencil, concentrating.

"Wait for me," I told him firmly. Then I took Morrisey's arm and began walking him back to his car, parked around at the front of the house in the circular drive.

"So what do you think?" I asked.

Morrisey stopped to kick a rock from the gravel

path. "Oh, I don't know. I think he's contrite. Just doesn't know how to show it. He knows he screwed up, leaving that stuff around, and it's embarrassing him."

"You make it sound so accidental, like some kid just saw the chance and started our fire for fun."

"I don't mean to say that. Not at all. Too many coincidences, what with all your current involvements. Someone was in your garage planning to put you in harm's way. Maybe to warn you and maybe to accomplish something more. Whatever, those pesticides were just too inviting." He stopped, took my hand from his arm, and turned me to face him.

"You must watch your step, Grace. Really."

"Yeah. Okay."

"Has anything more turned up about the Delacroix murder?"

"I was about to ask *you* that."

"Nothing on our end, though we're working on it. Seriously, what *are* you up to? Anything I should know?"

I told him about our interview with Del and caught him up on everything that had happened since our last talk. We talked about Eli Finer, how the arrest had harmed his professional life.

"What could we do? The ring was found in his place. I'm sorry. He seems to be a good man, but even good men can lose it. Look at the circumstances. Vichy France, his family underground. I read a lot of professional journals that study circumstances vaguely similar to his. An ordinary man faced once in his life with a situation that leads to an extraordinary reaction. Maybe everyone's capable of murder."

"I don't believe it, I really don't."

"Let's not test it out. So be careful. What are you planning next?"

"I have a date with Arlene, Delacroix's daughter, this afternoon. After that…" I shrugged. "I'm running out of fresh blood."

Morrisey got in his unremarkable blue sedan, a car apparently chosen to be ignored in traffic. "We're starting to check on Carla Correa. Asking around. If I learn anything, I'll let you know."

After a few more warnings, he drove off, tires scraping against the loose driveway gravel. I gathered my courage and headed back to the yard where Jesse Leake was waiting with his bill. It was time we had a little talk.

Ever since our discussion about Lawrence, I'd been agitated thinking about the boy's future. Intelligence, perhaps, is never lost but it can go underground when the world fails to value it. Surrounded by all the wrong people—people like his father who fail to understand his son's gift—Lawrence might dumb himself down just to survive. And that would be heartbreaking. An enormous waste.

Leake had his bill in hand when I rounded the corner into the back lower yard. He looked at me expectantly. "There's no hurry about this. You can pay it whenever." The way his eyes followed the paper as I folded it into my pocket, however, let me know he hoped I'd pay it soon.

I hadn't decided yet whether to fire him or not for his inadvertent part in the fire, but right now it was more important to save Lawrence.

"Jesse, I want to talk to you about your son. What you did with your chemicals was stupid. What you're about to do to… 'Larry' is beyond stupid. It's criminal. I've offered to see that he receives financial help, enough to allow him to go to college and use that fine mind of his, and you're making noises like you won't allow it. I find that outrageous.''

Leake rolled his eyes, a pointless gesture since there was no one but me to see it. Then he just turned angry. ''Mrs. Beckmann,'' he growled, ''I really don't think this is any of your business.''

''It *is* my business. A talented young man like that is the world's business.''

He looked like he wanted to kick something. The color rose in his pale face, infusing the scalp. His hair was so short, it turned suddenly red. His eyes wandered to my pocket where the considerable bill was tucked. I could almost see the wheels turning while he wondered how far he dared go and still be paid for his work. Apparently he decided discretion was called for, though the idea made him choke.

''I'll...think about it, okay?''

It was the best I could do. I didn't even say good-bye, just turned and walked quickly toward the house before he could see that I was gritting my teeth. I didn't want to say anything that would keep Lawrence from being able to spend time at our house. He needed us.

As it was to turn out, we needed him too.

TWELVE

THE LITTLE WHITE RENTAL was an ongoing irritation, in part because so many things I kept in my Aurora of blessed memory were gone. I'd replaced the cell phone. Some things one can't do without. But the extra pair of prescription dark glasses, the electronic parking cards, *Penzance* tape and CDs, coupons to cover overdue books at the library—all burned up with the car and none of them had been replaced. Maybe, once Albert got home, we'd have time to go look for new wheels.

I pulled into the hospital lot, not, for once, having to wait for the automated arm to decide someone had left, there was room for me, and it could lift itself up. My car as well as Albert's had staff parking stickers on their back windows, allowing me access to primo spaces, but, of course, the rental didn't. I didn't mind the longer walk, though. I was a little early for my appointment with Arlene and the teaching hospital always made me nostalgic.

When we were young marrieds and Albert was a house officer, meeting him here for a quick lunch was like a secret tryst. I was taking graduate courses in English and working part-time in the wedding department of the city's largest department store, racing back and forth to be prompt for my classes or work. Albert was rarely off his feet and rarely slept. By the time we converged in our small apartment at night, we were both so exhausted, we could barely stay awake long enough to wave. The lunches of usually dreadful institutional food were like a hot date. And how many people care what they eat on a hot date?

The halls of the main building were a maze of cream-colored walls, full of turns and reverses, studded with an occasional brass plaque to help place you in space. Hansel and Gretel's bread crumbs. With or without them, I couldn't get lost here. I could get to the cafeteria blindfolded. I was just rounding the last turn before the elevator when I ran into Eli Finer.

He was with a younger man, both wearing white lab coats and both carrying folders. The Research Fellow, as I assumed him to be, smiled absently before checking his watch and hurrying on down the long hallway. Eli, of course, stopped, embraced me, and planted a sweet kiss on my cheek. Americanisms were invading his European gestures, but the underlying warmth remained the same.

"Looking for Albert?" he asked, making a stab at peering around. "I haven't seen him for a couple of days, but he's probably around somewhere."

"No, actually he isn't. In New York. But he'll be back tomorrow."

Eli slapped his forehead, taking care to tuck the folders under his arm first. "Oh, of course. I knew that." Then he frowned. "You're not sick, are you?"

"No, no, fat and sassy."

"Sassy, anyway."

I smiled at the gallantry. "I have an appointment to meet Arlene Masters at three. We haven't talked since last week. Thought it was time for an update."

Eli's face seemed to lose its tone. The muscles sagged, allowing jowls to form and make him look old. "A nice-enough woman, but every time I see her in the halls, I wish she worked somewhere else.'' I didn't know what to say. ''She makes it hard for me to forget the trouble I'm in. And how frustrating it is that there's nothing I can do to help myself. I feel out of control. Like the Fates or something are playing with me.''

''I know, Eli. I'm just so sorry this happened.''

''The thing is, people in the hospital have heard. I can tell. They stop talking when I walk up. They know I've been in jail. Imagine! In jail.'' He shook his head, rubbing his eyes with a free hand. ''It's one of the worst things that has ever happened to me and some terrible things have certainly happened to me. This is right up there.''

I rubbed his shoulder, ending with a gentle pat. I couldn't help him. Not only that, I had the feeling that my presence was as upsetting to him as that of Arlene Masters or Detective Morrisey. Time to move on. I threw him a kiss and found the elevator buttons nearby. Eli, looking ineffably sad, walked away.

Arlene was waiting at the door to the cafeteria, several floors down and just beyond the elevator. She looked, I thought, like the perfect nurse, the one I wanted for my own if I ever had to be in a hospital. Other than having babies, I'd so far managed to avoid that reality, but the day would doubtless come and when it did, I wanted Arlene to take care of me.

Her straight dark hair had been cut since last I'd seen her and swished cheerily a little above her shoulder. She smiled but only briefly. Then her face returned to its serious expression and remained that way, the dark eyes firm and unblinking. Albert said she was very, very competent. She looked it.

I glanced at my watch. ''Am I late?''

"No. Early, actually. But so am I. Let's get something before we sit down. I'm famished, and I don't get off till eight."

We took trays and went through the line. By mid-afternoon, there was little left of lunch, though cold sandwiches were still available. Arlene took a roast beef and Swiss with a soft drink. I poured myself a cup of coffee and, after losing to temptation, added a piece of carrot cake. This detective business seemed to entail more than three meals a day. Pretty soon, "fat and sassy" would be right on the mark.

We took over a corner table, both of us choosing to face the wall, partly in the interest of privacy and partly to screen out the tacky surroundings. Hospitals, in my experience, seem to feel that allowing staff eating areas a touch of graciousness is somehow inappropriate. Don't want our people to dawdle now, do we? The large portable metal shelving, too close to ignore, was still stacked with uncleared trays and the remains of many unfinished meals. Now and then, I caught a whiff of leftover onion from the day's meat loaf special. At least there was no canned music to assault us.

"Here," said Arlene, after taking a tiny bite from her sandwich. "See what you make of this." She handed me a large manila envelope, its clasp unsealed.

I moved my coffee away and carefully removed the contents. As promised, it was a copy, black-and-white, from what had probably been a colored cover and the pages of a piece of sheet music. A single song, Rodgers and Hart's "Bewitched," was all there was. I flipped through it quickly and looked up at Arlene. "This is it?"

She wiped the corner of her mouth and nodded. "All she wrote. Would it help, you think, to see the original? I did as you asked and just brought a copy."

"I don't know." Nothing jumped out at me. I flipped through it once more, smoothed it out, and put it back in the envelope. "I'll look at it more carefully in a minute. First I want to catch you up on our progress. Or rather, lack thereof."

She knew, of course, about Eli's arrest. The whole hospital did, she said. He was right about that. The arson attempt on our house was news to her, however, and she was suitably horrified.

"Oh, Grace, that's dreadful. Terrible! I feel so guilty. Do you think your helping me with Dad's murder caused that?"

I shrugged. "Not to worry. And besides, Eli needs our help, too. It's not just you. All we know about the fire is that Detective Morrisey—you talked to him, didn't you?—thinks it might have been a crime of convenience."

I went on to tell her about Delacroix's probable abuse of Carla Correa and my interview with Martin Hazlett, leaving her almost as distressed as the story of the fire. "He was some piece of work, my father," she said, shaking her head sadly. "A batterer, a cheat. A big-time cheat, too. Really, what he did to Hazlett was literally criminal. He's lucky he didn't land in jail."

I didn't tell her what we suspected about the Finer family money and jewels. I figured what I was about to check out with her would be trauma enough.

"Did you ever think that your father had anything to do with your mother's death?"

"What? You're kidding. Of course not. She died in a car accident."

"I had lunch with your brother. My kids and I. That's his theory."

She pushed her plate away angrily, the sandwich half eaten. Of all the unpleasant information I'd had to dump on her, this was clearly the worst. "That would be the last straw if I believed it, but you can't trust anything Del says. He's been a liar all his life, even before he became a drunk. He'd blame Dad for germ warfare if he could."

"But you did know she was planning to leave him, that she'd been packing up for a week before her car failed."

She sank back in her chair, defeated. "I don't know. I was very young. I guess I knew that's what Del thought. I'm repressing it. Here." She wrote a name and telephone number on a clean paper napkin and handed it to me. "That's my mother's sister, Natalie Burns. My Aunt Nattie. She was very good to me after Mom died. Talk to her. They used to confide in each other, my mother and her, talked on the phone when my father was out of the house. He didn't like the fact they were close, so they tended to talk sort of secretly. She might know what Mom's intentions were back then. Though what difference it could make today I can't imagine."

I didn't tell her that a mother's murder could be a motive for Del himself to take revenge, even after all these years, that stranger things have happened. A table of noisy house officers had taken a table near us, and they were talking loudly about a new admission. Why was quiet such a rare commodity? I folded the enscribed napkin and put it in the paper money sec-

tion of my wallet. Arlene was casting sullen glares at
the residents, looks which did nothing to dampen their
decibel count. I finished my coffee, the last crumb of
the cake (alas), and returned my plates to the tray.
Then, with the deck cleared, I looked again at the
music.

It looked like ordinary piano music, the kind I'd
had fun with as a kid. Guitar notation plus banjo and
ukelele chords marched above the treble clef lines,
with the song's words taking the space between the
two staffs. Copyright 1941, it said, and I guessed,
from the look of the copy, Delacroix had owned it
almost that long.

"Boy, they don't write 'em like they used to," I
said, humming the chorus under my breath. "I remember hearing this tune years ago. Did your father
play the piano?"

"No. My mom. This was probably her music."

"I'm looking at a copy, obviously, but does the
original you have look like it might have been pretty
old?"

"Yeah, really. He must have kept her sheet music,
for some reason. I can't believe he didn't trash it. He
certainly threw out everything else without even asking us kids. I remember, after she died, going through
the garbage when he wasn't looking and picking out
little things of hers that he'd heaved. A comb with a
real silver back. A compact like women used to have,
with loose powder that smelled like her. Some pa-
perbacks with twenty-five-cent price tags. Hid them
all. But I didn't see her music."

I shook my head, puzzled. "'Bewitched.' Does that
mean something to you?"

She put her head between her hands. "Not even

slightly. It hardly describes my parents' life together.''

I looked through the pages again. ''Okay, I'm going to read the lyrics of the chorus out loud. Stay sort of, well, associative, I guess. Tell me anything that strikes you.'' I found a streak of sunlight, positioned the pages in the middle, and started reading....

I looked up expectantly. ''Well?''

''Are you kidding? Lyrics sound so stupid when they're just read. Absolutely nothing sounds... What did you say, 'associative'? I can't relate that to anything my father would have felt, though I'm probably missing something. He did, after all, underline parts of the song.''

''What?'' I looked at the music again. ''You mean these lines under some of the words are his? I thought they were printed. Unusual pedal markings or something.''

''That's because you're looking at a copy. Those lines were drawn there in blue ink but you can't see that. Hey, maybe my mother made those marks. Maybe she sang this in a school show or something, and those were accents. But frankly...''

The rowdy crowd at the next table left, after a great screeching of chairs across the linoleum, and the room was suddenly silent. I studied the music again. ''Arlene,'' I said finally, ''there has to be something here. I remember watching when your father handed this to Albert. He was very intense, very serious. I just really believe this music is important somehow.''

Albert had said that Arlene Masters was a very bright woman. Watching her focus, eyes fixed on a crack in the table, I could believe it. She sat back.

"Okay, read me just the underlined words. Maybe *that* will pattern out."

I chased the patch of sunlight that was moving away from me till it illuminated the music. "Here we go. '*Sim*pering, *wim*pering.' And '*Could*n't sleep, *would*n't sleep.' And here's one under 'Lost *my* heart.'" I flipped through the three pages again. "That's it. I don't see any more markings."

I looked at her and then, inexplicably, we both started giggling. "Oh, good grief," she said. "I can't believe two grown women are wasting their time like this. Would you like anything more to eat or drink? I'm going to have to get back to the floor."

"I have to go, too." I stood up and gathered my belongings, taking care to put the music back in its envelope and fasten the metal clasp. The sunlight through a window across the room was starting to deepen, turning gold as it sank toward the mountains.

Arlene, by now also on her feet, hesitated for a moment and then put a hand on my shoulder. I stopped what I was doing. "What?"

"One more thing. It's possible someone broke into our apartment."

"Oh, Arlene! And you waited till now to tell me?"

She looked embarrassed. Then she started to walk toward the exit and its nearby elevator. I followed her quickly. "The thing is, we can't be sure. You know we haven't been married for all that long, so we're not that sure about each other's habits. I just thought maybe Perry had left a drawer open. He thought I'd forgotten to lock up. It took us a while to figure it out. But now we really do think there may have been someone in there."

"Did you call the police?"

She shook her head no. "Nothing that we could see was missing. We couldn't be absolutely sure, in spite of our hunches. I could just imagine how we'd explain all this to the police."

My thoughts flashed back to the night of chemicals and smoke. I could smell all that again, hear Millie and the kids as we raced through the house groping for the outdoors. I felt a flush of heat that had nothing to do with the hospital hallway. The elevator came but I pulled Arlene away from it. "Don't take it. Now look, there's a real possibility that the person who murdered your father may have been looking for something. Everything, and apparently I do mean everything, was taken from his FBO. All the drawers had been stripped and the contents removed. Shelves wiped clean, except for a few doodads that he used to sell. Anyway, that's what the sheriff said. So why wouldn't the murderer search your place? Your relationship is no secret."

"But we don't have anything! You know I hadn't seen him in years till he suddenly showed up at the wedding. He wasn't the type to remember birthdays."

"A wedding present?"

"Money. A hundred dollars, can you believe? Daddy Warbucks."

"Where was this piece of sheet music?"

"Actually, I kept it here at the hospital in my locker. Your husband left it here for me and I just never took it home."

"Hmmm." I stared, pondering, at an old cigarette receptacle full of sand. Once, when smoking was allowed everywhere including hospitals, those containers were necessary to keep people from entering elevators still lit up. Today they were an anachronism.

Like old Rodgers and Hart songs. "Whatever he—
I'm assuming *he*—was looking for, he must not have
found it in all the junk he took away from the murder
scene. So this music has to be it. It has to be. Anyway,
do leave it here. And be super careful when you walk
into your empty apartment."

Arlene took a step toward the elevator and then
hesitated, turning. "I have to ask you, Grace. Do you
think it's possible that the killer only wanted my dad?
I mean, that he isn't a killer at all in the usual sense?
That once he shot my father, he'd be unlikely ever to
be violent again?"

"Are you kidding? It seems to me that anyone who
could kill once... Well if you mean that you don't
really have to be afraid even if you were to walk in
on him or her going through your things, forget it.
That's crazy."

"But there hasn't been any other violence."

"Arlene... Okay, I wasn't going to tell you this,
but the sheriff said your father had been tortured with
a knife, that there were wounds all over his body.
Does that sound like the work of a sane, nonviolent
killer?"

"Oh, no. Oh, no." Her eyes were wide with horror.

"I'm sorry. I didn't want to tell you that."

In tears, she nodded. "You had to. I'll be careful."

We parted, each absorbed in her own thoughts. I
despised what I'd just done to Arlene, despised the
killer for making me do it. And I despised James Delacroix for being the kind of no-good human being
whom someone hated to death.

THIRTEEN

ALBERT'S WEDNESDAY NIGHT string quartet group had been forced to replace him with another violinist yet again. Try as he might, there was no way he could get in from New York before Thursday morning. This had been going on ever since his sabbatical had assumed its present shape, and he wasn't happy. His ensemble playing was suffering and no amount of solitary practice could replace the weekly gathering. Usually, when Albert was in town, they played at our house, which meant I could neither run nor hide. Since they were working on something by Schonberg, I figured, philistine that I am, that it didn't much matter whether he practiced or not.

He arrived late Thursday morning, hauling a bulging briefcase and the ubiquitous rolling carry-on behind him. He had this commuting thing pretty much down to a science, leaving his car at the airport and packing the barest minimum for each trip. Still he was dragging, jet-lagged, and glad to be home.

He checked his mail and phone messages automatically, facing the worst before he'd allow himself to relax. "Rats," he muttered, dropping all the paper back on the sideboard.

"Trouble?"

"Always. I need a nine-day week. Seven days to work and two days to play. Anything new here since I talked to you last?"

"Too much to tell you quickly but not enough to brag about."

"You mean you haven't solved the murder yet? You're losing your touch. But, of course you've convinced Spence to change his mind about college, the house has been completely cleared of fire damage, and the garage is rebuilt, right?"

"I did all that before breakfast. And threw together two hundred manuscript pages on natural resource development in Raratonga."

"Good work."

Albert disappeared into the kitchen to say hello to Millie and find something to munch. Walking through the door created automatic hunger pains in all of us— the old Home from School syndrome. By the time he found me in the great room, the boys had come in and were sprawled in front of MTV, which was on at top volume. I think, knowing their father was home, they turned it on just for the predictable result. Nor were they disappointed.

"Off! *Off!* OFF!" he roared, coming through the door. "Turn that garbage off and try to restore what's left of your hearing."

"Hi, Dad," they called more or less in unison. "And nice to see you, too," Paul added as he turned off the set. Had Albert been one of those fathers who shared their enthusiasm for things adolescent, they would have been truly disappointed.

He came up behind them and gave their shoulders a squeeze. "To what do we owe this pleasure in the middle of a weekday?"

"Camp hasn't started yet," said Spence. "At least, the kids haven't come."

"But we haven't been idle," added Paul. "We've

been working on the 'Delacroix at War' problem. You'll be impressed.''

Albert sat down near them, leaning forward, elbows on knees. With the television mute, the day seemed suddenly and unusually quiet. The usual ambient noises were gone. The men working on the garage had taken off on a break, so all the machines were silent. The boys had our full attention and took advantage of it.

"First of all, how did you approach it?" asked Albert, always open to learning more about computers from the generation that was born to it. "Did you go on the Internet?"

"Well, sure," said Spence. "What did you think? There are all sorts of ways to tackle this, and when we ran out of ideas, Lawrence knew of lots of others. He was great with this, by the way."

"Good. But really, tell me what you've been doing. By the way, do they mind you working on the camp computers? If so, I can probably find you something fast enough around the hospital. They'd let you use it off-hours, probably."

"No, the camp people figure the more we learn the better for them. And heck, when we told them we were trying to solve a murder, well…"

"They were awed?"

"They thought we were hallucinating. But they didn't stop us."

Millie chose that moment to show up at the door. Her hair was out of its clips, strands creeping down one cheek. She was flushed and annoyed. "Okay, I give up. I went to the cupboard to get some canned tomatoes for a soup and all the cans are either black or funny shaped. I just threw everything out. And you should see what else has happened in there. I never thought to check *inside* the cabinets. I have about five hours of soot cleanup that I hadn't counted on…and the last thing I need to deal with right now is lunch.'' She dared us all to look hungry. ''And I'm going to have a shopping list from here to next Tuesday to replace all these ruined staples.''

We fell all over ourselves telling her that it was no problem, we'd go out. Albert was on his feet immediately and headed for the kitchen, going with her to see what she was up against. Behind his back, he signaled for us to come with him. Millie, we knew, needed to share the disaster. It.wasn't going to be enough for us just to disappear and make her job easier, she needed some appreciation in advance. I could understand that. What always surprised and, I admit, pleased me about Albert was the fact that he could, too.

We promised to bring her back some *chilis relleños* from a Mexican restaurant, and that mollified her somewhat. They weren't up there with bratwurst as her favorite food, but they made the top ten. Our restaurant of choice was a bit of a drive from home but only a short walk from the city's medical school and teaching hospitals, which meant the food didn't necessarily have to be good for the place to survive. Hungry, tired young docs would eat anything that didn't eat them first, but as it happened, the cook was first-rate.

It was early for lunch but the small café was at least half full when we arrived. The smell of fajitas frying in the kitchen mingled with that of fresh lilacs on each table, cut, no doubt, from the owners' own bushes. Brilliant, somewhat primitive, painted designs adorned every inch of wall space, earning for their artist, I suspected, a lifetime of free enchiladas. Owners Victor Ortiz and his wife, Joaquina, greeted us with the enthusiasm reserved for longtime customers. We waited till our lunches arrived to place the to-go *rellenos* order for Millie in hopes they'd stay warm. Albert knew most of the other members of the lunch crowd and took a moment or two to greet them all. Only then could we sit down and invite the boys to tell us what they'd been up to, so finally they were able to debrief. And not a moment too soon. They were about to explode.

World War II, they informed us, has a major presence all over the Internet. Military forums are everywhere, handling queries and searches, often for people missing in that long-ago and distant war. The boys had left messages on a number of them and checked back often. Web sites, too, had begun to spring up on a number of specific battle zones and areas. They were struck, they said, by how many new ones were being added even as they explored what was out there. As for interactive online sites, they were legion and the people who used them were, they decided, totally amazing. Encyclopedic minds and huge files of records. People had stories of finding long-lost relatives still alive and the graves of those who hadn't been so fortunate. The Web sites were human interest treasure troves.

"You could find article ideas here, Mom."

"C'mon, guys, cut to the chase. What have you turned up?" asked Albert, the weariness beginning to catch up to him.

"Well, we've found that nobody named Delacroix ever fought at Bastogne."

I groaned. "Terrific."

"And," Paul added, "no one named Delacroix was stationed in England. At least not during 1944 or 1945."

His brother joined in. "Except for a Mary Delacroix. An army nurse."

"We can eliminate her."

"Well…" I looked at Albert. "What are we supposed to make of that? That the guy was a total liar along with everything else?"

"Mom," said Spence, half leaning across the table in his earnestness. "Del said he thought he was telling the truth. Carla thought he was telling the truth, at least about his war record. These are people who knew him better than anyone. I think we should assume they're right."

"Then his name at the time must not have been Delacroix." The minute I said it, I knew the thought was inspired but no one else at the table seemed to have heard me.

"At least he wasn't named Smith," said Albert, reaching over with his fork to snag a bit of leftover chimichanga still on my plate. "Then we'd have gotten incredible noise. Too many false positives. In a way, it's lucky Delacroix is a fairly unusual name."

"Great, Dad," said Spence, "but where do we go from here? It's taken us hours, actually *days* of work on the computers to come up with these two dry holes. A negative answer may be better than no answer, but it doesn't exactly move us along."

Joaquina arrived with two cups of her trademark bitter coffee. Albert could never handle it without cream, so he poured in a liberal stream of white and stirred. "Let's assume, just for fun, that he changed his name," Albert speculated.

"Oh, you did hear me," I said.

"Hear what?"

"Forget it."

"As I was about to say, we could hardly check every male Delacroix in the world to see if he was born with the family name."

"But since we're assuming, let's assume he really did fight at Bastogne," I tried again. "And/or, really did serve in England at some point."

"Okay," said Spence, picking up on the game. "Then here's a big 'let's assume.' Let's assume that he kept the initial D."

"Why assume that?" asked Paul, feeling perverse. He hated to have Spence jump too far ahead of him.

"Because think about it, dumbhead. When people change their names, don't they almost always have the new ones start with the same initial? Maybe they like their monograms to match."

The acidity of the coffee made me pucker. "Strangely enough, I sort of agree with Spence. What would happen if you tried for all the men with the initial D who fought at Bastogne?"

"Oh Mom, get real."

"Well, how about D and E together? That would narrow it. Paul, who, unlike you, Spence, may take French in college and become slightly educated, will learn that *de* and *la* are French for 'of the.' Maybe there's a connection there."

"And *croix* means cross. We had French in eighth grade. I don't need college for that," said Spence with an attitude.

The sound of the booming voice made us freeze,

cups halfway to our lips, napkins in mid-swipe. "If it isn't the famous Beckmanns, parents and child. Children." He was upon us before we could react, his beautiful white hair curling over the collar of a silk-and-mohair jacket. Albert was instantly on his feet, greeting the man I recognized from too many faculty parties as the head of cardiac surgery.

"Dan, how are you? You remember Grace, I know. These are our boys, Paul and Spence. Kids, this is Dr. Xavier. We're almost through here, but join us anyway." He pulled a chair from another table and everyone moved around to make room.

I wondered if that was what he really wanted to do but Albert had left the poor man no choice. "Well, all right, if you don't mind. I just stop in here sometimes for their iced tea and a couple of *sopapillas*. I don't have a lot of time." Joaquina, serving a couple across the room, felt the vibes. He caught her eye. "The usual," he mouthed silently.

While professional small talk swirled about, I tried to remember what Albert had told me recently about Dan Xavier. He flew too. Was that it? He piloted his own twin because he had a clinic, or a hospital affiliation, somewhere in New Mexico. Used the plane to fly down there once or twice a month rather than rely on commercial aircraft. I think I heard the work was, at least in part, pro bono. Heart surgery, the kind that was probably saving lives, was far too expensive for the natives of some of the more remote areas of that wild and beautiful state. He could give of his time and expertise, allowing himself the pleasure of altruism and the joy of having an excuse to fly his own plane. Altogether a win-win situation. Albert considered him basically a good guy, if not one without a substantial ego.

I waited for a break in the conversation and then asked, "Ever stop over at Copper Creek in your plane?"

He looked at me oddly. "Often, actually." Then he brightened. "Oh, right, you're involved in that business down there, aren't you? I heard something about it. Yeah, I knew Jim Delacroix. Used to let him fill me up on occasion. Too bad, what happened."

The tea and a basket of *sopapillas* with honey arrived, so quickly I suspected Joaquina kept a supply ready just in case her distinguished customer came in. She also left a package on the floor near my purse, Millie's *rellenos* I guessed.

Albert was leaning forward, the chair's back legs in the air. "Ever see him professionally?"

Xavier shook his head. "Nope. But he did send me a woman he was seeing. Can't remember her name. Nice-looking gal, a certain age. Said they'd been seeing each other for years. Know her?"

Albert nodded. In fact, we all did. "Carla Correa. Problems?"

"Bad ticker. Untreated childhood strep, I suspect. Wanted to operate, but she said she'd have to wait till she had the money. She's one of those, you know, who fall through the cracks of our superb medical business establishment." His voice was pure irritation. "I offered to do it for expenses, the operating room, hospital, and so forth. She wouldn't hear of it. Proud woman."

I couldn't help being intrigued. Carla had seemed to be relatively well off, but relatively was the oper-

ative word. Without good insurance, open-heart surgery could do a number on the finances of all but the
megarich. "Dan," I broke in as gently as possible.
"Did she talk to you about…oh, you know, anything
at all? Anything of a personal nature? Did she talk
about Delacroix?"

Daniel Xavier broke off a piece of *sopapilla*,
dipped it in honey, and popped it in his mouth. Not
soon enough. A drizzle of yellow slipped out one corner, but he was quick with a napkin. Long practice.
"Now and then," he offered in my direction. "I
asked her once if he could help her out with the sur-
gical expenses. The guy didn't seem rich exactly, but
he didn't seem poor either. Always had that new Cadillac parked by the building. You see it?"

Albert laughed. "Yeah. The last time we saw it, it
had what you might call an unusual roof adornment."

"Oh right. I heard. Anyway, she said he wasn't that
generous. Not usually. I think she was a little afraid
of him, actually. Just the way she acted when his
name came up. She said she had nine or ten guns in
the house and no one was going to fool with her, at
least not more than once. Had the feeling she was
referring to him."

He'd finished his messy snack and started fishing
in his pocket for a credit card. I didn't want him to
go. Staring at him, I willed him to remember something critical, or at the very least something useful.
"Think, Daniel, please. Did she ever say anything
else?"

"You really care, Grace, don't you? Oh…that's
right." He turned to Albert. "His daughter is one of
your nurses, isn't she?"

"And Eli Finer's involved."

Xavier smiled ruefully. "Of course. Okay, let me think." He stared unseeing at the wall of designs. "Well, there was this."

We all tensed.

"We got into a discussion of murder once. I think I said something like, she wouldn't ever really *fire* any of those guns at anyone. She responded that murder was less foreign, less exotic than most people realize. That I probably knew at least one murderer. She said it really pointedly. She didn't mean it as an abstract idea."

"Did she imply *she* would be willing to shoot someone?"

"I asked her. She said some people deserved to die. In certain circumstances, she wouldn't hesitate to fire. Of course, at the time I wrote that off to her melodramatic instincts." He frowned. "You don't really think she killed Delacroix, do you?"

None of us answered. I thought back to that night and morning in her pleasant home, at how impressed I was with her style, her independence. And how I wondered what on earth a woman like that was doing in a tiny town, a place with so little to offer.

Xavier stood, brushing crumbs from his handsome jacket. "Better go. I've probably violated some doctor-patient privileges as it is, but murder is murder. On a brighter note," he said to Albert, "how's the instrument training going?"

"Tricky sometimes," he answered. "Of course, you're way past that. You've been flying now for, what, twenty years?"

"Just about. But I remember having to learn all that stuff, too, flying under the hood and missing half the instruments I was supposed to be scanning. Who's your teacher?''

"Gillian Morgan. Know her?''

"Sure. Cute, blond.'' He grinned. "I could handle having her flying right seat. She's been around a while too, hasn't she?''

"One of the many flying and waiting for a chance at the big time. Nice gal, though. I think I have a lesson with her coming up, don't I?''

He was looking at me, his appointment secretary. I couldn't blame him, really. This sabbatical bit was throwing every routine off. "Tomorrow.''

"When?''

"I don't know if she said.''

"I'll call.'' He got up and shook Daniel Xavier's hand. "Once I'm through with this project I'm involved with in New York, we'll have to have lunch. Talk about flying, of course.''

"You're on. I'll try to talk you into moving up to a twin.''

Albert smiled. "Never. I want to live.''

Later, when it was our turn to go, Victor followed us to the door, commenting on how big the boys were getting. We'd been coming here since they were in kindergarten. Joaquina ran up to us, waving the *chilis rellenos* bag I'd managed to leave on the floor. Millie would have been justifiably upset.

My slacks, not all that clean when I'd started the day, now sported a salsa stain right by the zipper. The meal was worth it, though. I felt we'd learned something, something that, in due course, would become clear. At the moment, however, it didn't mean a thing.

FOURTEEN

I COULD HEAR Albert on the phone early Friday morning asking the linemen to pull *Romeo* out of the hangar. He hadn't been able to reach Gillian last night and she didn't return his message, but they usually flew at 9:00 a.m., so he assumed she'd meet him out there. He had his flying case waiting on the couch. His hood, the oversized visor, he kept in the plane's backseat at the ready.

Without being able to see a horizon out the window, and that would be the situation in a total cloud cover, it wasn't always so obvious what direction was down. Or up. Instincts could fool you. Hence the instruments and hence instrument training. Without that rating, a pilot could only fly VFR (Visual Flight Regulations). It was okay with me if neither of us ever flew in a pea-souper, but I admit I didn't mind my personal pilot knowing all there was to know. Besides, it wasn't like Albert to quit a project before it was finished.

The boys were gone before I turned off the shower. I envied the fact that they could give so little thought to what they wore. Jeans, a T-shirt, and they were off. Clean was good, but not essential. Today, that comfy uniform wouldn't do it for me. I needed something other than my grungies, since I had an appointment to see Arlene's Aunt Natalie at the retirement complex where she lived. She sounded pleasant enough on the phone and far from elderly, though putting what I knew about her together, I figured she must be about ninety. Jeans would have been, well, disrespectful. My skirt choices were very short or very long. Nothing in between. I decided on very long, with tiny flowers on a black background, worn with sandals. The effect wasn't bad. I knew because Millie gave me an approving nod as I walked out the door.

Jeans, as it turned out, would have been fine. Aunt Nattie was legally blind. She met me in the complex's sunroom where she had been taken by an aide and left to await me. Unfortunately, she had to wait longer than I would have liked. The complex was just that, a number of separate buildings servicing different levels of need, from people like Nattie, who needed minimal care, to locked Alzheimer's wards. Lost as always, I stumbled through most of them, wandering aimlessly. Smells of perfumed sprays and detergents fought each other in the halls and both lost. No one knew where to find my lady. Many of those working in the complex spoke very little English, looked at me, and shrugged. I was beginning to feel like a character out of Kafka, powerless in the face of an unknowable bureaucracy, when I hit a pleasant solarium and saw the solitary figure.

She was old but by no means frail. Her hair was a color-enhanced white and professionally styled; her nails were manicured, long, and very red. Her outfit, a slim, navy blue dress with matching jacket, would have been at home in a boardroom. Sitting in a padded armchair, her legs crossed at the ankles, she had the hinged lid of her watch up and was feeling the hands. She looked annoyed. I hurried over.

"Mrs. Burns, I'm so sorry. I got lost in all these

buildings. I'm really ashamed to have kept you waiting so long. I'm Grace Beckmann.''

She put out a hand in my general direction and I took it, shaking it firmly. "It's not like you're keeping me from something I should be doing," she admitted a bit tartly. "But old habits, like punctuality, die hard.'' She sat up straighter. "You're here about Delacroix, aren't you? Terrible person. Terrible man. Someone should have killed him long ago.'' She expected no contradiction and got none.

I pulled a straight chair over and sat directly in front of her, our knees almost touching. "Yes, you're right, of course, probably on all counts. Was it you, by the way, who reported the words between him and Dr. Finer at the wedding?''

"No, that must have been someone else. I wouldn't do anything to help find the murderer of that man. More power to him, I say.''

"Oh, dear," I said. "I understand how you feel but I hope that doesn't mean you won't be willing to talk to me. Arlene said you might be able to help. She thinks the world of you, by the way.''

Natalie Burns smiled a bit at this, turning her head toward the window where the sun was so strong she seemed to sense the light. "And I her. She's a survivor, that one. Her brother wasn't so fortunate. Her mother either. But she has pluck, that girl. I helped her with her education, with nursing school, but she would have made it without me.''

"I don't know about that.''

"I do. I only wish my sister could have seen what a fine person she turned out to be. It would have given her life some meaning, which it certainly didn't have at the time she left it.''

I patted the unnecessary skirt over my knees, hedging. "Well, actually that's what I've really come to ask you about."

She snorted lightly. "I'm aware of that. Arlene told me. You want me to tell you why I'm sure that you-know-what killed her. Well, he did. Take my word for it. She was about to hightail it out of there and he got wind of it. He wasn't the kind of man who ever let a fox escape a trap. Or a woman he felt he owned. He'd rather see it, or her, dead." Her head shook with old fury.

"And she told you she was planning to leave him?"

The woman, her rage temporarily spent, reached out with one hand and felt around on a nearby table. She found a roll of Life Savers and, after offering me one, which I declined, slipped one in her mouth. "Lemon. It must have been yellow."

"It was."

"Blindness is a nuisance, but one can work around it much of the time. Yes, she said she was taking the children and sneaking away right after Delacroix left for Denver on a long weekend, which he was about to do. She said she had it all planned. And then..."

"I know. I'm so sorry. But tell me, if you don't...well, if you don't think I'm prying too much...tell me, why did she marry him in the first place? From what Del said, she was a cultured woman. I assume she was bright as well, as, obviously, are you. So why...?"

"He bought her."

"Excuse me?"

"He bought her just as sure as a rancher buys a heifer. Bought and paid for. See, he'd always had eyes for her, even in school, but she wasn't having any of the likes of him. Then our father, well, he got himself in a lot of trouble. Himself and all the rest of us. It was right after the war and the government was going after anyone suspected of dealing in black market goods. We didn't know anything. Papa went off to work in the morning and came back at night and we hadn't any idea what he did. Not really. Then suddenly there were huge fines to pay and he had to sell our house. We moved into this tiny rental hardly big enough for two, let alone a family of five. But we were more than uncomfortable. We were mortified. Hid from everyone we'd known.

"That's where Jim Delacroix, which was what he called himself then, found us and I swear it pleased him. What do they say on the radio these days, it 'leveled the playing field'? It did, too. He figured he was, if anything, better than Papa. Even then, though, Lois wouldn't have given him a second look, but..."

"Wait, Mrs. Burns." I hated to interrupt the flow of her story but I couldn't let that comment go. "What do you mean by what he called himself then?"

She moved herself awkwardly in the chair, flinching when something seemed to hurt. "Oh, he'd changed his name for some reason. She'd known him from school, but he didn't call himself by his old name. I have no idea why. Bad memories, maybe. Wanted to change who he'd been."

I was elated, but tried to keep the triumph from my voice. "Any idea what his name had been in school?"

She shook her head. "I don't. Sorry. Usually I can remember the old days, but that name's gone."

I knew it had probably been too much to ask, but at least we were on the right track. "Please go on."

"Well, that's about all, really. He paid off Papa's loans, his fines. He seemed to have come back from the war with money. In return, he got Lois. It wasn't quite as simple as that, but I'm telling you the way it was in fact. She knew if she said no, the rest of us would be stuck in that little house, and in that even smaller town where everyone was shunning us. The money let us leave, set up in a big city. We thanked her and never looked back." A tear fell down the thin cheek. "And she paid the price for our freedom with her own. He bought her outright and never let her forget it."

We talked some more, about Nattie's own life, her good but childless marriage, and the joy that her niece, Arlene, had brought her. Busy as she was, Arlene came once a week to take her out for a ride or lunch, and that hadn't changed since her recent marriage. She had gone to the wedding, with a favorite aide from the retirement home to keep her from being a burden during the ceremony and party after. She knew Delacroix was there. Her niece had told her she'd invited him as a gesture and she thought, at one time during the reception, that she recognized his voice even after all those years. If he recognized her, he never said a word, never came over.

"He was afraid of me even then, an old, blind lady. He knew Lois and I were close and that she talked to me. Well, too bad. It's okay with me if he realized I knew what her life was like. Mean as a three-legged bull, that one, and a wife-killer. But no fool. Nobody ever said he was a fool."

I thanked her for all the help and, with her cane,

we walked back toward the residential part of the complex. She directed me by rote where to turn and when. Her little room, sunny but chock-full of furniture and doodads, had pictures everywhere, pictures she could no longer see.

"There's a picture in here somewhere of Lois and Jim with their kids. I'm not sure where they put it. You probably think it's silly to have pictures in a blind lady's room, but I remember they're there and it makes me happy."

I saw it right away. A young James Delacroix, slimmer and with dark hair but bearing an unmistakable likeness to the body on the Cadillac. His wife was lovely, a slight, beautiful woman not yet destroyed. Del and Arlene were very small. It broke my heart.

I found my way out much quicker than I'd wound my way in. Driving off in the white rental, I tried to consolidate what I'd learned—which wasn't much. And yet it was everything. I'd managed to confirm our hunches, about the murder of a wife, about a name change. It was helpful, though, to learn why the two of them had married. I needed to know that a woman long ago dead, a woman I'd strangely come to admire, had not walked willingly into the hands of a monster.

Albert was home when I got back, which surprised me. He didn't look happy.

"She never showed up! I got to the airport, the plane was out, I was ready, and no Gillian. She's never done this before, at least not without calling."

"Did you fly?"

"Yeah, but...I wanted to do instruments. I called her place again and got the answering machine again.

I wonder if something's wrong. Incidentally, non seq, you look nice. Should I remember where you've been?''

I couldn't resist. ''You mean I only look nice under extraordinary circumstances?'' I proceeded to tell him about my morning, a story which took the edge off his own disappointment, but only for a minute. He was still distraught.

''I'm starving.'' I said. ''Let's eat a bite of lunch and then I have to stop at the library just for a second. If you want, we could drive over to Gillian's apartment on the way. Maybe one of her neighbors knows why she hasn't been answering her phone. Maybe she's out of town.''

The idea appealed to him. ''Good idea. I do have to get to the hospital sometime today, but... Well, I'll go after we do the Gillian thing.''

Thus, fortified with a bowl of Millie's clam chowder and good bakery sourdough, we drove down toward the central part of town where Albert said Gillian lived. Fortunately her number was in the book under her somewhat unusual first name. Otherwise, we'd have never been able to find her in the lists of Morgans. The area, once the habitation of the old city's mining elite, was now filled with block after block of apartment houses, some new, some made from divided turn-of-the-century mansions that had long ago lost any vestige of their former panache. Parking in the congested streets was a matter of luck, a question of stumbling on a car just pulling out. Albert found the building that matched the address we had and, with pure serendipity, found a space right across the street.

The building was perhaps twenty years old, a little

faded, the bricks chipped in the corners. Judging from the name tags on the call boxes, the clientele was predominantly Gen-X, or so we assumed. The little white squares with names typed in showed a predominance of male and female cohabitants with different names, a designation we took to imply youth. Gillian listed here only as G. Morgan, unit 530. No one answered our ring. The security door obligingly opened at that moment and Albert helped the mother of twins maneuver her double stroller through the doors and out to the sidewalk. I kept the latch from locking behind her. We were in.

Inside, the common areas looked freshly redecorated and clean, but even the pale wallpaper couldn't alleviate the darkness. No natural light entered from any doorway, so the only thing keeping the hallways from total blackness were a few forty-watt bulbs. Up on the fifth floor, accessed by an elevator so small we wondered how it had managed to accommodate the mother and her stroller, several of the ceiling fixtures had burned completely out, throwing everything into shadow. We knocked on the door of 530. No one answered. We weren't surprised.

"Okay, now what?" I asked. "Planning to break in?"

"Let's try to see if anyone on the floor is home. She must be out of town and forgot to tell me. Maybe she asked someone around here to water her plants or something." Albert headed down the long, narrow hall, knocking on doors as he went. I could tell, probably by the fact that he didn't wait for an answer, that he figured the odds of finding anyone home in early afternoon were slim to none.

We both turned when we heard the click of a door

being unlocked and opened. A slim, handsome young man, shirtless, stuck his head through a door about midway down the hall and looked around to locate the source of the disturbance. He registered Albert and then me, one of us on each side of his unit.

"Yes?"

"Hi," I offered with a touch of apology. "Sorry to bother you. We were looking for Gillian Morgan. She hasn't been answering her phone and we wondered if she was out of town. Any idea?"

"Oh, you want Gill." He glanced toward her apartment and then down at his naked chest as if seeing it for the first time. "Gee, excuse my clothes—or rather lack of them. I've been writing." He ran a hand carelessly through his thick, gorgeous hair. "Hey, I don't know. Didn't say anything to me about a trip. Are you sure she's not there?"

We both shrugged. "We're not sure about anything," said Albert. "Do you know her very well?"

"Yeah, I guess. We've gone out some. But we both go out with a lot of people." *Too bad, Gillian,* I thought to myself. *You have to share him.* "Incidentally, I'm Bob." We exchanged handshakes. "If you're really into this...like worried, I mean, maybe we should get the manager to open her door. What d'ya think?"

"No...well, I don't know," said Albert, at war with his curiosity. "Maybe we should just come back some other time."

"Oh no." My feet were starting to hurt and I wasn't about to do all this again. "Hey, why don't I try a credit card? It might work."

"Yeah, you bet it'll work," said Adonis, aka Bob. "These locks are made of tinfoil."

"Worth a try, then," I added before Albert's law-and-order mentality could set in.

"Well, wait a sec. Let me at least call downstairs." Adonis disappeared for a moment and came back shaking his head. "The manager's not there. No one answers. He has a tendency to disappear this time of day. I think he has his own stool at the bar around the corner. The ferns come out at five o'clock when the Yuppies descend. Before that, the place is there for the neighborhood's heavy drinkers." He had a plastic card in his hand, though not, I noticed, a major one. On the chance that it was going to be destroyed, why ruin your credit along with it? "Here, let me try."

He slid the plastic down through the space between door and frame. The lock clicked open. "See what I told you? Is that a cinch or what?"

Albert and I both held back. Breaking into locked doors was a little beyond our comfort level. We let Adonis do the dirty work, which happily he was pleased to do. He eased the door open an inch and called in, "Gillian? Gill, baby? You in there?"

No answer. He looked at us questioningly.

"Open it," I said.

"No way, not without you guys standing right here beside me."

Which was why, when the door was pushed open, all three of us saw Gillian's body at the same time.

It looked like she had surprised a burglar. That he had killed her and left her lying on the floor as he continued to search the small apartment. She was partially covered with ledger pages, miscellaneous envelopes, and junk that had apparently been unearthed from all the open drawers. For some reason, I just assumed a man had done it, murdered her and continued to search her place for whatever she had that he wanted. A woman, I decided irrationally, wouldn't have been so messy.

Everything I'd heard about Gillian was, if anything, understated. She obviously had been very beautiful. Her beauty was the fresh, natural kind that in life would have needed no makeup to look wonderful. Her long, straight blond hair, loose of any constraints, fell thick across the oversized T-shirt she must have slept in. The long legs were tanned. Her feet were bare. Did that mean she'd been awakened during the night? The room light was on, so perhaps that's what had happened. She'd heard something and come to look. There was some blood, though not a lot. I walked in, far enough to see the entry wound on her forehead, before stepping away. Bob, after a moment, backed completely out of the apartment. I followed to make sure he was all right but all he did was sit down in the hallway and put his head between his legs. He didn't look much like Adonis now.

Albert, after hesitating, went to his now former flight instructor and bent down, checking her pulse and eyes. He looked up at me, shaking his head. When he started to say something, the words stuck. His eyes were unnaturally bright. "Call Morrisey, would you? I don't think I can do it."

"Does it have to be Morrisey? Wouldn't just 911 do?"

"Do you think this is a coincidence? I was supposed to fly with her this morning. Call Morrisey."

"Okay, but first I'm going to look around."

"Gracie…" Albert was sitting on the floor next to Gillian. I felt terrible for him, being the one to find the body of the instructor with whom he'd shared many special moments in the air. His voice was thin. "Maybe you'd better just wait."

I peeked out at the hallway to check on Bob. He was gone, the door to his apartment closed. I came back into the room and shut the door of 530. "I didn't know her. This is a heck of a lot easier for me. I'll call, but then I'm going to look around. You just stay there and don't worry."

I phoned in orders for the police to come and to bring an ambulance as well, though it was obviously too late. Then leaving Albert sitting motionless on the floor next to the body, I headed for Gillian's bedroom.

Her bed linens were those favored by young women just starting to build their own nests. Nothing really matched, having probably been picked up at garage sales or flea markets with prices to bargain over. The nights were still cool here, even in May, and she had used an Indian madras spread to keep off the chill. Three teddy bears, which must have lived on the bed when it was made, were propped in a small wicker chair in the corner of the room, waiting for caresses that would never come again. A maudlin thought, suitable for a corny poem, but I couldn't chase it away.

The room was tiny, big enough only for the bed and a small chest of drawers, but it had been ran-sacked. Everything in the drawers and closet had been emptied and thrown to the floor. I searched through the underwear and sweaters, hoping Morrisey wouldn't notice that they'd been further disturbed. I checked under the bed, but the burglar had checked first. A large box that seemed to have lived there had been pulled out. Gillian, obviously a neat person with a pilot's eye to detail, had apparently used the space under the bed to store out-of-season clothes. I felt around without much enthusiasm. All I learned was that she skied.

The floor of the closet was much more interesting. All her clothes had been hurled from their hangers and dumped, but I wondered if a man would know how to check them. I was forever tucking things into any pocket I could find, and so were most of the women I knew. An outfit without pockets was cause for despair, so I never bought one unless it was an evening gown. Evening gowns, alas, don't come with pockets. Fortunately, I spend as little time as possible in them.

Working fast, I checked the pockets of Gillian's entire spring wardrobe. Nothing. Well, not exactly nothing, but tissues, cleaner stubs, gum wrappers, and pennies didn't really count. I looked at my watch. It had been about six minutes since I'd left the message with the police, so I had to hurry. Did this one-bedroom apartment have a coat closet?

The fact that every drawer, every surface had been searched made me feel that the burglar had failed in his mission. If he'd found what he wanted, he would have stopped the destruction. But maybe he missed the coat closet, assuming there was one.

He hadn't. The floor of the coat closet looked worse than the bedroom. Coats, boots, gloves, hats were a jumbled mess. And whatever pockets I could find were essentially empty. Was there anyplace else she might have hung a jacket, somewhere for an item too grungy for guests to see? I wandered into the kitchen, which was small but serviceable. The burglar had opened drawers but had not emptied them, probably because their contents were so easily assessed. Apartments of this vintage usually had a broom closet, something to store long-handled tools like dusters and vacuums. I felt around the walls till I found it, an odd corner arrangement that a burglar might have missed. It looked almost like an architectural detail but swung aside at a touch. Sure enough. There it was, a flyer's battered leather jacket, draped over the end of a dry mop.

And in the jacket pocket was a little black appointment book. I just had time to flip through it, long enough to note that it was filled with Gillian's small, neat writing, when I heard Albert at the door. Morrisey's voice was unmistakable. I slipped the black notebook in my own skirt pocket and closed the door of the broom closet arrangement just in time. The detective peered into the kitchen, took a quick measure of the situation, and said sweetly, "Okay, Grace, what did you find? And may I see it, please?"

He's worse than Millie.

FIFTEEN

MORRISEY WAS followed in due course by all the members of the violent death team, so many officers they were tripping over one another in the little apartment. The medical examiner, forensics specialist, and all those who turned the killing of a young, ambitious woman into a textbook exercise were crowded together in a space no more than twelve feet square. I couldn't watch.

The detective, whom we now privately referred to as our friend in the murder business, told us to wait for him outside the apartment. Banished, we headed down toward the end of the hallway, passing Bob's digs. The door remained firmly closed, though we knew he must have heard all the commotion.

We found a place on the floor and squatted down cross-legged like first-grade children at story time. This apartment house could certainly have used some guest furniture, though chances were they had probably tried it once and found themselves ripped off by acquisitive tenants. Morrisey located us there after a few minutes and, having checked in vain for something to perch on, joined us down on the floral carpet. He looked ridiculous but then so, probably, did we.

He sneezed from the dust of wool pile, pulled out a huge white handkerchief, and blew his nose. "Nice spot you found here," he said, sniffling. He stuffed the hanky in a pants pocket and from another retrieved the black notebook I'd found and been forced to relinquish. "So tell me, you two, what do you think this is?"

He started to hand it to Albert, who waved it away, pointing at me. "She found it. Give it to her. Right now, all I know is that I've lost a teacher and a friend. I can't deal with the details. Have your men been able to determine anything yet?"

"Just that she was killed with a large-caliber bullet to the temple, probably at close range. In that apartment, of course, everything's at close range. We think she woke up and found him in her living room. The odd thing is that, while he rifled her bag, he left the credit cards and even a small stash of bills she had hidden behind the coin purse. He didn't seem to be after money or, for that matter, jewelry. She had diamond studs in her ears, nice ones too. Must have slept in them. He left them alone, and a ring, too. Not the usual MO for a burglar."

"What about the entry?" I asked. "Did the burglar force the lock, or maybe a window? I know we're on the fifth floor, but I haven't looked out the back. For a fire escape or something, I mean."

"Nothing's been forced. He, or she, may have had a key."

"But you said she must have surprised—"

"Those things are not mutually exclusive."

Albert straightened his legs trying to get comfortable on the floor. It wasn't working. "Has it occurred to you, Detective, that the one constant in all these recent traumas is *us?* This woman was my flight instructor. We were going up today. Now look, our house almost burned down. My colleague Dr. Finer ended up in jail. Even Delacroix had the misfortune to run into us...or maybe it was us to him. Whatever." He looked totally frustrated. "I'd hoped, at least, that Gillian was killed in a simple robbery and now you're telling me that's unlikely." He studied the dingy carpet flower under his hand. "Somehow, I can't help thinking I caused this."

Morrisey, who might have tried to deny that depressing thought, chose not to. Instead, ignoring Albert's earlier protest, he threw the black notebook into his lap. "Take a look at this and see if it makes any sense to you. I have a hunch your wife thinks this was what the killer wanted."

He was right, of course, but I didn't know how he guessed. I don't think poker will ever be my game.

Albert opened the notebook and flipped through it quickly. Then he backed up and started reading more carefully. "This is her daytimer, her schedule book. The appointments she had with clients. Funny, though, she just used initials. I guess it was her own particular shorthand."

"When did you say you had an appointment to fly with her?"

"Well, the most recent one was this morning. Nine o'clock. I tried to fly with her once a week when I could, and particularly since we were working on this rating." He turned to the page with the day's date at the top. "Here. It says...well, at nine it says 'D.'"

"That's nice. 'D.' Who's 'D?'"

Albert thought a minute. "Oh right, that's me. She called me Doc. She had nicknames for all her students, it was just her thing."

"Wonderful," said Morrisey. "That makes our lives so much easier. Nicknames. Does anything else in that book make sense?"

Albert studied the pages for a minute or two while

we waited. The light was so bad in the hallway, he had to squint, tipping the book from side to side to catch some illumination. "She seems to have noted when the pilot was going to do a cross-country. There are destinations marked here and there."

"Anything ring a bell?"

"Sure. They all do. There are only so many places a small plane, and particularly a small plane with an inexperienced pilot in it, would go from here in a day. Oh…"

"What?"

"Here's an interesting notation. 'CCR.' That's Copper Creek. How about that, someone took a student plane to Copper Creek. What a coincidence." He glanced at both of us to be sure we appreciated the irony.

"Who?" asked Morrisey, excited now. "Can you tell?"

"Of course I can tell. 'S.' Good old 'S.'"

"Well, there must be a ledger or something somewhere that has her student list or her accounts receivable, something to expand on this."

I realized in a flash what had happened. "And here I thought I was so clever, finding what the killer was looking for. Wrong. I may have found a small piece of it, but he found the important part himself. Now we know she flew someone down to Copper Creek but we'll never know who. He got her student list."

We sat in the darkening hallway, mired in our solitary thoughts. Could it have been so important to kill the only person, Gillian, who knew about the Copper Creek visit? Yes, if that person were to realize the connection with James Delacroix. Gillian was probably not murdered because she surprised a thief. Her

death was an end in itself. If she hadn't heard someone and come out to the living room, she'd have been
killed in bed. She was a witness, albeit an unwitting
one, to the events leading up to another death. Someone flew down...when? I flipped the pages of the
notebook till I found the Copper Creek entry. Someone, 'S,' flew down there in mid-April and saw James
Delacroix. He must have. There was no other place
to land. And that was the beginning of the end.

I shared my idea and we discussed it, still sitting
yoga-style like a group of aging flower children. The
more we talked, the more plausible the theory
sounded. Finally, we hoisted ourselves up from the
floor and stretched.

"Have you learned anything else since last we
talked?" I asked Morrisey. "You did promise, don't
forget, to keep us on top of things."

"Did I promise that?" He feigned innocence.
"Okay, so I promised. Maybe one thing. We've
known that Carla Correa left her house about a week
ago and hasn't been back. Her car's gone. Now we've
had a sighting. Apparently, she's here and has been
for a while. An old business friend of hers gave her
up. So that places her in the city where some nasty
things have happened." He turned to me. "Is that
good enough?"

"It's a start."

"You realize, of course, that you're probably in
considerable danger. I'd like to think that mattered to
you...." He shook his head. "But hey, I'm not too
old to learn."

"We'll be careful," assured Albert.

There was no way my husband could go to the
hospital after this and deal with mundane things like

mail and phone calls. We headed home in the late-afternoon shadows, wondering what disaster would be next.

The boys were outside lobbing balls into the tattered old hoop at the side of the house. It had been a joint birthday gift when they were eight and it was a rare evening in all the years since when they hadn't gone out to shoot a few. Albert had his pepper vodka in hand, I had my tonic water with lime. The boys had a basketball. Tyler Oates, their longtime friend, was with them and we greeted him warmly.

"I waited to see you," he said after enduring my hug and Albert's manly shake. He reached for the backpack he'd left on the ground. "My folks are having company for dinner and I have to go but I wanted to stay long enough to say hi."

Tyler wasn't into computers the way the twins were this year and their friendship had become less intense as a result. Still, going back as far as they did, the threesome still looked natural playing together in the waning light of day. He and the twins made preliminary plans for a rock concert not scheduled till midsummer and, after lots of good-byes, he started toward the path to his house. Then he looked back. "By the way, I moved that wire. We were tripping on it. If somebody looks for it, it's there against the wall." He pointed behind us, turned, and was off. A roll of wire leaned where he had gestured.

"What's that?" asked Albert.

"Beats me. Probably belongs to the men doing the garage." I glanced at the boys who were rounding up the balls. "Nice to see Tyler. But where's Lawrence?" I was more than a little worried that my offers of help might have made him uncomfortable around me. "Has he given up on us?"

"Good question," said Spence, wiping the sand and sweat off his hands. "He wasn't at camp today. We called his house but no one answered. They don't have an answering machine. If we can borrow a car, we thought we might drive over there after dinner, just to see if something's wrong."

Albert was shaking his head. "Huh-uh, I don't think so. Not tonight. And after we tell you why, I think you'll understand."

They did understand, only too well. Dinner was a sad and sober affair. The boys had never met Gillian but they'd heard Albert talk about her and had, on occasion, answered the phone when she'd called. Paul, the sensitive one, put it together and asked with some alarm, "Dad, did you want us not to go over to Lawrence's tonight because you think something might have happened to him, too?"

"No, no. It's you I'm worried about. I just don't want you driving around alone for now."

"Oh, don't..."

"Look," said their father. "Just indulge me, okay?" His tone said they didn't have a choice.

After supper, Albert and the boys headed for the computer as if it were an ordinary night. I had so much paperwork to do, I didn't really mind their being otherwise occupied, but a part of me needed to know what they were up to. Three people and one computer is bad enough; they didn't need four. I watched them go. "Okay, I'll back off and let you guys have your fun," I called. "Just tell me where you stand now. With the search, I mean."

"Not bad," said Spence. "Of course, if we had a

name, there'd be all kinds of ways of finding this guy.
Voter registration, car licenses, real estate listings—
but you need at least a surname for all those. If he'd
been in some conventional career, which he wasn't,
that might have done it. But this name change bit
makes it really hard. We've been running lists at the
camp computers whenever we can, but we're getting
too many names. We're basically trying to find anyone who fought at Bastogne with a name starting with
a D apostrophe or a DE. A 'DeLa' would have been
nice, but there weren't any. We're really messing in
the dark here. We don't even know that Delacroix's
real name started with a D in the first place. Meanwhile, we're learning an awful lot about the Battle of
the Bulge.''

I really needed to hit my desk, but Spence's com-
ments were too tantalizing. Forget paperwork. I
walked over to the computer and leaned over the three
of them, watching as the preliminary menus came up
on the terminal. ''Well, tell me the sort of names you
have so far. See if anything makes my intuition kick
in.''

''D'Costa. DeAngelo. DeAngelis. DeBello. De-
Boer. Debroisse. DeCarlo. Those are a few. We're
printing them out. Do you really want us to read you
all the ones we have? There could be hundreds and
hundreds before we're through.''

''No, I guess not. Debroisse has a French sound,
like Delacroix. Could that mean something?''

''Mom...''

''Okay, I'm going. Anyone but me want some
background music while we work? I'll even break
down and turn on classical.'' They nodded vaguely,
already into the zone.

At least my desk was in the great room, as was the computer. We could work together but apart, in a musical silence of sorts. That way, I could hear if something exciting was happening which, for the moment, it wasn't. For quite some time, Mahler's Fourth was the only other presence in the room. Albert and the twins muttered too quietly for me to hear. I paid bills, made donations, set up new tax files. Now and then, breezes sent a branch slamming against the house. Something thudded at a distance, an animal knocking something over in the far yard. Finally I finished the most pressing chores and could stand it no longer.

"All right," I said, walking over to the group across the room. "Now what do you have?"

"DeFelippo. DeFiori. DeFord. Like any of those?"

"DeFiore is 'of the flowers.' That's not bad. Not French, but not bad. Sounds Italian."

"Oh, you want Italian now?" said Albert. "We can do Italian. What have we found, guys?"

Paul looked at his notes. "DeCicco. DeCroce…"

"Wait…DeCroce?" I felt the beginning of my buzz, the electric surge that goes through me sometimes. The surge that signaled *Listen*. "DeCroce! Don't you see, that means 'of the cross.' At least I think it means 'the cross.' Like Delacroix. Maybe the guy was religious. Or superstitious. Wanted to keep that part of the name, just in case."

No one said anything. They were obviously trying to decide if I was inspired or delusional.

"What about a first name?" I asked. "Can you get it?"

"We'll have to go back," muttered Spence, "but it's doable." He sounded like he thought the idea was hopelessly lame, but behind the put-down lurked a hint of respect. His mother had been right before, though he'd have endured a thumbscrew before admitting it. Boys who are trying to separate from their parents have great difficulty with respect.

I stood impatiently behind the men at the computer while rows of print cycled down the screen. Now and then, one or another would suggest something in a low voice and there'd be a quiet discussion. Finally, the scroll slowed and then stopped.

"There it is. 'Jimmy,'" said Paul. "Jimmy De-Croce. He doesn't list as James, but maybe he thought James was too namby a name for the army. Or maybe his parents really named him Jimmy and he wanted something fancier later. Whatever, it works...sort of. What do you think?"

"I think you guys should find out if a Jimmy DeCroce was in England just before D-Day, that's what I think. Any way to do that?"

This was Paul's specialty, though Spence was good, too. Both understood the trial-and-error method of computer work better than Albert, who hadn't been born to it. "I think the best way would be to put a message in a military chat room, preferably one that specializes in World War Two, asking if anyone who'd been in England at the right time knew a Jimmy DeCroce."

"But then what?" asked Albert. "Let's say you get a yes. What else do we want to know? Might as well ask for everything at the same time. We don't want to take too long." There was a tension in his voice that only I could read. After so many disasters, he was beginning to run scared.

I knew what *I* wanted to know, anyway. "Ask if

anyone knows who he worked with. I have this hunch...."

"Okay, spill it, Gracie."

"I think that Delacroix, or whatever his name was then, worked in that mail room during the war when the Finer family's package arrived and that he stole it. That's pretty much a given, after all. Don't forget his ring, the one that Eli recognized. And the money he had after the war to 'buy' his wife. And I think that maybe he didn't do it alone or, if he did, that someone else found out. What if someone knew what he'd done and chased him down? That someone might very well have been a soldier who worked with him in England. What do you think?"

"And what if his name wasn't DeCroce? And what if no DeCroce ever worked in England?" Albert, ever the party pooper.

"Maybe," added Spence, who chose to ignore his father, "that's why Delacroix *had* to change his name. To keep away from...whoever. Whomever," he amended before anyone could do it for him.

We were all beginning to rev up with the new possibilities. The twins, with only occasional input from Albert, devised the message they were going to send, writing it off-line and editing as they went. Then it was time to send it on its way. They typed it in, pushed the right buttons, and sat back. Albert got up from the desk chair that hit his back in the wrong spot, rubbing the sore spot. He headed for the bottles of designer water in the cabinet under the bar. The boys, after some discussion, arranged to spell each other while they monitored the responses—on the outside chance they might get some. Military chat rooms were busy places, largely but not exclusively the province of the young.

Forty long minutes later they struck, if not gold, at least a form of pay dirt. JockO, or such was his electronic name, sent a reply, their first. "I have a friend who was in that part of England at the right time," he wrote. "I'll call him and see if your name rings a bell. He's not a computer type, so I'll answer for him. Watch this space tomorrow evening. I'll get back to you."

That was the first. There were to be three more, none of whom had memories good enough to answer off the cuff, but all of whom promised to check their files and reply soon. Albert would have preferred an immediate response. He was starting to pace the room. Ever since Gillian's death, this mystery had lost all elements of a game.

When we finally turned off the computer for the night, all of us were wrung out. I was in the process of making my usual resolution yet again to master the Internet. "I have to admit," I said to my now-weary sons, "I'm impressed. If you get an answer, I'll consider that machine a legitimate part of the family. How did you know how to go about finding these military sites? How did you know where to start looking? Were you born with that much intuition?"

They just smiled.

It was late, the night sky through the windows moonless and dark. We began our ritual locking of the doors and turning off of the lights, each with our own thoughts. For some reason, I started worrying about Lawrence, why no one had seen him. Earlier, the boys had let me know he'd told them about the offer I'd made for college.

"That was really nice, Mom," they'd said.

Yeah, I thought ruefully. *So nice we haven't seen him since.*

SIXTEEN

ARLENE CALLED AT the stroke of seven the next morning, obviously waiting till she felt it was okay to disturb us but not holding off a single minute more. She'd been at the hospital late last night and her husband, figuring there was no reason to come home on time, had stayed at the office to get some work done. When he did finally return, around ten at night, he'd surprised a woman in their apartment. She'd managed, head down, to shove him away and push past him through the door without his getting a very good look. Their place was partially torn apart. What should she do?

Morrisey, we knew, was taking the weekend off to fish his secret mountain stream. Rather than recommend she call someone else, we promised to be right over. The boys were sleeping in, a Saturday morning indulgence. We told Millie we'd be back eventually and headed for the Masterses' apartment.

Perry and Arlene looked like they'd missed much more than a single night's sleep. I suspected they'd never actually gone to bed. Arlene, in particular, was shaky and deeply apologetic. "We hated to wake you so early this morning but we just couldn't wait any longer to call. This has been so scary."

Perry Masters was a small, gentle man who seemed happy to let his wife speak for him. I wondered if he was actually much younger than the competent woman he'd married or if his shyness only made him seem so. "Can I get you some coffee?" he offered softly. "We just put on a pot."

Our acceptance meant he could disappear, at least temporarily. He jumped at it. We turned to Arlene, still in the flowered smock from the night before. Nurses looked a lot less formidable these days, having traded their starched uniforms for more cheerful garb. "So did the mystery woman find the music?" I asked immediately.

Arlene smiled, probably the first smile she'd allowed herself in quite a few hours. "Nope. Had it nicely hidden, and I don't think she'd been here too long before Perry walked in on her. But you can bet that's what she wanted, whoever she was. We're not exactly Mr. and Mrs. Moneybags. Our earthly possessions are worth, maybe, ten grand max. She wanted the music."

Albert had been looking around at the mess in the apartment. The drawers in the rough pine desk had been left open and rifled and chair cushions were askew. "Is Perry absolutely sure it was a woman? No chance he was wrong about that?"

"That's what he says."

Perry was returning with mugs of steaming brew. I accepted the coffee gratefully, the first of the day. He'd heard the question. "Yeah," he said, passing cream and sugar in homemade pottery bowls that looked like wedding presents. "It was a woman. I'm sure of that. She was wearing some kind of scarf or something that hid her hair, but hey. You know a woman from a man no matter what they're wearing. I do, anyway."

"Didn't you guys say you thought someone had been in here before?" I asked.

Arlene nodded. "Yes," she said, "and I've had it. You take the music. I'm tired of worrying about it. You have a big house and we just have this little place. You can protect it better than we can, not that I can figure what there is to protect." She and Perry went over to an armchair at one corner of the room and moved it away from the edge of the rug. Then, with Perry holding up one end of the chair, she reached beneath the Navajo-style carpet and removed the original manila envelope. We both recognized it as the one James Delacroix had handed Albert the last time we'd seen him alive.

She handed it to Albert, who regarded it a moment before carefully pulling out the music, watching the edges. It was, as I remembered, a simple C Major rendition, probably made easy for amateur pianists. My husband, the musical one, started singing under his breath. And then stopped. "Is this the same sheet music we have a copy of?" he asked.

Arlene and I both nodded. "'Bewitched.' You saw it."

"But this has Morse code."

"What?" We all gathered around, leaning over to see where Albert was pointing. He had the loose sheets spread out on a coffee table side by side.

"See?" he said. "Here. And here. And again over here where the chorus repeats." He was fingering the dashes we'd seen on the copy, but here on the original something else was suddenly visible. I looked at Arlene, startled.

"You didn't tell me there were dots there. See, between the dashes? And here, in front of one? They didn't pick up in the copy at all." I stared at the lyrics between the staffs. "Either I just didn't see them or I thought they were copy blurs. Little blobs of toner."

Arlene looked stricken. "Oh, Grace, I'm sorry. The dots…" She thought a minute. "I don't remember. I think I noticed them. Maybe. Not that I thought they mattered." She grimaced. "They do matter, don't they?"

Albert nodded. "I should know Morse code. I did as a kid, and of course dealt with it a little when I was first learning to fly. Didn't rememorize it, though. Do you have the code table anywhere in the house, in a book or something?"

"Don't think so," said Perry.

"Wait," I said. "What time is it? After nine?" I'd left my watch at home in the rush. When Albert nodded, I located the phone and started dialing. My memory for numbers was notoriously good, but the number of the library's reference department was certainly etched in my brain, as it was with every freelance writer. "Quick," I said to Arlene as I waited for an answer, "hand me the music's coded sections."

Moments later we had the answer. Dash dot dash dot was C. Dot dash dot was R. But what was CCR?

"That's easy," said Albert. "At least one possible reading is that it's the VOR signal for Copper Creek. You know, the radio keeps sending out those letters in code to let pilots know where they are?" His face turned rueful. "I remember that one rather well, actually."

"That's all?" I was shattered. I hadn't been this disappointed since the boys asked for money instead of toys for their birthdays. "Break-ins, secret codes, all this high drama, and all the man gives us is his own address? And here I thought he was trying to tell his daughter where to find...well..." I stopped, realizing that I was about to say he was trying to tell Arlene where he'd hidden the Finer jewels and money he'd stolen so many years ago.

Arlene was way ahead of me. "It's okay, Grace. I know what you're thinking. I realize what my father was. But if there was something illegal there, what good is he doing telling me it's hidden in Copper Creek? Of course it would be there. Why not? That's where he lived. Can you imagine someone breaking in here trying to find this silly music and then realizing my father went to a great deal of trouble to tell us something so obvious?"

There was no denying her point. From the excitement of discovering the code to the letdown of realizing what it said had been a matter of only a couple of minutes. We were all disgruntled.

"Guess we'll just clean the place up," muttered Perry in annoyance. "No point in worrying about this break-in."

We did our best to talk him into calling the police, but our hearts weren't in it. "Whatever," I said. "You people really should go back to bed and start the day over."

They saw us to the door, their weariness suddenly overwhelming. Perry looked like he wanted to say something but couldn't give birth to the idea. Finally it came out in a rush. "Mrs. Beckmann, Dr. Beckmann. Thank you for anything you can do to make this stuff stop happening to us."

His plea pulled at our hearts. More than he knew, we wished we could.

"Think the woman was Carla?" asked Albert as we hurried from the building.

"Sure. Who else could it be? We know she's in the area. I liked her, too. Your wife, the great judge of character."

The drive home was unusually pleasant on this Saturday morning, the traffic light. Everyone, it seemed, was out jogging or biking or playing soccer in the parks but the mood of spring couldn't penetrate our gloom. I wasn't that thrilled to see the trucks of the construction crew parked in our driveway when we arrived home. I wanted the new garage, but come on. It was a weekend. The head of the crew was waiting for us as we pulled up, which meant he probably had hit yet another snag of one kind or another. We parked and wandered over to where he was waiting.

"How's it going?" asked Albert.

The foreman was holding the roll of wire that Tyler Oates had found the evening before. He had it looped around one wrist, wearing it like a giant's bracelet. He held it out to us in a kind of gesture. "Any idea what this is, sir?"

"None at all," said Albert. "Isn't it yours?"

Another workman who had come over to join the group looked pointedly at the foreman and shook his head. Only the crew head, a squat man with a firm jaw, did the talking. "We were a bit worried about this when we saw it, so we started looking around. Hope you don't mind, but I have to be careful for my men." He regarded the wire still circling his wrist like an alien object. "This isn't ours. We decided to go checking your property. Didn't like the looks of things." He met our eyes dead-on. "Seems like someone's trying to wire your house and yard. Anyone you know want to blow you up?"

To say we were shocked doesn't get it. When we

finally caught our breaths and were able to ask the right questions, the story came out. Wire, a great deal of it, was snaking through the trees on the property, hiding in the grass, circling trunks, burrowing between shrubs and small plants. The far end began toward the back fence line, a good acre away. The trail stopped about twenty yards from the house, but it seemed apparent to the men that the final roll of wire would have made it to the outside wall of the great room. He must have run out of time and planned to be back. I felt my knees go weak.

Albert continued talking to the men but I went inside, needing to see the boys, Millie, my house, everything I loved. A wire running through the yard felt like a poisonous snake creeping up on us, ready to destroy with a single snap of the jaw.

I told Millie, who was waiting for us in the breakfast room. I felt I had to. She was the one who was almost always home, the one who had to be aware of the danger. And it was her life, too. She took the idea that someone might be trying to set explosives around the house with a rare equanimity. Probably felt her fate was, by now, completely out of her hands.

The boys, on the other hand, barely bothered to listen to the story, so full were they of their own news. Possible explosives hardly compared with their surprise. They had finally reached Lawrence, they said, and he'd been offered a job. Not just a job, a career. Here he was with a full year left before he could graduate from high school and a computer company, impressed with his tremendous talent, was offering him fifty thousand dollars a year to be creative on the computer. Design software, primarily, but also Web page work and even graphics. Fifty thousand dollars!

And they said he could finish high school on his off days, that the salary wasn't even for full time. It would go up very quickly when he was ready to work a full-time job. Wasn't that unbelievable?

"For a seventeen-year-old?" I gasped. "You might say so. In fact, I don't believe it. Too fanciful. Maybe he has some agenda he's keeping from you."

"Mom, it's true. Computer companies have people working for them as young as *fourteen*, though there are laws about hours and stuff at that age. See, we're better than older guys. We've learned directly by fooling around on the Internet, taking after-school classes. Mostly, we spend hours just dreaming things up. That makes us worth more than people who just do what they're told."

News like that knocked even danger out of the picture. The owners of the computer camp had tipped off the company, apparently, and they'd come asking. I wondered what Jesse Leake thought of that, his son being offered a salary probably larger than anything Jesse had ever made. I suspected he must have been seriously rocked by such an idea. And here he'd wanted "Larry" to work with him.

"Lawrence must be incredibly thrilled," I said. And at that the boys became quiet.

Paul finally smiled at me a little sadly. "He doesn't want to take it, Mom," he said. "He wants to go to college."

"Can you imagine?" asked Spence. "He gets an offer I'd kill for and he wants to go to college."

Poor Lawrence, I thought. Such an appealing kid. Here I was trying to help him with his college tuition and a computer company was trying to give him more money than his family had ever dreamed of. I could understand why he might be miserable.

Albert joined us, far from happy. Normally careful, he was tracking mud from the construction work outside all over the carpet. "You told the boys?" he asked me. When I nodded, he said, "Unbelievable. Bomb threats yet. We're through fooling around with this thing. I want some answers, whatever it takes to get them. Come on." He gestured to the boys. "We're getting on the computer. If we can't get some names today, we're hiring an expert."

While the twins booted up the machine and made the necessary connections, I told Albert about Lawrence's job offer. "I think, if you're looking for an expert, you probably have them already sitting in front of you. Tomorrow, *they'll* get the job offer."

"Okay, Dad, here we go. I'm putting out the word as an emergency in the military chat room. If we're really lucky, some of the people we exchanged with yesterday will be reading it and answer. Should I tell them someone is threatening to blow us up?"

"Sure. Why not? Anything to get some action."

I hadn't had time to shower or clean up this morning, since we'd raced to the Masterses' apartment. This, I figured, was my moment. I left them huddled around the screen and headed for the bath, snagging an oversized towel and some shampoo. The hot water was copious and soothing. I let the strong spray run over me for much too long, hoping it could wash away the considerable tensions of the morning. Drying my long hair helped, too—all that heat aimed at my head and neck, releasing tightened muscles. By the time I returned to the great room, restored and clean, the rest of the family was sitting on the couches, the computer off. Sitting is perhaps the wrong word. They were perched on the edges, hands between their knees. Defeated. Or so I thought.

"Nothing, huh?" I asked.

Paul answered. "Not nothing. Something. Something really bad, really horrible." He looked like someone in mourning. "I just wish we'd never searched for it. The pits."

Teenagers did have a way with hyperbole. I sat down with them, resisting the urge to put my hands between my knees to look like everyone else. I waited for the rest of the story, but no one said a word. Finally I exploded. "All right, does anyone plan to tell me what you discovered or would that ruin the fearful symmetry of the moment?"

Albert straightened up, coming out of his trance. "Okay, here it is. The chat room came to life, all right. All the seeds we planted... People remembering, people telling us what they found when they went through their records. Old soldiers, some of them, or old soldiers' kids. Some remembered DeCroce from Bastogne. They didn't have much to add. Said he was an ordinary guy. They were all too busy then to do any deep analysis. People were dying. No help there. But one man, and he joined in later after we were beginning to get discouraged, had more. See, we needed to find that a DeCroce had been in England, too. This guy, one of the survivors of D-Day, remembered him. Said a DeCroce worked in the mail room before the invasion. In England, where the mail was, you remember, disrupted then. Anyway, the reason this man remembered DeCroce was that one of his buddies, a guy from his hometown, worked with him."

"Oh, wow."

"Said his friend's name was Leake. Charlie Leake."

Silence rolled into the room like a front-end loader. I didn't want to hear it. I almost whispered, "Does anyone know...?"

"Yeah, Mom," said Spence. "Lawrence showed us an old dog tag once. He was real proud of it. His grandfather's. The name on it, we're pretty sure, was Charles Leake."

"But surely he's dead by now."

The boys looked at each other and shrugged. "Why do you think that? James Delacroix was still alive."

Of course, that was foolish of me. The war ended over fifty years ago, but the men who fought it could have been in their late teens. Time had moved so fast since then, so many changes to absorb, I forgot that a lifetime could easily have contained a Bastogne and a World Wide Web.

"I'll tell you one thing," I said. "It could explain all the wire they just found. Who's always in our yard? And it could explain the surfactant that set our fire. Jesse knew it was there, of course, since he put it there."

"And Lawrence picked up the rest of his supplies one day after the fire, remember?" said Paul. "Oh gosh, do you think Lawrence was in on this?"

Spence was angered by his twin's perfidy. "*Im*-possible. Just *im*possible. Lawrence wouldn't do anything to hurt us."

"He would if, maybe, he has a grandfather and he told him to."

"What about the woman who's breaking into the

Masters place?'' I asked. ''Does Lawrence have a mother? I don't think I've ever asked you.''

The boys looked at each other again. ''I guess so,'' said Paul. ''Don't know, really. We were at his house once, but it was empty. We've never met anyone there. Never asked about his mother. He never said anything about her.''

''One thing we do know,'' said Albert, coming back again after departing some time before for outer space. ''Lawrence was always here and we spoke freely in front of him. He knew about everything we were doing. I mean, look over there.'' He pointed to Spence's chart taped up on the wall. ''He could have reported back to his family about everything we had scheduled, everyone we planned to interview. He heard Eli Finer that night we had dinner at our house. Lawrence has always been around at the appropriate moments.''

Spence jumped to his feet. He'd had enough. ''Lawrence is our *friend*. He's a *good guy*. What are you talking about? Do you think this...kid... murdered Delacroix and then for good measure dispatched your Gillian, too? For no reason? Lawrence? I mean, get *real*. He's practically part of the family. Mom even wanted to pay his tuition, for Pete's sake.''

''Gillian,'' said Albert. ''Where does she fit in?''

''I have an idea,'' I said.

''Me, too,'' echoed Albert. ''The airport. We have to go to the airport.''

''Are we flying somewhere?'' asked Spence.

''Nope. We're going to find out who Gillian's students were. Those coded initials she had in her black appointment book must have a counterpart some-

where. People had to pay her. Maybe she has old
records in a desk or something. Anyway, we're going.
Now. You kids can come or not, whatever you want.''

''We're coming,'' they said almost in tandem.
''Before something terrible happens to Lawrence,''
added Spence. ''Before you have him arrested or
something.''

I knew it wouldn't come to that, at least not for
now. But just at that moment, in my pressed slacks
and silk shirt, hair washed and clean, feeling reason-
ably right with the world, I wondered why I felt so
totally betrayed.

SEVENTEEN

NOT BEING SURE where else to start, we headed first for our hangar and the all-knowing Jack Potts, hoping he'd be around with time to talk. This was a search with an overwhelming chance of success, since Jack Potts always was around. He never went home. He never left for lunch. He lived, loved, and vacationed at the airport. And indeed he was there, rubbing down the Cessna that shared our space. *Romeo* looked so clean, we knew it had already been groomed for the day. My kids had never been so spiffed up, even on holidays.

While Albert cornered Jack to see what he knew about Gillian and where she hung out, the boys and I wandered through the large hangar doors to check out life on the tarmac, always colorful and diverse. Clouds gathering in the distance looked ominous for flyers but today, since we were grounded, they didn't bother me. One or two students were talking with a flight instructor and, beyond them, someone was inspecting a private jet that seemed to have just pulled in. When he turned, I caught sight of the unmistakable red hair. Martin Hazlett. I told the boys to stay with their father and walked out to meet him.

He greeted me like an old girlfriend, with a hug and kisses on both cheeks. I didn't really think a single lunch qualified him for such a demonstration, but this was no day to quibble. Anyway, his good spirits disappeared fast when I told him about finding Gillian's body. The word had reached most of the airport, as we were to find out, but somehow it had missed him. I watched blood drain from his face, leaving the freckles in bold relief. If that was an act, he was *good*.

"She was a sweetheart, that girl," he said, reaching in a back pocket for a handkerchief. His eyes were bright. "Loved her students. They loved her. Some instructors can make their novice pilots feel like airheads, if you'll pardon the pun, but she never did. I suppose this is a colossally trite question, but is there anything I can do?"

"Lots, actually. We can find out who killed her. In her own apartment. So awful. Albert and I are out here trying to see if we can find bookkeeping records or a list of students or anything that might give us a clue." A tail-dragger nearby started its propeller, peppering our faces with sand and dust. We backed away and began to stroll toward the hangars. "Do you happen to know where she operated her business, such as it was?"

"Certainly do. She officed in my place. *My place*. That's why I can't believe no one told me about this. I let her use a desk in a corner of my building over there." He pointed behind him. "That's why I sort of..." He watched the tail-dragger start toward the runway. "We were pretty good friends. Nothing more, unfortunately, but we really liked each other. I think she liked me, anyway."

"Did you ever fly with her?"

He waved absently at a gnat. "Maybe. I think so. But not recently."

It wasn't the answer I wanted. I already knew Hazlett himself had flown down to Copper Creek at least once because he told me over lunch about the day he confronted Delacroix. I wanted to know if he'd gone down recently with Gillian, maybe on a business trip that would have prompted her to enter his initials in her book, but that lucky I didn't get. I asked him if he'd mind meeting us at his headquarters which wasn't far away, maybe a couple of hundred yards down the road. He agreed readily and I went to retrieve the family.

Hazlett's building was a handsome, sprawling one-story with real landscaping somewhat out of place in the row of hastily built metal shells. In spite of being so outrageously cheated by Delacroix, the man had obviously made his money back and then some. A secretary was on the phone when the four of us walked in, talking to a contact in Ohio. The furnishings were luxurious, Berber carpeting, chenille couches and chairs, decorator touches throughout. I introduced Albert and the boys, who hadn't met Hazlett yet, and we were shown to a small, cluttered desk in a cubicle off the main room. Gillian's, he told us.

Feeling a little like cat burglars, we began a methodical search of drawers, file folders, even the still-unemptied wastebasket. I knew Morrisey wouldn't be happy if he knew what we were doing, but it was his own fault, going fishing when we needed him. Hazlett was another story. He stood by watching, his eyes narrowed. Despite his offer of help, he looked angry. I couldn't tell if he felt we were "dissing" her memory or if there was something he didn't want us to find. In any case, there was no nice black book conveniently waiting with a record of names and fees paid. That was what we expected, what we hoped for, but not what we got. In the bottom lefthand drawer,

a narrow little thing with dividers made of wood, we
found her bank statements and canceled checks.
Maybe she kept her flying accounts separate. We
could hope.

The envelopes contained only the canceled checks
she'd written, returned by the bank. No surprises
there. Checks for upkeep on her own plane, gasoline,
taxes; she paid her accountant for tax services and
even paid Hazlett a small monthly stipend for use of
his space. What we couldn't find was any record of
who had paid *her*. It was Spence who spotted the
critical sheets of yellow paper in the back of a drawer,
the kind of paper with self-carboning copies.

"She seems to have kept her deposit slips," he
said, surprising me. I didn't know he would recognize
a deposit slip if it bit him on the foot. He handed us
the small stack. We received the narrow yellow slips
as if they were fragile ivory carvings, holding the
pages by the edge, trying hard not to smudge the car-
bon. The copy was bad, barely legible in many places,
but we could make out the numbers and most of the
words. The name "Beckmann" popped out in several
spots on each monthly deposit and with difficulty we
could read the amount of Albert's lessons. Other
names were there, none of them meaning much. Then
I heard Spence's breath catch in his throat.

"What?" I asked.

He walked away, turning his back to us all. I
looked at the paper he had been studying and saw it.
Leake, it said. And the deposit was high, two hundred
dollars, certainly more than the fee for a single lesson.

"How extraordinary! Of course there are lots of
Leakes, but..."

"That looks like a cross-country, maybe," said Albert when I pointed to the figure. "But let's see if there are other Leake entries."

There were many, though some were so hard to read, we could only guess. "He seems to have taken a lot of lessons, maybe two or three times a week for a while there."

"Why do you assume it's *our* Leake? Why do you assume it's a he?" challenged Spence from across the room. "Maybe a *woman* named Leake took those lessons. Maybe it's a total stranger."

I didn't want to make light of his unlikely take on the situation, since Spence was so clearly hurting. Instead, I pulled out Gillian's appointment book from my purse, grateful again that Morrisey had let me keep it. "Let's see what initial repeats most often here."

Hazlett watched while we worked our way through the pages of the small black notebook I'd found in the broom closet of the murdered woman. The correlation with the deposit slips was obvious. "*S,*" said Paul as Albert nodded. "*S.* But who's *S?* It could be any Leake. It could be no Leake."

"See, you're trying to make it look like Lawrence," accused Spence. "S for student. Or for Smarty. Who knows how she assigned her nicknames?"

"*S?* Oh, I know who that is," said Hazlett. "I used to overhear her sometimes on the phone. I knew, for example," he said to Albert, "she referred to you as 'Doc.'"

"So who's S?"

"'Spray Baby.' Pretty dumb name, but that's what she called him. Some guy who always smelled of chemicals when he showed up here. She said he was in the bug-poisoning business. Didn't like him much.''

So there it was and no matter what Spence did or didn't want, S was Jesse Leake. Squinty-eyed, irritating Jesse Leake, who looked so much like a victim. We had every reason to believe that Spray Baby, aka Jesse Leake, was our murderer. He learned to fly with Gillian, flying with her to more and more distant destinations including, probably, Copper Creek. Gillian knew he'd been there. It wasn't just us he needed to silence. He had to get rid of this woman who knew he'd found James Delacroix. Maybe she'd even seen them arguing.

Jesse must have discovered that Albert was one of Gillian's students, and that Albert would be able to add things up if she happened to mention Jesse to him. Who could have guessed that the Beckmann family would have been the ones to find Delacroix's body? Jesse Leake must have railed against the coincidence that he and Albert shared Gillian as a teacher, though in fact it wasn't such a coincidence. There weren't that many flying instructors around, not really. Whatever, he didn't like the connection. Who could blame him?

We had to get out of there for any number of reasons. If the police happened to show up in the course of investigating Gillian's murder, I imagined they could arrest us for obstruction of justice or something. Hazlett was clearly relieved that we were through mucking around in the dead woman's things. With his okay, we took the deposit slips with us. He decided to box up everything she left behind in the building and just store it, awaiting the unlikely possibility that someone would show up to claim it. We promised to return the slips before Morrisey could get to Gillian's desk.

The drive home was all speculation and plot. Everyone had an opinion about what had happened and the opinions didn't always mesh. The think-tank system worked, all of us freely percolating ideas. I started off, throwing out postulates.

"Okay, so where does this story begin?" I pondered. "I'd say its seeds were planted fifty years ago. More. Charles—Charlie—Leake and a young guy named Jim DeCroce are doing grunt work together in the Army postal service in England. They're bored, wanting to see some action, wanting to be heroes."

"Why do you make them sound so ordinary, Mom? We know what kind of a creep DeCroce, as you call him, became. And a wife murderer, maybe."

"Evil itself can be very banal. But okay, maybe they weren't ordinary. Maybe they were jerks from the get-go. Maybe they'd been opening and stealing from GIs' packages all along. What could they have found? Cookies? Socks? Everybody else was getting ready for what became D-Day, the invasion of Normandy, and they were left out of the action. Maybe pilfering gave them a buzz."

Albert's look was not supportive. "Grace, dear, have you considered fiction?"

"Bear with me. So these guys, they're doing their thing, checking to see if any of the boxes look a little interesting and they run across a package sent from the Finer family to their contact. It seems a little heavy for cookies. They'd know that, having spent their days handling mail. They open it, finding a false bottom in it, and when they get a private moment and a private place, wow, their eyes bug out. What a stash! Money, obviously valuable jewelry, and they know someone must be waiting for it.''

''Don't you think they'd know what it was for?''

I thought a minute about Paul's question. ''Hard to say,'' I said finally. ''First of all, information on what we now know as the Holocaust may not have filtered down to the Army's rank and file at that point. Certainly not in the horrific detail we know now.''

''My father's family, some of them anyway, were trapped in Eastern Europe and we never got news of them at all till after the war,'' added Albert. ''We tried everything we could think of, but they couldn't get word out to us. I suppose we could give Delacroix—or DeCroce—the benefit of the doubt here. He might not have known the money was a matter of life or death.''

''Oh you guys.'' Spence's tone was close to a sneer. ''I can't believe how naïve you are. Don't you realize there are some genuinely rotten people in the world? I can just see these fools looking at all this money and saying, 'Gee, Jim, this must be meant to buy someone's freedom. We can't take it, no, no. Shame on us for even thinking about it.' Yeah, right. That's what must have happened.''

''Okay,'' I said. ''Point taken. So they looked at all the swag and had no moral issues about keeping it at all. What did they do next?''

''Hide it? Split it?''

''If they split it,'' said Albert, ''why was Delacroix considered a rich man, why did he drive Caddies and own FBOs? And why has the Leake family, apparently, worked so hard for whatever they've had?

Looks to me like Delacroix made off with the goodies."

"Yes!" said Paul, raising a clenched fist. "There you go. DeCroce hides it and Charlie Leake never finds it." His voice dropped off. "But how could he manage to elude his inseparable old pal?"

"He went to fight at Bastogne."

"So?"

"And *changed his name,*" said Spence.

"Oh, I don't know, Spence," I said. "That sounds almost impossible to do right in the middle of the fighting."

"But Mom, we know he *did* do that—or anyway, we strongly suspect it—so it *was* possible, q.e.d. I can imagine a lot of ways he might have managed it. He had a super mind for being devious, we've learned that. It's a special talent and he had it."

"Dog tags? Papers?"

"Couldn't those things have been lost during battle? Maybe there really was a dead soldier named Delacroix, though that seems like a long shot. My guess is he just invented the name. It was, in its way, close to his own."

All we could hear for the next few minutes was the bump and whirr of tires on a high-speed highway while we mulled over the evolving story. Finally Albert broke the silence. "All right, Gracie, keep going with your scenario. What happened next?"

"Well, DeCroce, who now called himself Delacroix, finally saw the fighting he craved. He became one of the heroes of Bastogne…. No, no wait. This isn't working. He must still have called himself DeCroce at that point, because no one could find the name Delacroix in the lists of that battle. Remember? The boys couldn't. And Carla looked for it.''

''Yes, that's right. She did say that. He was probably still DeCroce then, but in the midst of such fighting, it wouldn't have done Charlie Leake much good to look for him. In fact, it doesn't much matter exactly when he made the switch,'' said Albert. ''The point is that Leake lost him and the loot. Leake was stuck in England till the end of the war...maybe. Then he came back and started searching for a Jim DeCroce and failed to find him because by then he had changed his name. So, Charlie gave up his dreams of sudden wealth and life went on.''

''Till when?'' asked Paul.

I took it from there. ''Let's say Charlie Leake gives up on his share of the money and jewels but he never forgets how he was cheated. One day, in a rare moment, he tells his son Jesse the story. And Jesse internalizes it.''

''Oh, please. Save us from the armchair psychology, Mom.''

It would, I thought, be easy to disinherit Spence. ''All right, adorable child, he doesn't internalize it. He just remembers it, okay? But his father, Charlie, has died and there's no trace of a Jim DeCroce and he forgets about it. But he's resentful and bitter, sick of coveting the lifestyles of the people whose homes he services. And then his precocious son comes along and he begins to see the possibilities that computer searches have opened up. Now he thinks again about finding the man who cheated his father.''

''Yeah, but Mom, look how hard it was for us to do that search. And do you really think Lawrence had already made the search and was lying to us? Don't forget, he was trying to help us.'' Paul's voice cracked for the first time in a year.

The thought of sweet Lawrence being duplicitous was more than I, too, could handle. I found a way around it. ''No, I agree. Impossible. But there are libraries with computers in them. Librarians who are better than just about anybody at handling search engines. Let's for the moment assume that Jesse did in fact discover the name change. Now what would he do?''

Spence, up till now Mr. Hyde, had turned back into Dr. Jekyll. I couldn't keep up with his mood changes. ''It's no big deal to turn up every Delacroix in America if you want to. Lots of ways to do that on the computer. You can figure he found that one of the men with that name lived not so far away in Copper Creek. And what he did for a living.''

''I don't think it matters how he found him,'' picked up Albert. ''Just that now he needed to find a way to check him out. And one way or another, he turned up enough info to suspect he had the right person. The man he zeroed in on owned an FBO. If he learned to fly, he could eventually land at that FBO and case the area. Don't forget, he's trying to find a missing treasure of money and jewels, which may or may not still exist. Flying into that little landing strip was the best way to check things out. So he signed up for flying lessons. And found Gillian.''

''Do you suppose when he landed he introduced himself to Delacroix as Jesse Leake?''

''Absolutely,'' said Spence. ''He said 'Hi, I'm Jesse Leake, the son of the man you robbed blind. Nice to meet you.' ''

The restaurant we sometimes stopped at on the way

home from the airport loomed up on our right and
Albert pulled into the lot. The effort of working out
our theories was exhausting and we needed a break.
The men found a table while I used the car phone to
call Millie and tell her we wouldn't be home for
lunch. For once, she had nothing to report. We didn't
pick up our theories till after we'd refreshed our bods
with thick deli sandwiches and a bucket of cole slaw.
The café was almost empty, so we had no compunc-
tions about staying there to nurse our soft drinks. It
was almost too pleasant to contemplate tragedy. Almost...

"Okay, now where were we?" I asked.

"Jesse Leake has made contact with Delacroix,"
said Albert. "When do you think he really did tell
him who he was and what he knew?" He answered
his own question before we even had a chance. "I
wonder if he heard about the scene between Eli and
Delacroix at Arlene's wedding. When Eli recognized
the ring, and incidentally, wasn't *that* a piece of dumb
luck, Jesse would have felt that the game clock was
running out, that he no longer had the luxury of time.
But how could he have heard about it?"

"From you? From Gillian?"

"Maybe from Gillian. It's possible. I think I may
have told her about it and she could have passed it
along to Jesse. They'd flown together to Copper
Creek. She might have thought he'd be interested."

"In any case, Jesse obviously told him sometime
before that fatal weekend," I said. "Don't forget, the
phone rang that Sunday we were there on the way to
Carlsbad. The call scared Delacroix, or at least it
seemed to. It must have been Jesse. That was when
he gave you the envelope for Arlene."

"And that call wasn't very long, so Delacroix must have known who Jesse was. He already knew what was going on."

"So we flew off and sometime before Tuesday morning when we landed en route home, Jesse also flew to Copper Creek and killed the man who had cheated his father."

"Yeah, but wait," said Spence. "What about the knife wounds? And why make him climb on top of the car?"

Paul was rocking on the edge of the chair, a habit that drove me crazy. "I know. Well, I think I know. Part of it, anyway. He used the knives to try to find out where the money was. Don't forget, the ring was gone from his finger when the body was found. Jesse suspected the jewelry still existed somewhere. He wanted whatever was left. But he was one stubborn old guy, that Delacroix, and I think he was tired. He probably didn't much care any more if he got killed."

"Does anyone ever *not* care?"

Paul considered his brother's question. "Well, maybe he was just such a mule, he wouldn't have given Jesse the satisfaction of thinking he broke him. So Jesse killed him. End of story."

"Not bad," said Albert, musing. "Not too bad."

"No," I said. "Too many holes. What about this woman who keeps trying to find the Delacroix envelope in Arlene's apartment? And what does the sheet music have to do with anything? Why kill Gillian? And why our fire and why the explosives at our house? Why wire us for extinction?"

"I guess," said Spence sadly, "that's where Lawrence comes in."

EIGHTEEN

WE ALL LOOKED AT Spence as if he had just announced he was going to make his living dancing flamenco. He'd been spending every moment defending his friend from any hint of wrongdoing. Now he seemed to be indicting him.

"I *know* he didn't do it intentionally," he said, unable to meet our eyes. "He wouldn't have. But when you asked, Mom, how we knew about military chat rooms, I was too tired to tell you. It was Lawrence who taught us. He knew all about them, and I bet he learned helping his father find Delacroix. Maybe he didn't have the details, but he was beginning to get it. Starting to wonder. Don't forget, he saw all our stuff. He must have carried tales, must have told on us. I don't think he confides in his dad, but he may have told his mother. He probably does have one and she probably said something."

"Jesse would have picked up on all of it," I said. "And then he must have grilled Lawrence every time he came home from our house."

Paul was listening intently. "Do you think he knew the whole story, Mom? That his father may have murdered a man? Lawrence is no meathead, after all."

"Not *if* he knew, idiot." Spence answered for me. "*When.* You know he must have put things together at some point. Remember when his father had him remove the surfactant from our garage? Well, anyway, I'll bet it was the surfactant. We never found it. He must have realized eventually.''

"If we're right, can you imagine how he must have felt?" added Albert. "Think about it."

We were a sober group on the way home. The minute we hit the house, Spence headed for the phone. "I'm going to call him," he said grimly. "Lawrence. He must be back by now. Ask him to come over or something. Tell him we got something new for the computer. A new game, maybe. Anything. Just get him over here so we can ask him some questions."

None of us felt like stopping him. Our curiosity, by now, was too great. We watched Spence disappear into the back of the house where he could make his call in private. And we watched him return. He was clearly distressed.

"This time he's really gone," he announced. "I got his mother. She said she'd been trying to reach us to see if he was with us. She said they haven't seen him since last night. That he seems to have left and taken some things with him. When I told her we hadn't seen him either, she started crying." His face crumpled. "I thought I could hear his miserable father yelling in the background. This is really awful."

"Don't forget we thought he was missing before."

"Yeah, but that was different. This time his family can't find him."

We were all quiet. I tried to picture one of our boys facing such a choice of betrayals and could well imagine him running. It was too much for a kid. Albert headed for the bar and designer water which he poured over a glass of ice. He polished it off and emptied another, the effect of salty corned beef and chips. "I guess you know what we're doing first thing tomorrow morning,'' he said, pointing the glass in my direction.

"Let me guess. You're surprising me with a trip to Paris and reservations at the Georges V."

"Try a trip to Copper Creek and reservations at the Delacroix FBO."

Was he kidding? "You're not really planning to sleep there, are you?"

"Not really. But we will if we have to. Something's down there and we have to find it before Jesse Leake does. Once he has it, nothing will stop him from adding us to his victim list."

"He's already tried twice. What difference does finding the loot make?"

"I have a hunch he's decided we now know where it is and will lead him to it. He's waiting."

Spence wasn't missing a word. "We're going, too, right?"

Albert shook his head. "Not on your life. I don't know what—or who—we're going to find down there, but I don't want you kids anywhere around."

Both boys howled in protest. "Not fair! We've been part of all of it till now. We did all the computer stuff. You owe us!"

"Sorry. The decision's not negotiable."

The twins tried mightily to change their father's mind but to no avail, and they spent the rest of the day in a deep funk. They were no happier watching us prepare to leave the next morning.

In spite of Albert's threats, we didn't take anything for overnight. In fact, we didn't take anything that might add extra weight. We hoped someone had taken over the functions of the FBO, most importantly being sure there was gas available for tanking up, but just in case, we hoped we could get down and back on a single fill-up. We tried to leave our angry sons as calmly as we did for more conventional flights but we probably weren't fooling them. Both of us were more than a little frightened and, I suspect, they were scared for us.

Albert had called ahead so *Romeo* was waiting for us out on the tarmac. It was a beautiful, cloudless day, perfect for flying, and there were more cars than usual at the general aviation airport. Out near the runways, a dozen planes had been removed from their hangars and were awaiting their owners. Our Turbo Arrow, immaculate as usual, stood small but proud outside our hangar door. It gave me little pleasure to see it looking so fit. No reprieve in sight.

Jack Potts was waiting to greet us, emerging from the washroom drying his hands. "Going someplace nice today, Doc?" he asked cheerfully. He nodded at me. "Mrs. B?"

"Back down to Copper Creek," said Albert. "Doubt that it'll be too nice."

Jack frowned. "You sure you want to do that? Think it's been pretty well deserted since the old man died."

"Whatever. Long as this weather holds, we can land without help. It's not that busy. The plane's the least of my worries." Albert thought a minute. "Jack, got a favor to ask. We'll file a flight plan, but even so, if we're not back here by tomorrow night, and if we haven't called you to say where we are, could you please call this number for me?" He handed him a slip of yellow paper. "Ask for Detective Morrisey. Okay?"

Jack glanced at the paper and then pocketed it. He

looked none too happy. "Sure. If you think that's what you want."

I did appreciate being married to a good detail man. He wasn't likely to forget anything important. I mentally rehearsed the route to Copper Creek, taking comfort in the fact that we could avoid turning west till the mountains were no longer a major factor. Waiting while Albert performed all his many functions and strapped himself into his seat, I climbed on the wing and into the plane. No point in spending any more time in there than necessary. Some buckling, a "Clear!", and we were off.

Half an hour into the flight, we picked up a significant head wind. I don't need much to make me panicky in a little plane so the head wind did nicely. It would cost us gas, bucking the current, and we had no idea if we'd be able to refill at our destination. It felt like an old story problem in math. If a man is rowing upstream at six miles an hour and the current is charging downstream at six miles an hour, how far does the man move in thirty minutes? Ask me. It felt like we weren't budging. Besides, more wind equals more time in the plane, where I didn't want to be. The fact that we might, maybe, have a tailwind coming home didn't help. The return trip was far away. This trip was now and now was going to last forever.

A good twenty minutes later than we'd estimated, we finally saw the single runway of Copper Creek, its witch's hat VOR nearby guiding us in. Below us, I could see the little FBO where Delacroix had lived and died and beyond that, the lone hangar, and a shack or two at a distance. This time we weren't quite alone. Several other small planes were scattered about. I wondered if any of them spent time in that gray, windswept building. A far cry from *Romeo*'s immaculate digs. Not every pilot had a Jack Potts.

No one responded to the radio, not in the air or on the ground. The runway was at angles to the fierce wind, so Albert, his concentration total, sideslipped into his landing. We were blown from one side of the airstrip to the other but, thanks to my husband's good calculations, we weren't blown off the edge. Usually I was so happy to land, I didn't care how he did it, but today was different. I had no idea what awaited us here, but memories of the last visit were vivid. Dread plus the sideslip landing brought the taste of what TV liked to call "acid reflux" into the back of my throat. I fought it down while Albert maneuvered the plane to a space not far from where we'd landed two weeks ago.

While he secured *Romeo,* I looked around. The wind was still whipping dirt across the ramp, making me squint. I felt in my pocket for dark glasses. Not a soul appeared at the FBO door to greet us and offer gas and a cup of coffee. A car was still parked beside the building, but this one was far from a new Cadillac. Blue, rusted, and with a major dent in the back bumper, this old two-door huddled embarrassed against the gale. The entire airport area appeared deserted.

Once out of the plane, we walked toward the building cautiously—and apart. If someone was hidden there, we'd be an easy, open target, easier if together. The broken blind still hung crookedly across the top half of the door which was closed and, in due time we discovered, locked. Walking slowly around the building, we tested every window. No luck. In the back we found one with a fist-sized hole which we stopped to consider. It looked like some kids had tossed a rock through it for fun. At least it looked like that till we noticed that the hole was directly beneath the window latch.

Having the smaller hand, I pulled my shirt sleeve down as far as it would go over the wrist and reached in. The latch was too high. My fingers just missed connecting. Albert found a large rock near the car in the back and, panting from the effort, managed to carry it to a spot below the window. That did the job. Standing on it, I could turn my hand far enough to catch the old-style flange. With some difficulty, I moved it parallel and pushed up. The edge of the glass bit into my shirt but missed tearing the flesh beneath it. The window lifted an inch from the frame.

Albert took it from there, getting his fingers under the bottom and hoisting. With that leverage, it opened easily. Too easily. Someone, I guessed, had used this entry before us.

Standing on the rock and with Albert adding a push here and there, I jimmied my body through the open window, hesitating only for one heart-stopping moment when my jeans pocket caught on a protruding nail. I landed in the back office near Delacroix's desk. This was a bit too simple and I stood poised and listening till I was sure I couldn't hear anyone else breathing. My partner in crime at the window was listening too. Finally, satisfied that we seemed to be, for now, alone, I moved to the front door and let Albert in.

All life had gone out of the place. The glass cases were covered with dust and emptied. No more gruesome scorpions embedded in plastic. Every drawer hung open, all of them emptied. We walked around checking everything, not really knowing what we were looking for. I was sure there'd been an intruder, that the baby-faced sheriff hadn't been the last one here, but even so I wondered how thorough a search he'd made. Just in case, we removed every drawer completely from its housing and checked under, around, and behind it. We lifted the worn carpet in the front room, rolling it back until the obviously undisturbed dirt discouraged us. I leaned over, picked up a hairpin, and studied it curiously. It had been years since I'd seen this kind, used mainly these days to restrain a chignon or a simple bun. I pocketed it and went to the back office.

Glass from the broken window lay undisturbed on the floor. I'd managed to avoid it climbing through. Surely the sheriff wouldn't have left that lying around. Had the person who broke in found whatever it was we were looking for? We stripped the desk, moved it to look below, tapped with a hammer Albert had brought all over the walls and floors. Nothing.

The search had taken the better part of an hour and turned up zip. Discouraged, we walked out, welcoming the sun. The wind, still significant, had died down a bit. It would be just our luck to lose it on the trip home. An old wooden bench, dry and splintered, leaned unevenly on some weeds. Probably the place Delacroix sat to watch the world go by when there was no action in the sky—and that must have been most of the time. The air smelled of wild tarragon and hyacinth, patches of which we could see around us. We sat down and stretched our legs.

I was tired from moving furniture but too nervous to relax. "Now what?" I asked. "We're stymied."

Albert propped a heel on the bench seat and we

heard the wood crack. He put his foot down quickly. "We could check the hangar. The base of the wind sock. The gas carriers themselves if we can find them. Where would you have hidden money and jewels if you were Delacroix?"

I thought a minute. "Underground, I guess. Dug a hole for them. There's nothing but miles of open land here."

"Right, but how would you find the spot again? Twenty steps right and turn sixty-five degrees to the north? The man didn't strike me as a Long John Silver type."

"Oh, I don't know. Look at the music he sent Arlene. Morse code, for heaven's sake. There's a touch of the romantic in that."

Albert shook his head and then stretched again till the bench groaned in protest. "That makes the least sense of all. Why bother using code to tell us where he lived—which we already knew? There's really not all that much Morse code used in piloting, so why did *he* choose to use it?"

"Seems to me I heard something on your radio once, while you were flipping that gadget around, that sounded like a telegraph operator. Lots of dits and dahs."

"Yeah, the VOR sends that out. But no one really listens to it. Makes you appreciate how fast the early guys could react to those signals."

"VOR?" We'd seen it so recently, for once I didn't have to ask what it meant. "The witch's hat? That thing?"

"Yeah. I…"

He didn't get a chance to finish. I was the first to jump up. Albert was on his feet a moment later.

"Ooooh boy," I said. "Oh, wow. That's it! The witch's hat!"

"Of course! Arlene's name for it—and her father knew it. The code was the tipoff to look near the VOR. And his choice of sheet music... He hoped she'd figure it out."

We were giddy with the joy of discovery, dancing around like dervishes on holiday. We started to act like idiots, laughing and singing the song like two drunks at a karaoke bar. After "Bewitched," we tried a few choruses from *The Wizard of Oz,* the ditty about the wicked witch being dead. We couldn't stop giggling. The sun seemed to add heat, and nature in all its wonder was celebrating with us. We had it! We knew where the hiding place must be. Those jewels, or whatever, were as good as in our hands. Arlene would have money for...whatever. Or did they belong to Eli Finer? Well, we didn't have to decide that right now. The important thing was we'd get them safely back home. As for Jesse Leake...

"Where is it?" I stood on tiptoe, shading my eyes and staring back the way we'd come. "I can hardly see it from here."

Albert was beside me. "It's in this general direction. We flew over it on the way in." He looked back at the dilapidated car at the side of the building and apparently decided against trying to use it. "Let's just hoof it. It can't be more than half a mile and we'll see it as soon as we get over this little hillock."

The New Mexico countryside looks like no other, a mix of mesquite, creosote bush, and yucca that grows, to my knowledge, almost nowhere else. We could see a paved road leading in the right general direction, but we'd have to detour to take it. Instead, we chose to trudge through and over the uneven ground, finding the distance much greater than we'd thought. The red soil was working its way into my sneakers and I had to stop occasionally to empty them. Finally, at the top of the tallest hill, we saw it.

Being so close to an answer at last, I didn't even notice the sweat collecting around my hair. By the time two drops rolled miserably down the back of my neck, we were there.

The VOR itself looked underwhelming up close. The small rectangular structure was built of metal siding, its walls pierced on two sides by air conditioners going, on this hot day, full blast.

"Something in there is more comfortable than we are," I said, wiping the sweat from under my eyes.

"The avionics, probably. Those radios. They can't stand too much heat."

Crowning the building, which was circled with antennae, was the cone, the white witch's hat, made of what looked like high-impact plastic.

"Why is there a locked fence around this thing? Do you think Delacroix had a key?"

"We're in trouble if he did, but I think—and, mind you, I'm not sure about this—that only the FAA or their subcontractors can get in here. Anyway, I'm not about to break in and find out."

"What are you afraid of? You think it's Tut's tomb? Enter here and die?"

"Actually, I'm afraid of shutting the system down. I read someplace there's a magnetic field around these things. You can't drive a car too close without bolixing it up. Someday, everyone will probably have a Global Positioning System in their planes and we won't need these babies anymore, but for now, they're the basis of our navigation. If it's okay with you, I'd like not to be the one to blow it out.''

I looked at the unprepossessing structure. A navigational system rested on this? It had the abandoned look of buildings that had spent too many years out in the elements with too few visitors.

"We should have brought a shovel," said Albert, annoyed, the elation following our breakthrough idea now long gone.

"Gee, how could we possibly have forgotten to pack one? What dolts."

"We could walk back. See if there is one someplace."

I wiped my face with a tissue I found in a shirt pocket and emptied my shoes yet again. My quads were aching. "Forget that. Let's look around here. Maybe something will turn up."

There were few hiding places amidst the low-growing vegetation, but we started making circles around the area, our eyes on the ground. Albert was the one who got lucky. "Here, how's this?" He held up a metal spike with a flat top, perhaps a foot long and fairly thick. "Now who around here could have used that? Must have been left over from the construction of this thing."

After arguing about where to begin, we started piercing the ground around the VOR's fence, a job that turned out to be much more work than we expected. Without tools, we were forced to start the spike with our ungloved hands, following that by stepping on the spike head and driving it in. We'd left our little hammer back in the FBO, not that it would have helped much. When the spike failed to touch anything but dirt, we had to dig it out with our fingers in order to try again. Within moments, my nails were embedded with red crud.

"This is ridiculous," grumbled Albert, his face covered with dirt where he'd accidentally swiped at it with his hand. "For all we know, the box, or whatever we're looking for, is inside the gate, maybe even inside the VOR itself. Which is locked. Even if Delacroix didn't have a key, this approach is very unscientific. I should go back down and try to find something to use here." He stepped on the spike head one last time, transferred his weight to it, and almost fell.

We both heard the spike hit metal. At that moment, the right tool ceased to matter. Using the spike as a pickaxe of sorts, we both started digging on our hands and knees. The soil itself was not completely packed down. Delacroix himself, or someone else, must have been digging here within the last few months. Whatever, we were grateful for the fast progress. It took no longer than five or six minutes before the top of an old-fashioned steel lockbox showed through the soil. We had it out of the ground in no time, working with both hands.

The box was perhaps eighteen inches wide, a foot deep, and six inches high. Its weight was significant. I shook it. Nothing rattled but it was obviously not empty. It was, however, like everything else around here, locked.

After some consultation, we decided to try to force the lock right there rather than take it back to the place closed, using the ever-dependable spike. I decided, if we succeeded with this venture, I was going to save that ersatz tool as a memento. Without a hammer to work with, we had to reverse the usual procedure. Albert would insert the point of the spike into the lock mechanism while I held it in position and then together we'd turn the whole box upside down and pound it against the ground. It felt more than slightly absurd. How many Beckmanns does it take to open a locked door? A hundred. One to hold the key in place and the other ninety-nine to turn the house around. The fourth time we turned the house around, something gave way and the lock opened.

We'd been making so much noise, down on the ground with our backs toward the direction in which we'd come, we'd failed to hear company. I was the one who sensed hard breathing behind us. Before I even turned around, my heart dropped into my shoes.

Jesse Leake was standing no more than a yard away holding a shotgun, the kind one might take hunting for quail and other small birds. Probably the only weapon he could get his hands on fast. It was pointed at us.

He looked like a different man without his work uniform, without his subservient air. He looked like a killer. "Thanks," he snarled, gesturing toward the box. "But that happens to be mine. Throw it over here."

Albert started to get up but Leake shoved him back down with the butt of the rifle against his chest. "Sorry, *Dr.* Beckmann," he said with bitter sarcasm. "I'm the boss here."

NINETEEN

"OVER THERE," Jesse said, pointing with the rifle to the chain fence around the VOR. "And push that box here to me. Carefully."

We did as we were told, scooting on the ground till our backsides collided with the metal. Jesse, the gun propped under his arm but still aimed at us, squatted against the hard soil and pulled the chest the rest of the way toward him. When he opened it, we both leaned forward.

A grin of sorts crossed his face, never making it to the watery eyes. "Oh," he said, "you want to see what you found for me? Sure. No problem." He turned the box toward us and tipped it up so the contents were visible.

If we'd expected cash, we would have been disappointed. If we'd expected a fortune in jewelry and gold coins, as in fact we did, we would have been right on. Delacroix must never have been able to convert all the contents of the original box into cash. Surrounded by wads of cotton and old rags to prevent the contents from rattling around, the gems and coins were tucked in every crevice, glinting where the sun hit them as if grateful for a chance to shine after so many years. There were no loose stones, at least none that I could see from a few feet away. All the diamonds and sapphires, the gems I could make out, were in what looked now like antique settings, ex-

quisite and distinctive. And hard to sell without alert-
ing authorities.

"What do you suppose those other coins are?" I
asked Albert, gesturing at a cluster of protected but
ordinary specimens.

Leake answered for him. "Those gotta be the rare
ones, the collector coins my old man told me about.
He said they were better than the gold ones. Worth a
fortune." Suddenly angry, he stood up and let fly with
one foot at a piece of loose granite which arced into
the air and landed thirty feet away. "Coulda made us
real comfortable, my ma and us kids. Dumb. Stupid
fool. He said when him and DeCroce—Delacroix—
opened the box for the first time, they both knew what
they had. Difference was, my old man believed everything his 'good buddy' told him about putting the
stuff in a safe place for the two of them to share.
Yeah, you bet. Then suddenly, my old man looks
around and he's gone. Box is gone. Couldn't find him
in the middle of a war and after... Well, you figgered
out he changed his name." Leake rubbed at his eyes.
The spring pollens—that or too many insecticides—
were getting to him. "Wise guy, huh, that *Mr.* Delacroix? Well, he wasn't such a wise guy when I had
a knife to him. When I forced him to crawl up on
that fancy car and poked him a few times. Not so
wise then, was he?"

I interrupted, not a smart move. "Why the car?"

"Shut up." Sudden rage twisted his look. "The car
bugged me, that's all, and I'll tell you what I want to
tell you. Then I'm going to do to you what I did to
the wise guy. There's no one out here for twenty
miles in any direction so you can just forget someone
comin' out here to save you." His head picked up as

if he'd heard a noise. He turned back stroking the rifle. "No one could hear him and no one will hear you."

"So you tried to make him tell you where the good stuff was. And he wouldn't."

The rage attack subsided abruptly, replaced with a kind of pride. He needed to let us know who we were dealing with. "The pig. I knew there had to be plenty left, that he hadn't been able to get rid of it all. Or maybe he just wouldn't want to. Probably afraid, even after all these years, that the coins and jewels could be traced. My old man told me, before he cashed it in, to go find him, get his share back. He never got over it, the old man. Dwelled on it, ya know? Reason we moved here, he'd heard a rumor that someone had seen DeCroce in the state. Made it my job, to do what he was too dumb to do. But Delacroix wouldn't talk, even when I cut him. Wouldn't tell me where it was. Dared me to shoot him. So I did." He looked away, remembering. "It was a real pleasure."

I had no idea how we were going to get out of this spot alive, but every moment we could keep him talking increased the chance that someone, anyone, might just happen to decide to fly in and land at Copper Creek. This was, after all, the only landing strip for miles. Maybe they'd see us from the air, maybe they'd see the rifle pointing in our direction. That's what I told myself. In fact, I just needed to know. I didn't intend to die with unanswered questions.

"So did you find him when you learned to fly? Is that what happened?"

Jesse let me know he was disgusted with my stupidity. "You got it wrong, lady. Backward. I thought you were supposed to be smart. I learned to fly *after*

I found out where he was. Heard some guy in a bar talking to a woman about a slimeball named Delacroix and the name sort of, you know, rang. The slimeball part did too. This guy, he said, had a habit of disappearing—right after he fleeced you."

"Was the man you heard, could you tell if his name was Hazlett?" Things were suddenly coming together.

He shrugged. "I was doing the trees for the airport. You know, them juniper by the front gate. Guy seemed to be involved. Hung out around there."

"Mm-hmm," I said. "Hazlett." So it wasn't Lawrence and his computer genius that fingered Delacroix. I hoped someday I could let him know.

"Planted the ring, too. In that foreign guy's apartment. That was a good touch." Jesse was getting into it now. He'd loosened his grip on the rifle and let it point at the ground near our feet. Memory and the need to talk about his victory now that the treasure was in his hands was too great. He wanted us to know how smart he'd been.

I shifted positions, which made him straighten the gun. The ground was getting hard under my tail. I sat up straighter, no longer leaning against the VOR fence. "I still don't understand. So you decided to learn to fly to, what? Confirm that Delacroix was the man you wanted? Couldn't you just have driven down to Copper Creek and taken a look?"

"Flying gave me the excuse I needed to hang around him. Thought I'd be able to tell what was up just by being there." He gestured back toward the airfield. "I knew it was the right guy the day that woman, Gillian, and I flew down here the first time.

I had an old snapshot my pa had given me. I recognized him right away."

"And Gillian?" I looked down, seeing her body, the small apartment, the sad waste of a young life.

Albert, who'd been listening silently, picked up on the Gillian image. Losing his icy composure, he turned on Leake. "Did you have to do that? That lovely young girl? What did she ever do to you?"

He stared back. "Like you don't know? Had to play big shot, right? Ask questions? Well, that's what happens."

"How did you get in her apartment?"

"Real tough. Rang the bell. She knew me, remember?"

Poor Gillian. She'd probably told him to hang on a minute and started toward the bedroom for a robe. *Finite*. The wind, now just a breeze, was churning up plant matter all around us, sending a wild scent into the air. I moved again and this time Jesse's rifle sagged.

"Delacroix must have known you were after him," I said finally. "He was tense that day we landed here."

Jesse hunched over down near the box. "Oh yeah, he knew all right. I called and told him I was coming to get what was mine, what should have been my old man's. He just laughed."

"He didn't laugh that last day, that Sunday. We were here when your call came through. At least I assume it was your call."

"Yeah. Maybe."

In the distance, we heard an engine cough into life and rev up. Leake heard it too and started. We were no longer able to see the airport from here, our sight lines impeded by too many tall hills, but the sound seemed to be coming from that direction. The man with the gun saw me exchange glances with Albert and look toward the sky. He smirked.

"Think one of those planes down there on the ramp is about to save you? Well, for starters, one of them is mine, the one I flew down. A rental. The other needs new parts. I asked the owner weeks ago about it. No one's going to spot us here even if there is a plane back there. They'd be taking off in the other direction." Still, just in case, he turned the strongbox toward him again and began closing it up, tying it with a cord he'd brought for the purpose. The rifle hung under one arm.

The engine sound grew louder. We all looked up, scanning the sky. Nothing. The air was clear. Rifle or no rifle, we began to look wildly around. Suddenly, there it was, the battered heap from the side of the HBO, racing up the hill toward us with more force than we could have guessed possible. The steep ascent didn't slow it at all. Those old eight-cylinder engines may have burned fuel like crazy in their day, but they were never short on power.

Jesse Leake was on his feet instantly, the rifle aimed, but the car kept coming straight at him, bouncing over the uneven ground. Far from decelerating when the driver saw the gun, it sped up, hitting the bumps so hard, the aging sedan was all but airborne.

Leake's first shot, not a good one, hit the front bumper. Albert and I were both on our feet. The car seemed, for a split second, to be suspended above ground and in the briefest moment of time, we saw the woman behind the wheel. And we saw the weapon in her hand.

Leake saw us as he saw her and in the time it took
to decide which of us to kill, he lost his edge. Just as
he raised the rifle to shoot again, Albert and I leaped,
Albert tackling him around the knees. I pushed his
arm upward so that the shot, when it rang out, missed
the car entirely and went straight up into the cloudless
sky. Leake fell to his knees, arms flailing. I fell with
him, tripping over his feet and lower legs, losing trac-
tion in the red dust. I rolled over, prepared to fight.
The memory of the shot seemed to echo against the
sudden stillness, a stillness caused by an engine that
had stopped running.

Leake, on the ground, was lying still. Albert, dazed,
had fallen to one side. I tensed, waiting for the man
to make a move but his body was flaccid, quiet. The
rifle had fallen from his hand and lay beside him,
pointing off into the distant shrub.

I looked at Albert, amazed. "What did you do to
him?"

"It wasn't me." He bent down and turned Leake
onto his back. That's when we saw the bullet hole in
his chest. Blood was oozing from the wound, but not
spurting, not propelled by a beating heart. That heart
would never beat again.

By the time we realized she was out of the car, she
was standing above us, the automatic still in her hand.
It looked like a moment she'd been rehearsing for all
her life, the starring role in some postmodernist play.
In leather pants and tall boots, her hair tied back by
a red ribbon, she belonged in a western art museum,
reproduced in wax. Carla Correa's years added character to her fierce beauty. She stared at us, taking
everything in.

She nodded toward the metal case. "So he found the jewels."

"Actually, *we* did."

"Whatever. At least he saw them, finally. He'd been waiting a long, long time. But then, so had I. I was watching you and him. Saw where he was headed. He is dead, isn't he?"

Albert, still on the ground beside the body, tried for a pulse one more time. Then he nodded. "He's dead. And you're some shot, from a moving car." He looked at her with admiration. "You almost certainly saved our lives. He wanted to kill us. I don't think he'd have backed down."

Now that the immediate danger was over, I stood up and discovered I was shaking. My jeans were torn where I'd fallen. My shirt was stuck to my shoulder blades with a sweat I hadn't even realized was there. At least we'd been able to move quickly when we had to, both Albert and I. One can't practice for a crisis.

Carla had transferred Leake's rifle as well as her own automatic to the trunk of the car and tied the lid to keep it closed. We piled into the backseat, sitting on shredded upholstery that had long ago lost its filling. She drove. None of us had much to say.

Once we arrived at the FBO, Albert called Sheriff Tim on our cell phone, the office phone no longer being connected. While he was busy finding someone to pick up a body at a location he couldn't describe exactly, Carla and I sat together in the two front room chairs.

I was able, at last, to shake off nerves. "So when did you know?" I asked.

"About what? About the jewels? The coins? About

what kind of man Jim Delacroix was?'' Her laugh had a bitter edge. "Little by little. And by the time I realized how dangerous my knowledge was, it was too late. He'd have never let me get away alive.''

"Actually, I meant about Jesse. When did you know Jesse Leake was here, that we were here?''

"Oh, not so long ago. Leake landed pretty early this morning. I saw him. I've been coming here every day to make sure no one else had found what I couldn't find. I've been looking too, after all. I knew about the chest and, once Jim was killed, I felt it belonged to me. Can you believe that creep wouldn't even pay for my medical care? Those stupid baubles meant more to him than my life. I put up with him all those years. His daughter didn't. Why should she get all that money? Or his no-good son? I deserved it. I earned it, Lord knows.''

"And that's why you broke into Arlene's apartment?''

She nodded. "To find that envelope. I knew about it.''

I didn't tell her that Jesse Leake had also decided the contents of the chest were his by right. She'd have to stand in line. Even Del and Arlene didn't really have a moral hold on this treasure, though they might have a legal one. Though all the principals were long dead, Eli Finer probably had legal ownership. I had a strong hunch that this problem would take years in the courts.

Albert was still in the back room. I could hear him trying mightily to find some legal authority to contact, periodically groaning in frustration. Carla and I, by mutual consent, brought the chest from the car into the room and spread its contents across the top of the dusty glass cases. Even in such inauspicious surroundings, nothing could dull the luster of the wonderful old pieces, the huge, finely cut gems. I could imagine them around the necks and wrists of prewar European society, elegant women who wore them while listening to the melodies of Kurt Weill or gazing through opera glasses at performances of *Le Sacre du Printemps.*

"I hope you can take something, Carla."

She looked up at me, surprise replacing the look of someone who's seen everything at least twice before.

"Yes, really," I said when she didn't reply. "You saved our lives. You have a gun. You could have run away with the whole lot. It's going to be a very long time before anyone has clear title to these beauties and chances are they won't go to you." I slipped a huge ruby on my right ring finger and admired it before, with a sigh, removing it. "You could probably make some kind of case for a common law marriage, maybe. Stretching it. But it's not likely to stick. You should have something, a ring or...something."

We were suddenly like adolescent girls, playing with the extraordinary baubles, running them through our fingers. She held a necklace up to her face, checking the reflection against the front window. Then she tried the rings. But what caused a small gasp, a lingering look, was a bracelet, eighteen-karat gold, with blue-white stones trapped in an ornate weave. It was gorgeous and tasteful. She caressed it, put it down, and shook her head. "I can't," she said. "It feels like stealing."

I didn't push it. Just quietly resolved that, one way or another, I would see to it that the bracelet found its way to this mysterious woman. It was too late for these magnificent jewels to save the lives of the people who should have had them. Perhaps someday they might save hers.

IT'S MIDSUMMER NOW, the hot days of late July. Albert's still fighting TB, commuting to New York, and that's enough flying for him in this weather. He doesn't like to fly his own plane when it's this hot. Too hard to get lift. I've been trying to work on this assignment for the new magazine but it's difficult when the house is full of workmen redoing the kitchen and finishing the last of the garage. Millie, at least, enjoys the company. She finds excuses to bring cold drinks and sandwiches to the sweating men who would like to be pampered this way for the rest of the summer. I suspect they finish work at less hospitable houses much faster.

The boys have enjoyed teaching younger kids to master computers in a way their parents never will. Senior year is still ahead, but college is all they talk about. That is, Paul and Lawrence talk about college. Spence goes mum at those times. We're no longer making an issue of it. What will be, will be.

Lawrence's mother found him where he'd run, to the home of an understanding aunt. He returned without argument when he heard about his father. He'd known the truth, of course. Not right away, but eventually. I wonder what would have happened if Jesse had lived. Lawrence, that complicated young man, would have been all but destroyed by conflicting loyalties.

Strangely enough, I ran into Del yesterday. He was

selling newspapers outside a supermarket. I don't think I'll ever forget that lunch we had. I bought a paper from him and said hello. He had no idea who I was.

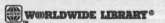

Dead Man's Fingers

Barbara Lee

A Chesapeake Bay Mystery

Maryland real estate agent Eve Elliott has left Manhattan
for a more peaceful life along the shores of the Chesapeake.
Once there, Eve discovers greed, corruption and murder
rock the calm waters of Anne Arundel County.

Both Eve and her aunt/business partner, Lillian, find
themselves scapegoats in a heated controversy over zoning.
Development scams, crooked politicians and unhappy wives
with dangerous secrets add fuel to the fire. Soon, sinister
threats and the murder of an attractive, ambitious
environmentalist warn Eve she's digging too close. Now the
murky issues are becoming frightfully clear: her life...versus
a killer's deadly intent.

Available December 2000 at your favorite retail outlet.

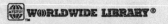 **WORLDWIDE LIBRARY®**

WBL369

THROUGH THE EYES OF THE DEAD

MELISA C. MICHAELS

AN AILEEN DOUGLASS MYSTERY

Chalk it up to the heat…or to hormones, but when
San Francisco P.I. Aileen Douglass catches the sexy
young Gypsy man trying to hot-wire her car, she doesn't
call the cops. Instead she gives him a lift to Oakland…
and lands herself in a twisted case of murder.

Nick inhabits a dangerous world, as Aileen quickly
learns, when she stumbles across a dead fortune-teller,
then dodges a hail of bullets. Next, Aileen's only paying
client is murdered, her office ransacked and
her partner drugged.

And she discovers these cases are connected…
by a missing $100,000.

Available December 2000 at your favorite retail outlet.

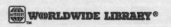

WMM370